To Norma—
whose journey has
not been easy
but whose wisdom
has grown strong.
With love,
Carol

little ways: an artists tale

It's hard to know what makes a person shut down, and harder still to recognize the mechanisms that offer rescue. *Little Ways* follows an artist's journey to understand her present by examining her past. It is a story of secrets, abandonment and revelation.

Abigail Lynde was born with her arms wide open, ready to embrace the universe and to love everyone who came her way. In the beginning, she had a mind that saw all things new and delighted in magical places. It wasn't hard to be happy. Born in Brooklyn, New York, during the golden years of American wealth and prestige, she had the comforts, interests and opportunities to become the person she wanted to become. Surely, she was graced.

Unfortunately, the innocence and egocentricity of youth can't know the layers of a complex universe. When loss and shame came her way, they were buried rather than faced, and scar tissue formed in the corners of her mind, silencing any words that may have led to healing.

From this silence she found the language of painting.

...thirty years of mud and dead insects were scraped off a newly accessible window, one that allowed a token of natural light into the darkness, even a breath of fresh air. This sacred corner soon held an easel, a table, shelves, a high stool and a flood light. In no time at all her muse appeared.

In this private space where ancient earth cooled sturdy granite walls, she would squeeze tubes of paint onto her palette, mix them with a flat knife and grow nearly drunk from the joy of it. She loved combining colors, the alchemy when they became something else, and the smell of the glistening oils and turpentine. Her canvas was a world she climbed into, where she was delivered from the ordinary, the very ordinariness she had believed she wanted...

little ways

Also by Carol St. John

Anchors of the Soul
Taproots: Where Ideas are Born

little ways

Carol St. John

Tusaints Press

"It's not love's going that hurts my days,
but that it went in little ways."

—from "Little Ways" by Edna St. Vincent Millay

First edition, published 2008.

Editing/design/layout by Jill Buchanan, ZoomConsulting.net

ISBN 978-1-6064-3-458-1

Acknowledgements

Thank you to my first readers, who were kind enough to offer encouragement and smart enough to help me hone my words. Kent Bader, Virginia Hall, Glenda Martin, Lucy White Mueller, Joan Frank, Martha Schuyler, Eileen Mueller and Patti Willis are women I respect deeply and see as representative of the future readers of *Little Ways*.

Joanne Michos was a fellow writer with whom I shared my initial ideas. We began our novels side by side, but Joanne did not live to complete her story. Her inspiration and friendship are still with me, and I cannot pass on these pages without mentioning her influence.

I especially want to thank my editor and book designer, Jill Buchanan, with whom I have shared the intimacies of creative pursuit and the issues of womanhood. Together, we explored the effectiveness of this story. Not only was her expertise as an editor exceptional, her dedication to this project made its fruition certain.

Carol St. John

1

Chaos

Abigail MacKenzie was delivering her last and largest painting to the Field Gallery when a blast of cold wind almost sent the precious cargo down Prince Street by itself. In order to cross SoHo's busiest intersection and arrive at the gallery intact, she ignored the sooty sheet of newspaper that had attached itself to her foot. At the gallery entrance, using her backside as ballast, she leaned the rest of her one hundred and twenty-eight pounds against the heavy steel door, opened it, and went inside.

Immediately, she stripped off the artwork's heavy, brown corrugated wrapping to inspect the gilded frame and its contents for bruises. Satisfied there were none, she continued into the interior gallery and placed the piece against the showroom's wall. Only then did she think to lean down and remove the annoyance of newsprint from her shoe. Princess Di's crinkled face looked up at her. The shock of her senseless death still hurt. The Brit she loved best, gone forever.

But she could not be distracted by her death, not now. Instead, she crumpled the paper into a wad and stuffed it into her parka pocket. The presentation had to come first.

No one seemed to have noticed her arrival. She was grateful for the minute it offered to look privately at the paintings as a whole for the first time. Lined up around the room, the bright colors and bold shapes screamed, "Look at me! Look at me!" It was unsettling. These were parts of her, parts that had appeared like dreams to a fevered child. She had not anticipated their impact as a group. With their neediness so transparent, she wondered who would take them seriously. Her face smarted with doubt, but there was no way out. She was committed to this exhibit and had to follow through no matter what cruel criticisms might result. She owed nothing less to her friend, the gallery's owner/director, Kendra Field.

Kendra was no fool when it came to the art business. She was renowned for supporting the high end of edgy, contemporary art, and even though Abigail's paintings were a major departure from the style and genre of the gallery's stable, it was an honor to be hanging in such a prestigious space, one that had displayed the likes of Kline, Stella and Motherwell.

Leaning down to retrieve a small painting eclipsed by a larger one, she heard Kendra's voice call from the back room. "You made it! I knew you would! Sorry darling, but I was on the phone. Terribly important call."

As always, Kendra's energy filled the air. Abigail could almost see clouds of ions framing her words.

"I'm here, but I don't know if I made it!" Abigail smiled, wishing for still more time to sweep the hair out of her eyes and rearrange her paintings.

She tried to breathe naturally as her friend's narrowed eyes scanned the canvasses, but the nasty critic inside her head was yammering, scolding her for not placing her name consistently in the lower righthand corner of each piece, for putting too much varnish on some work and not enough on others, for frames that looked too common for SoHo.

Like a mind reader, Kendra said, "The frames are perfect Abby. Now, where to begin?"

Poised for rejection, Abigail assumed she was being asked to help decide which work should stay and which should go. She was wondering if it wouldn't be easier to just bundle the whole parade of embarrassment back into the bruised Dodge wagon. "What do you mean, begin?" she asked.

"Which painting would you like people to see first? I'm setting an easel by the door. What should be on it?"

Abigail looked at the small painting in her hands and said, "How about this?"

"What do you call it?" Kendra asked.

"*Chaos.* I could begin or end with this one," Abigail laughed. She was hoping to sound light, like her life wasn't depending on what happened next.

"*Chaos* it is!" Kendra said, taking the painting from Abigail's outstretched hands. "This certainly establishes the mood of the show. It's funny and colorful. Yes, this one will be perfect."

The comical painting of a startled woman being shot out of her clothes dryer into a cluttered garage had a cartoon quality. A child sat alongside the machine, detergents balanced precariously on their shelves, and a scraggly cat and rubber ducky watched the poor woman's flight.

Chaos was the first painting to have followed that crisp October day, when the last of the golden leaves released themselves from the backyard's maple and Abigail woke up one person and went to bed another.

It was Friday, her To-Do list was exceptionally long and then complicated by a missed school bus. She fought the instinct to rage at the bus driver for taking off without her children (he could have given them another minute) and skirted a foul mood for the remainder of the morning.

After dumping the two kids at New Horizons Academy and running three autumnal paintings to Primary Colors for its fall exhibit, she hooked up with some friends for a fast lunch at Twin Sister's. By one o'clock, she was making a dash-grab through Toys-R-Us in search of unique gifts to tuck into her children's hands for simultaneous birthday parties that evening. Turning onto Apple Blossom Lane, she spotted the vibrant red leaves of an oak. Thinking how wonderful they would look in the tall glass vase near the door of the gallery, she estimated the time it would take to snap and deliver them, and still be back in time to retrieve her son and daughter at the bus stop.

She just made it.

Home with only minutes to spare, she raced the children upstairs to strip, dunk and don them in party clothes. After their respective presents were wrapped, they were delivered with appropriate inanities to their festivities at opposite ends of town. This done, plus a pick up at the cleaners and a careening sweep through Wiley's Finest Foods, she was home in time to make dinner for her husband. But this Friday, he'd arrived home earlier than usual.

With tenuously thin grocery bags dangling off her fingers, crisply cleaned shirts slipping from her shoulders and the day's mail wedged between her teeth, she skirted around her husband's car and staggered from the garage into the kitchen. It was a typical attempt to conserve energy, making one trip from the car instead of two.

She spat the mail at the table, spilled her groceries on the kitchen counter and swore under her breath as an escaped can of tuna rolled to the floor and took refuge under the fridge. In her don't-even-go-there voice, she called out, "I know I'm late. I know the refrigerator is empty. I know the children's clothes are all over the place, so please don't make any pronouncements, okay?"

Hank, who was lurking somewhere in the house, didn't respond. If it wasn't for his shining black Porsche still warm in the garage, she might have doubted he was even in the house. She hated it when he got home earlier than expected. It exposed her ability to turn chaos into order in less than fifteen minutes.

To the invisible critic she called out, "Stephanie and Joshua are at birthday parties and I had to buy decent gifts and gift wrapping before the kids could go. I am so sick of these juvenile extravaganzas—pizzas, clowns, gifts for kids who have too much as it is. I mean it, I hate the whole thing! The Abrams even had pony rides. Really! They had the pathetic, scruffy thing waiting on the front lawn with its mane in fuzzy braids tied with pink bows."

He failed to answer. "Hank?"

Beyond the corner of the kitchen, she saw his profile reflected in the warped glass of the front hall mirror. His head drooped strangely, like it was too heavy for his neck. His face looked miserable or ill, his jowls deep, lips set in a straight, thin line.

"What's the matter? Hank, really. I had a busy day. I'll take care of everything in a minute. Let me get you a glass of Scotch."

"Don't. Don't bother, Abigail. I have to go. I'm leaving."

She met him face to face, but it was as if there was a wall between them. She could almost see the impenetrable plastic of it.

"What do you mean you're leaving? Where are you going?"

He was wearing the tie he'd said was too loud when he opened it last Christmas. She loved it for its Matisse design, thought it helped bridge the gap between his conservatism and something more playful.

"I'm going, Abigail. It's over. There's nothing left."

"Hank, what are you saying? Nothing left where? In the fridge? What do you mean, nothing left?" She did not need this, did not want to have an argument. But he didn't seem cantankerous, just tired. Well, so was she.

He rubbed his forehead. In a quietly resolved voice, he said, "It's over, I mean, if it even began. There's no more us. I'm not sure there ever was an us, Abigail. I'm leaving, and my decision is final."

"Your decision is final? Hank, are you having some kind of a breakdown?"

"No breakdown. No. I think I've just woken up. I'm facing the truth and helping you do it, too."

"Oh, this is ridiculous."

"I'm going, Abby. I'll call you as soon as I'm settled."

"Settled? What are you talking about?"

"I have to go. Now."

She felt the air press against her as he walked through the kitchen to the garage, ignoring the five starched shirts semi-draped across her right shoulder. She heard the door slam. His car revved and the cranky garage door groaned open, then the Porsche's tires squealed down the otherwise quiet street.

Stricken, she stood perfectly still for a moment, until anger hit and propelled her up the stairs. She threw his things on the bed and she struggled out of the purse that had wound itself around her neck like a feedbag.

"Screw you, you bastard," she screamed as she opened the closet door to hang up his clean shirts. Her voice reverberated from its hollow shadows.

He hadn't left one single item of clothing in the closet, not a tie, a shoe, a jacket. Nothing. She ran to the dresser and found only one foolish paperclip, a few pennies and a spare button in the bottom drawer.

She tried to remember an argument, signs that anything was wrong. Had the night before been different from any other? Last night, she'd made dinner as usual. She remembered little of the conversation, their quiet moods distracted only by the children and unsolicited phone calls. Had they watched the news together? She wasn't sure. He had, no doubt, fallen asleep in his recliner after dinner. She had, no doubt, cleared the table and asked the children to show her their homework. When they went to bed, he had followed them and kissed them good night, while she put their clothes in the hampers. With the TV's recap of a Sunday ball game blaring, she had spent the evening in her studio working on the new sunflower painting. Was he depressed? Sick? He hadn't complained or missed work or any other routine of his life. She didn't think so, anyway.

She sat on the edge of their queen-sized bed, with fear blocking her breathing. Her colon cramped, her thoughts knotted. No tears emerged, nothing at all escaped. Instead, a huge gulp filled her gut, and time slowed down to interminable seconds as she waited for... what? A call? An explanation? The sound of his car?

At seven, she headed out to pick up the kids. They ignored her presence, talking only to each other all the way home. As usual, she was simply the chauffeur doing their bidding. Back home in the kitchen, they refused the hot dogs she offered. Their stomachs were full of pizza, cake and ice cream; how could she have expected anything different?

Next, Stephanie battled her little brother in the living room over a broken sketch-o-graph set that she'd grabbed and sent hurtling to the edge of the glass table. It split open, exposing its barren interior. They were screaming when Abigail took over. "Take your book bags and go to your rooms. Do not come out until I say so."

Begrudgingly, they left the new toys behind and retreated to their private spaces. So did Abigail. She went down to the basement and tried to concentrate on her painting, but she could not care about the light that played on the yellow petals or the clarity of the sky.

She was sitting in a daze when Stephanie came down the cellar stairs. "Mom, where's Daddy?"

"He had to go away on business for a few days. Now, you go back upstairs and get ready for bed, alright?"

Stephanie, in a rare show of acquiescence, did as she was told.

A long night followed. By the time a slant of light began defining the horizon, Abigail had decided to extricate herself from the utter tedium of her life with Hank. It was she who should have walked out. She told herself what hurt most was that he'd done what she should have done years earlier. He was not worth her grief. She would not fight. She would teach him that he couldn't hurt her, that he was disposable. She willed herself into making a vow not to let him come back, no matter how much he begged. He would learn a valuable lesson and she would be free.

With this conclusion firmly in mind, she grabbed at least an hour and forty-five minutes of sleep before hearing the kids fight over the TV's remote control.

Four days passed before his first phone call. By then, she had ridden the rails of hurt, fury and desperation.

"How are Stephanie and Josh doing?" he asked.

"They're fine. I told them you're on a business trip," she answered.

"Well, that won't do."

"Listen, if you want them to hear something else, you will have to come and tell them yourself."

"I can't. I'm in Tucson."

"Where?"

"Arizona. I'm moving here. An easy transfer."

Where reality was hiding in his head was a mystery. She tried to control her voice and language.

"Easy? What is the matter with you, Hank? This is ridiculous. Have you lost your mind? You can't just walk out on two kids, a house and all your responsibilities."

"You will be fine, Abby."

"You're damn straight I will be fine, but your children need to be considered. You have to talk to them and help them through this transition."

She looked at the kids happily playing in their plastic fort in the backyard. They didn't look upset, but why should they? They thought their father was away on business. Little did they know he didn't care what they thought.

"I can't come now. It would be too hard. Give me a few more weeks."

"You can have the rest of your life, as far as I'm concerned," Abigail said icily, hoping his ears were frostbitten by her voice. He wouldn't get away with this behavior without consequence, but she wouldn't sink to threats.

She didn't slam down the receiver. She just carefully clicked it to off.

The next day, Abigail received a letter with a Tucson return address. Her fingers shook as they tore the envelope apart, anticipating explanations, but inside was only a check, a sizable amount, probably meant to assuage his guilt. Fueled with humiliation, she took it directly to the bank and padded her account, vowing that the best day of her life would be the day she could tear his checks into tiny pieces and return them that way.

A month from that moment, she ran into Kendra Field in the town parking lot. Kendra had been a "Glam Girl" in the New York Art School where they had been classmates for two-odd years in what seemed liked a century ago. Somehow, they ended up in the same burbs. Why a single woman without children had settled in Montmarte, the most boring of all burbs, Abigail could not understand. Kendra commuted to Manhattan practically every day and returned to Mom-and-Popsville each night.

"What's wrong with you, Abby?"

"Everything. Why do you ask?"

"Well, you look exhausted. Are you okay?"

"No."

The train's whistle announced its arrival. Amid its snorts and squeals, car doors opened and husbands and wives split in their ritualistic pattern. Smart briefcases swung beside legs lifting themselves onto the cars headed for Grand Central Station.

"Listen, we have to talk, but right now I have to catch that train. Let's make a date. How about dinner at Luigi's some night?"

"I have two kids, remember? Come to my house. Come tomorrow night."

"Fine, I could use some home cooking. Hank okay?" she called over her shoulder.

"Perfect," Abigail said, knowing Kendra was already out of hearing range.

Inviting Kendra for dinner was Abigail's deliberate initiation into reality. It was time someone knew what was going on. She certainly wasn't tempted to tell her sister or her mother of her circumstances. She deemed Kendra to be a better candidate, more distanced, less likely to overreact. She was a part of the bedroom community of Montmarte's inhabitants; those who worked in New York but liked to wake up to bird songs and go to sleep with a blanket of stars above their heads. Most had little time to become part of the fabric of the town. This anonymity appealed to Abigail.

The following night, Kendra arrived at Abigail's door perfectly put together. Her designer jeans, low slung and accented with a jeweled belt, made an otherwise common uniform look stunning. A tight, black turtleneck set off her white skin, skin made luminous by impeccably applied makeup. Tootsie, a droll little shitzu, peeked out of Kendra's large leather satchel, her chin resting on the neck of a bottle of vintage Cabernet.

Abigail fussed over the little dog, threw Kendra's leather jacket on the big suede chair that once cradled her husband, and wasted no time getting around to the truth. "Hank left."

Kendra didn't even blink. She acted like those were the very words she expected to hear. "How long has it been?"

"Weeks. Months. God knows."

Abigail handed the corkscrew to Kendra and pulled two glasses from the china cabinet. She glanced at her wedding pictures on top of the cabinet. Each gilded frame held the same optimistic smiles. She looked like a girl in full bloom and happy enough. Unconscious, maybe.

"Another little boy has walked?" Kendra said. "And I suppose you were the last to know?"

It hurt to hear her husband dismissed that way. "He wasn't a little boy. He was dependable and kind and as predictable as rain. I am in a state of shock."

She wasn't sure she could talk about her situation after all. She had no idea she'd feel so defensive. Obviously, Hank wasn't as predictable as rain.

"You had no warning? Seems like a childish way for him to handle such a momentous event. Of course you'll sue?"

Abigail didn't answer. The wine tasted slightly bitter. She started to collect the schoolwork that lay in disarray on the cocktail table. Stephanie's composition called "My Family" was started and aborted after naming the principals. She looked at the end table, at their family portrait, where four perfectly healthy, attractive people smiled at some stranger and pretended happiness. It should have worked.

"Record everything, every phone call, every letter. Everything. Get a detective on the scene immediately."

"What? Oh, Kendra. This thing is going to right itself. I don't think drastic measures are in order just yet." Even discussing legal action made her upset. She shook her head in confusion.

"I have a friend. Wade Barnstable. He's good, he's honest and at least he will find some answers for you. I think his price is fair and if I call him, I'm sure he'll take your case."

"I don't . . . I don't see that I have a case. I have a separation, but there's no point in going off and investigating the man. He's simply going through a mid-life crisis or something. I think spying on Hank would only exacerbate the situation. We've been through a lot. He waited for me when I lost it."

"Oh. You think he's coming back then?"

"I suppose so. But, I'm so angry right now, I can't imagine letting him back in. Unless it's something I don't know about, like his being terribly ill or at some kind of crossroads he isn't willing to share with me."

"Have you talked about that?"

"I tried. Maybe it's too soon for us to have a conversation. I might explode. He might fall apart."

"So what? Why shouldn't you explode?"

"I think that would be the wrong way to go. Maybe we both need a time out."

"Where is he?"

"Arizona. He moved to Tucson, Arizona."

"He went to the desert? How appropriate."

"What do you mean?"

"You know, it's the place to shed your skin. Christ, Mohammed, Moses, Abraham—didn't they all head for the desert when they wanted to get their acts together?"

"You think he's just shedding some middle-aged skin?"

"Not really." Kendra's voice didn't disguise her inherent judgment.

The drapes moved ever so slightly, letting in a last hint of sunlight on the window sill. Abigail rose and placed two candles on the table, struck a match and lit them.

Kendra took another sip of her wine. "Listen, Miss Innocent, there's more to this story than meets the eye. I can almost guarantee it."

Abigail thought, How dare she assume she knows what I don't? She is no friend of Hank's. People don't change. She's the same know-it-all she was in art school.

The discussion was too exacerbating to continue, so Abigail turned the subject from herself to Kendra, asking about her gallery and the New York art scene.

"It's alive, but phony as hell, and manipulated by a small clique of critics. If your art is even slightly 'mundane' you will be totally dismissed. It's the outrageous they love. Shock them, repulse them, frighten them, confound them and they consider it talent."

"Are you still painting?" Kendra asked.

"My stuff is piling up in the coal bin. It's compulsion, not art. I don't understand what drives me."

"Let me look at it."

"Oh no! Not under your eye. It's too personal."

"But you show at the Primary Colors Gallery, don't you? I've seen your name in the Gazette."

"I will not point out that you didn't make it to the opening. Plus this isn't the stuff I show at the gallery. It's primitive, childish."

"Come on. Take me down to your dungeon and show me your work. You've whet my curiosity," Kendra laughed.

Reluctantly, Abigail led her visitor down the crude wooden steps to the cellar. In the harsh glow of fluorescent light, Kendra began to pull paintings from the bin like files from a drawer.

"The colors! They just sing, Abby. Oh, this one is a treasure. The feet. It's all in the feet! Oh, I love this one, *Miss Lonely Hearts*! Been there, done that. For heavens sake! How long have you been pumping out these jewels?"

"Since we took out the old furnace. They represent about four years of hiding out."

"Well, they're going upstairs and into town. I think it's time to entertain some of those stodgy New Yorkers. We all need a laugh these days. These are marvelously droll, very witty. You've led me to the pot at the end of the rainbow. I never realized, Abby. All these years and I never knew."

"You really like them, then?" Abigail said, her surprise transparent.

"We just have to do something. I will start to introduce you into the gallery, a few pieces at a time, see how they fly. But they're fabulous, darling. Fabulous. And give up the sunflowers. Van Gogh already did that along with thousands of others."

"Sorry, but the sunflowers are a must, my tribute to Fibonacci."

"Fib Who?"

"Fibonacci, a mathematician. He believed there are underlying patterns in all things. I like to believe there's an underlying scheme to everything."

"Well, that's lovely, but may I suggest you stay with the figurative stuff. It's your best, most original art." Her long red fingernail pointed at the park painting. "Who else is painting hoola hoops and baby carriages? Really, Abby, you have something unique going on here."

Nothing inside Abigail had anticipated such a positive response. Of course, she had never exposed her work to Kendra. From what she'd seen, Kendra Field's idea of art was a gray clothesline wrapped loosely on a black pole. How could she have imagined her paintings would be taken seriously by this promoter of the avant-garde? Then again, perhaps this was simply Kendra's way of making her feel good about herself. That surely was it, Abigail thought.

"I don't really paint for an audience. I paint for myself," she explained.

Kendra clapped her hands. "Don't you see? That's the very thing that makes it work. An artist who paints strictly for an audience will always be mundane. This shows you are not. But don't tell me you don't care about an audience."

"I don't."

"You have to face the truth, Abigail. You're painting to be heard. Keeping your paintings in the basement is like screaming in an empty room, out of anyone's earshot. What good is that? Painting is communication. It needs a receiver."

"I think I'm receiver enough. I'm interested in what shows up on the canvas. I really just like being in my own head."

"But you need an audience. You need to have reactions, something to reflect upon. How else will your work teach you?"

Kendra didn't follow up on her enthusiasm or ask for any of the paintings for the gallery during the months ahead, but Abigail did not care. She continued to paint by the weeping granite wall, under the stairway of old pine boards, in her sacred space with only an occasional cockroach or spider for company.

The children functioned on automatic, dressing for school, making their own breakfasts and leaving her alone each day. She didn't bother to make the beds or go to the market, or check the calendar. She had been fired from those jobs. She was out of work and out of her mind. Feeding the cat was no more important than feeding herself. She put its food in a large bowl and left the kitty litter to build until she could no longer stand the odor.

After a second cup of coffee each morning she would go to the basement and sit in her corner to stare at a canvas. If one color wanted to replace another she would squeeze out a coin's worth of pigment, just enough to do the job and then dully study the results. She operated on instinct, because her mind was hard to find.

But she tried to work and think. In her first effort, the one that followed weeks of numbness, she began with a circle slightly to the east and south of the center of her canvas. Then, she put four walls around it. She considered the circle in the square. Was that she and Hank, a circle inside a square, two pieces that could never fit unless one was smaller than the other? With a pointed bristle brush and some yellow paint, she pushed a figure out of the circle, beyond the square. It only took a few strokes and a bit of orange and blue and red, and the shape became an emerging woman. Her arms were stretching, her mouth open, her eyes bulging, a green shirt identified her sex, some toning of the hair, and you could see her flight. Putting a lid beneath the dark circle, she turned the box into a clothes dryer. She decorated the edges of the canvas with a child, toys, tiles, tilting soap boxes and a bicycle. For a final touch, she put a plunger in the woman's hand and shocked her hair.

She was in shock. Her body could function no better than her mind. She found herself doing strange things like wiping a dish over and over as if to remove its design, or putting the butter in the bread box, or getting up at one in the morning, thinking it was seven. She would go to the window and look outside for something, but had no idea what the something was.

Newspapers piled up, as did leaves, then snow, then winter's waste. Time either did not go fast enough or it would disappear. She shopped out of town, at odd hours, and went to the stores in Nyack rather than Montmarte, wearing her hair down, dark glasses and a long coat, happiest on the cold days when she could cover up. Prepared foods, snacks and milk were all she thought to buy. She had never liked shopping. She didn't like cooking much either. She was going to do things her way, which was not at all.

Cooking was a chore that had gone largely unappreciated, anyway. Appreciation from a six- and eight-year-old could not be expected, and now, now she would be free, forever free, with no one beyond the kids to worry about, to wait on or fake it for approval. She knew now that marriage was just another illusion and would not come her way again.

Kendra did not abandon her, but remained blatantly unsympathetic. They found the present, politics and art to talk about on their rare get-togethers. It sealed their friendship, whereas pride and shame within Abigail's small coterie of Montmarte friends was crippling. She would ask herself why she should suffer shame. Hank had been the villain after all, but she found pity or imagined gossip unbearable. So she maintained a safe distance from all things local, and waited for time to heal and her mind to forget.

It annoyed her that scenarios of Hank's deceit kept popping up in the most bizarre circumstances. She'd be picking up a pizza and find herself wondering where he ate his meals during all those late nights of so-called work in New York. The thought would magnify itself into scenarios of food at another woman's table, clandestine dates in little restaurants on 57th Street or in Cold Spring Harbor. Maybe they didn't eat. Maybe they just went to a hotel. Jealousy and rage would set in for days. Her imaginings became obsessive, unconfirmed truths, the violation of her trust irrefutable.

Once, when she was looking for pieces to a jigsaw puzzle she asked herself which pieces of the Hank puzzle she had missed. She had to admit that his world of auditing and numbers had disinterested her entirely. She had no idea what he really did all day. If only she could have cared, had learned to care, and he had helped her to know his world.

And then she remembered how he had become irritable over the smallest things—the absence of a sock, a lid left off the toothpaste. In the scheme of things, these issues seemed inconsequential. Had he just wanted to have a fight, communication at any price? She had noticed he started to leave in the mornings without so much as a peck on her cheek. While they had been perfunctorily planted, they were significant enough to be missed.

She didn't miss their sex life, though, which had dwindled down to a weekly exercise, a biological function meant to keep things working. What kind of a woman did he need? What erotic tricks should she have known that would have prevented him from leaving everything he knew without turning back?

He was the one who wanted to go to the right dinner parties and join the social clubs. She had gone along. He was the one who believed the children needed competitive sports and toys from FAO Schwarz. She thought cardboard boxes and cans of paint, pencils and books were enough, but never got in his way. It was just a difference of perception. She complied with his conventions and told herself their differences of opinion made for a healthy whole. Obviously, he was anything but healthy.

When the air began to swelter and the children grew restless, she hired a sitter, a college girl who would take them to the pool and the library and play games with them on rainy days. Meanwhile, she continued to lose herself in the world of Grumbacher and Winsor-Newton. New colors of paint thrilled her more than any food or human being. The dioxazine purple, the bariums, cobalts, quinacridone orange and shiny metallics turned her on, but she always returned to her primary palette, the old faithfuls: cadmium red, yellow and standard blues. These were the colors whose chemistry she understood and worked best.

The number of paintings in the coal bin grew until her earliest paintings were virtually buried. But she threw nothing away, held onto them all, as Kendra's encouragement gave her a new sense of her work's value, in addition to having affirmed its quizzical style.

Stephanie and Joshua continued to grow. They asked little beyond the basics. There were incidents, but she did not dwell on them. Slowly, the house began to gain some order. By the end of the summer she was functioning less like a zombie and more like a single mother. It was something she had not believed she could do, but knew she had no choice if she was to keep their nucleus of a family alive and together. Hank would never redeem his children. He had not tried, but he would not dare, because she would never give him reason to hope.

Around the first anniversary of Hanks' leaving, Kendra called.

"I need to see your latest work," she said. "Are you ready?"

"For what?" Abigail asked.

"I need you. Mike McCarthy, my new protégé, has deserted New York. Rumor has it he fell in love in Majorca and is not coming back to the States. This leaves me with four empty walls for the holiday weeks. I'm desperate. Can you find framers and have twenty pieces ready for me by December tenth? Be a darling and just say yes."

"Kendra, I'm so flattered. I really am, but my stuff is so quirky. I can't imagine anyone finding it interesting."

"But if they do, you will earn fistfuls of money and you'll simply paint more. Really, Abigail, you must sell in order to grow. And be sure to have them photographed in the event that you want to make prints."

"Well, it would be nice to have the money, although my work hanging in SoHo could be humiliating. You said it yourself, those galleries pride themselves in negating all things ordinary."

"Girlfriend, your work is anything but ordinary." Kendra declared emphatically.

"Are we on, then? I need to know, now. I have to get publicity rolling. The more I think about it, your work will be perfect for the holidays. This will be my surprise gift to the stressed-out lives of my patrons. I just can't wait."

Without an affirmative answer, Kendra went on. "And by the way, I'm glad you took my advice and investigated Hank's whereabouts. I heard from Wade Barnstable that you contacted him; he thanked me for the business. I don't suppose you really needed him in the end.

"I made that call to Wade over eight months ago. He only corroborated what all of Montmarte knew before me. Hank, Jane Browne and her two children are living happily ever after in the Old Pueblo. But I'm sure you know that."

"Gossip is insidious, isn't it? People love to share the sexy tidbits. I heard about Jane Browne on the commuter line, during a mindless conversation about the real Montmarte, where people meet at lunchtime to fuck like bunnies."

Kendra's words stung. As usual, they were too glib for the circumstances, but Abigail pushed back the hurt and replied, "I don't know about the lunch hours around here, but Jane Browne is a fact. She walked out on her husband in the same manner as Hank left me. The two cowards deserve one another."

Abigail's initial reaction to Wade's confirmation had been unspeakable, a miasma of emotion. Jane Browne? The Little League mother she saw him laughing with that one time? She had appeared so "white bread," so undistinguished, a plump woman without style. But the image of them sharing a joke had stuck in her mind. It came up when she first heard her name. She remembered because Hank rarely laughed. She wondered what the two had shared at that moment to cause him to throw his head back and laugh so hard.

Abigail said yes to Kendra's invitation. The opening was set for December 12th, 1997. It would be called, "Introspective". More importantly, a seed of purpose was planted in Abigail, a raison d'être. She began to get her paintings ready, and this effort sustained her in the days that followed.

2

The Critics

Abigail arrived in town earlier than planned. Instead of the typically slow Friday evening traffic into the city, the roads were open and easy. Miraculously, she found a free parking spot on Spring Street, only a few blocks from Prince. Swinging a bag stuffed with dressy heels and a makeup kit, she hurried to the gallery. Facing locked doors, she repeatedly knocked and rang the bell, until she accepted she was first on the scene. Fortunately, Kendra had anticipated such a possibility and given her the code for the lock-box over the doorjamb. She pressed the correct buttons and heard the lock release.

Just inside the entrance, a clipping from *The New York Times Magazine* was already enlarged, framed and hung. Kendra not only managed to get her shows into the city's art reviews before an opening, she also made sure they were remembered after the fact.

"The joy that pours out of Lynde's paintings will scintillate any space..." the review began, already saying too much, Abigail thought, making too bold a promise for paintings yet to be tested.

She entered the exhibit hoping she'd experience a scintillating space, but all she saw were her children, from the youngest to the oldest, competing with each other in their bright Crayola colors. Her work was a direct contrast to the restrained elegance that had graced the entry, which was subtly lit by recessed lighting and grounded with mauve-streaked marble tiles. On the walls, black- and-white photographs memorialized the days of Warhol and gang.

The main gallery was bare except for the twenty Lynde paintings covering its walls. "It's your room," Kendra had told her only the day before. "This is about your art, not flowers, not food, not wine splattered on the carpeting. Your space will be sacred. Let the reception take place in the foyer where a reception belongs. Then guests will be able to move easily about the main gallery to view the exhibit to their hearts' content."

At five o'clock, Abigail made way for the Can-Do Caterers who evidently knew the entry code. Sparkling cobalt glass vases, filled with stalks of velvety red roses with baby's breath between the blooms, added seasonal color to the room. Abigail leaned into the flowers for a sniff while the crew placed their large silver platters of canapés on the banquet tables, and set out at least a hundred glasses.

Beyond the window, SoHo was winding down another workday, its history laced in the iron grillwork facades of the buildings. The neighborhood had come full circle, transformed from early nineteenth century streets lined with family mansions, to sweatshops that created a thriving textile marketplace by the turn of the twentieth century. Tragically, harsh working conditions led to its ignominious implosion and the area was condemned and abandoned for years.

The reincarnation of Hell's Hundred Acres began when hip artists saw opportunities in the empty lofts and low rents in this part of lower Manhattan. By the 1960's, some thought SoHo, New York, was the American answer to the more outrageous SoHo, London. But, insiders knew the name rested solely in its location, south of Houston Street.

The Field Gallery was a prime example of what happens when artists breathe a tenuous neighborhood back to life. It was only one of the many high-end galleries that moved into SoHo to capitalize on the energy of the creative spirits that came first. Soon, property values went up and artists were forced out, left to find other more obscure and affordable places to live and work.

Abigail hugged herself as the outside streetlights blinked on, illuminating the hubbub of subway-bound workers who shuffled past the window. Few paused to note the unobtrusive sign:

A. Benoit Lynde
"Introspective"
Opening Tonight

No art rested in the window. Kendra preferred not to have drop-ins. She didn't believe previews were meant for the simply curious. "Exclusivity whets the appetite and loosens the purse strings," Kendra explained, when Abigail asked which painting she planned to showcase.

After the caterers had left, Abigail pilfered a stuffed olive from one of the perfectly arranged trays. Eating the first olive made her stomach needier. She ate a second, only to succumb to a third, which meant she had to carefully rearrange the tray's remaining delectables and then find a place to brush her teeth and wash her hands.

Insatiable and anxious, she avoided the pressure of the empty gallery, used the restroom and entered the cluttered storage closet in the back, a perfect retreat where she could curl up like a cat and ensconce herself in a pile of wrapping paper and boxes. From this feline perspective she regarded the foam noodles, balls of string, bubble wrap and corrugated cardboard on the shelves above the wrapping table and hoped they would be put to good use tonight. It would be embarrassing to have nothing to compensate for Kendra's advertising and enthusiasm.

She lay back and fantasized herself emerging from the closet inconspicuously, obscured by elbows and shoulders, easing into a room fueled by the energy of others. She tried not to allow thoughts of a poor turnout to enter her head.

The minutes passed slowly, but her pulse raced when the clock read 5:45. Useless thoughts cluttered her mind. She asked herself if Kendra's lateness should be cause for alarm. Was she was caught in rush-hour traffic? She simply had to arrive before the first guest walked in. That's her job, after all, to be on time.

Kendra managed to arrive before the hour, and she was not alone.

From the storage closet, Abigail could hear two distinct male voices in addition to her friend's. She opened the door slightly and saw Tootsie the shitzu, jumping out of a gold lamé tote bag. The ball of fluff wore a piece of satin around her neck and a small diamond clip attached to a tuft of fur on top of her head.

"I hope that's a rhinestone. Tell me it isn't the real thing, Kenny," a bushy-browed man said. "Won't she shake it off?"

"Now, Max. Tootsie thinks it's the real thing and is quite vain about her appearance. Her diamond is as safe as this one." With that, Abigail could just imagine Kendra dancing her fingers before the man's eyes and flashing the engagement ring from which she had never disengaged.

"Oh, look at these treasures," Kendra exclaimed. "Come take a whiff of these roses. They're perfect. Now, you two let me put away my coat and then we can chat. You're dears to come. You won't regret it, I promise."

Abigail closed the door quickly and reached for her satchel, taking out the new Ferragamo heels she had purchased for the occasion.

As she put her down boots in the bag she heard Kendra call, "If you want to get rid of your coats, I have a closet back here."

Kendra opened the storage room door and let out an ear-splitting shriek upon seeing someone inside. Abigail screamed just as loudly, and both women fell backwards to the floor.

"Christ, Max, something is back there!" Fred said.

The two men rushed over and found the women doubled over.

Seeing the men's frightened expressions made them laugh even harder.

"We…you…I…" Kendra tried to speak. "If…if you…if you are trying to save me, put away your guns, boys! May I present our artist, the star of the evening, Abigail Lynde. She is not dangerous, I promise you."

Pointing from one man to the other Kendra introduced Abigail to the men. "Max Lewis, *The Times*, Fred Barber, *The New Yorker*."

"My God, Fred!" Max said to his colleague, his white hand trembling on his heart, his voice incredulous. "We could have rushed into a high crime scene! Do you think we have some hidden death wish? What's happening to our better instincts?"

Fred turned to Kendra. "Do you always keep your artists in the closet?"

"Only if they so choose."

"Well, lots of us choose the closet at first, dear," he quipped. "Wouldn't you agree, Max?"

Max nodded and stroked his moustache as if to calm a pet.

"I find being in the wings preferable to center stage," Abigail said, her mood considerably improved by the ridiculousness of the situation.

"Well, come on out of there, will you?" Max ordered, fussily waving his hands like palm fronds. He was wearing sneakers and a worn camelhair jacket over a slightly crumpled shirt. It looked as if he tied his bow-tie exactly as he tied his shoelaces. Abigail figured he must enjoy rummaging in closets, too.

"I'm afraid I need a minute to pull myself together," she answered. "You should have warned me about these early birds, Kendra. I could have found a better hiding place." She grabbed her purse and slipped into the lavatory.

In the mirror, anxiety sat in the shadows beneath her eyes and the pleats of skin between her brows. She checked her teeth again for olive bits, smoothed the blonde hair that was arranged in a loose knot and appraised herself. *I no longer look like a girl, but I'm not a girl. Why try to deny the obvious?*

Using the sink like a baptismal fount she tapped her face with cold water and then, with a few swipes of a damp towel, removed the dust that had streaked her black velvet skirt. She foraged in her makeup bag for the little tube of toothpaste, and brushed her teeth a second time. A dab of lipstick, a long deep breath, and she gave herself to the night.

The men were already taking notes when she appeared in the gallery. Fred Barber turned to her and said, "You've changed your name a few times, I see." His attention for details was apparent in the hair laminated in place, the conspicuous black-and-white checked handkerchief in his jacket pocket coordinated with the Lauren tie at his neck, and his wing-tipped shoes shined to a glare. Abigail wanted to say how observant he was, and considered explaining that the art world is a different story for women than for men, but surely he didn't need that information, she thought. He had to know it had been a boy's game from the dawn of time.

"I signed my paintings Abigail in the beginning because my art was just for me. It wasn't until I began to show my work that I became self-conscious about signage."

Fred nodded. "That's got to be true for most young artists. But artists should be forewarned from the beginning that their best works can emerge at either end of the spectrum. At sixteen they're as capable of producing extraordinary work as at eighty. Look at Picasso's boyhood portraits. No wonder he grew bored with realism! And at the other end, remember Grandma Moses—the poor dotty old girl—and her octogenarian forays into the landscape.

"Too many pieces of art are destroyed out of innocence and ignorance. So often the freshest, most untainted works, the works that tell the whole story, are lost. Of course an artist's defining piece can only be measured at the end of a life. Matisse's best and final works were done from his sickbed, the most elegant work of his lifetime. A grand finale of sorts, wouldn't you say?"

"Yes." She assumed he was talking about the collages.

"You agree!"

She was grateful that she had seen the retrospective and remembered the feeling of liberation it gave her, standing in the last room, in the midst of a circle of cutout stars and dancing figures whose simple lines and shapes defied gravity.

"They were splendid! Proof that good health has nothing to do with good art. Van Gogh's best work was produced during his most desperate years. And my poor friend Rothko simply went over the edge," he continued.

"What do you mean?" Abigail asked, afraid she knew too well.

"You know, he slit his wrists and made his final work with his own blood. His partner in the next room never had a clue."

"Perhaps all artists are on the edge," she responded, thinking her present madness might actually lead her to wilder more abandoned places.

He ignored the comment, removed his glasses and bent over to peer at another moniker.

"Ah. Now you are signing as MacKenzie."

"Yes. Identifying myself as a wife and mother." She figured she might as well make a story of it.

"But here we have A.L.M. Yet another phase, I gather."

"My transition period."

She started using initials after fellow women artists advised her to use an androgynous name, a name that would protect her from those who would diminish the value of women's work.

"My latest and last compromise is A. Benoit-Lynde. Benoit, is my mother's maiden name, passed on to me as a middle name. This is a signage I can use forever, fortuitous, too, as I plan to divorce Mr. MacKenzie."

The declaration surprised her far more than it did Fred Farber. He ignored her words while she felt more powerful for the telling.

It had only been a year and two months and yet it seemed like her husband had just left. It was a brutal ending, so brutal her food regularly became stale and voices in her head crowded out voices on the phone or in the stores. During the past year she had even considered mixing a bottle of Tylenol PM with a bottle of scotch and taking the easy way out. But she couldn't do it. There were the kids, and no matter how much she grieved, she was still curious enough to want another day. It was the call from Kendra that lifted her to action.

But the hot shame of Hank's departure was far from over in her day-to-day existence in Montmarte. She knew people were still talking about it. She imagined people liked to dwell on who he took with him—Jane Browne, an unlikely adulteress with two quite ordinary children of her own. Plain Jane. Round Browne, she had privately named her; a woman as unlike herself as he could have found, full of bubbles and freckles, a sloppy, chatty woman, too ready to put her hands on a stranger's arm or around a messy child's shoulders. Her Berkenstocks and tie-died shirts were better suited for Vermont than the burbs. Abigail remembered seeing her hold forth at the community house with grandiose schemes to enforce recycling or create halfway houses. The woman was one of those cheerleader types, in concert with every issue that wanted a spokesperson. She was obviously looking for something, Abigail just never dreamed it was Hank.

After he left, the kids pressed on her, questioning, bickering with each other, and whining about their meals and homework, until she finally exploded. It began with a watery reproach, "Why can't you two behave?" Escalated to, "What is wrong with you? I am doing the best I can, why don't you?" Then culminated in rage, with her fists trying to break through the living room walls.

At night, she screamed at Hank silently, asking him how he could have done this to them. Hank. Hank, the reliable, non-threatening, true-blue guy she'd chosen out of those who had come her way, mostly because he didn't intimidate her as other men had, those men who'd pressed themselves and their body parts on her before she could think straight. Hank, whom she believed would never engender the dangers of passion. She had thought that neutrality was the very backbone of their marriage. She believed they shared a healthy passivity that protected them from jealousy and pettiness, where neither asked too much or too little. She saw in this passivity a safety factor that would make a long-term relationship work. And it had worked until this breakdown or whatever it was that was going on. In the cocoon of their partnership, they had produced two children, established a decent home and made friends who provided a modicum of comfort. She had never dreamt their neat little package would come undone.

Recently, however, she started to recall the times he had said strange things like, "Speak to me, Abby. I never know where you are," and "Do you love me, Abigail? I mean, really love me?" Such questions from him were completely out of character. She now realized she should have explored what provoked them, and asked herself what she might have done differently.

There was the night he called down to her sacred space in the basement, "Still down there, Abby?"

"Where else?" she'd snapped.

"Just checking!"

Checking for what? She wondered, was this some meager attempt at communication? But, she hadn't asked, didn't want to interrupt her own concentration.

She thought she had given him the reassurance he was looking for. She had pointed out she was right beside him, wasn't she? She folded his underwear and cooked his meals, didn't she? She tried to keep the house straight and be a good mother to his children, hadn't she?

True, their lovemaking was marginal. Sometimes he asked her to talk to him during sex. "Say something, Abby," he would beg. "Tell me what you want me to do for you." She found it a disruption to whatever was going on in her head. Things like, did I take the meat out of the freezer? Can the children hear us? Is he ever going to finish? Passion was just not part of Abigail's expectations and she thought Hank had accepted that. She thought they both understood love was not sex or vice versa.

The closest she had come to passion these past few years was when she was painting. Painting turned her on, evaporated time, released her from herself. Her senses would rise from the very sight of colors oozing from their tubes. The umbers promised forests and country paths. Prussian blues made deep, blue-green seas. Ultramarines let shadows play on snow. The reds—cadmium, magenta, and alizarin—belonged on barns and in gardens. Buttery yellows spread summer sunshine. She loved rainbow colors and used them to describe the world inside and outside her head, the rich hues seemingly pulled by fairy hair to her canvas.

The perfumes of oil and turpentine made her high and the motion of moving her brush took her away, where she experienced orgasms of color. In her coal bin sanctuary, she could not get enough of the images that surfaced when she called on them.

And now she could not believe she was allowing strangers to see the creations she had yet to understand herself.

3

The Visionary

Max Lewis appeared to be taking notes as he studied *The Visionary*. In the large, cartoonish painting, a man is leaning out of an apartment window with his eyes focused on the horizon. It would not be hard to assume he had knocked the tumbling flowerpot off the window ledge and sent the cat flying. The cat's eyes are wide open, along with its mouth and splayed legs. But its assassin remains oblivious. An obscure woman, observing the disaster from behind, looks to be concealing a rolling pin, or at least ready to give her man a whack on the side of his head.

Max chuckled. He wasn't the first person to laugh seeing the soon-to-be-dead cat's fall. Kendra had laughed, too.

Max turned to Abigail and posed the question she anticipated.

"Why do you call this *The Visionary?*" he asked.

She put her hands on her hips and tipped her head. "Why do you think?"

"Are you poking fun at the man who is looking so far ahead and far away, he can't see what lies within arm's reach?"

"Exactly!"

She could like this man. He smelled of Old Spice and he was willing to play.

He folded his arms and considered the work a while longer. "An interesting indictment of those of us lost in the future, who don't deal with their sins or their blessings," he said. "Visionaries! You've got to forgive them their farsightedness. Love them for who they are. I'm a Buckyophile from way back, a prophet in his own time, that man. Dare to be naïve, he said. Do more with less. Yes, a marvelous mind."

Abigail was fairly sure he was talking about Buckminster Fuller, but didn't know if Fuller was dead or alive. What was clear, was that Max identified with him.

He went on. "And how about Isaac Asimov, the master of futurism, able to forecast new worlds, delve into sciences beyond the beyond? What brilliance!"

"The physicist?" she asked.

"Of sorts. Although I think metaphysics is too close to religion to legitimately call it physics."

Max was obviously adding his own meaning to her piece and she had no intention of dissuading him. He continued to rhapsodize.

"But of all the futurists, Ray Bradbury is still my favorite. I love the man. He can go faster than the speed of light in his head and yet he's afraid to get on a plane, says he wouldn't get on a plane if his life depended on it."

She didn't need to tell him that her painting had nothing to do with Bucky or Isaac or Ray. The only visionary she had ever known was her father. *Your father was a delusionary visionary*, her mother liked to say. She never questioned her mother's words because there was enough evidence to prove her right. The packet of letters he had written to Abigail during the nine months of her gestation described her future as riding on a cosmic rail, the stars aligned for a new generation of global awareness. He foresaw the internet, satellite dishes, the end of disease and cultural divides, the breaking down of religions and the building up of science, all bringing people together to create a safer, fairer world.

This child, he wrote, would reap the rewards of those who lived before. He believed in the potential for all things to heal. He trusted that the oceans would recover and the skies would grow clear. He predicted a future where prosperity was possible for all. He conveniently disregarded a world where five out of eight children went to bed hungry each night, dismissed the fact that the United States was on the brink of an all-out war with Vietnam; was assassinating its own leaders, and had enough nuclear arms to destroy the earth ten times over.

It only made sense that such an optimist had chosen the name Abigail, meaning father's joy, for his second child. He was no doubt confident the name would live up to itself.

The letters, a treasure trove of his thoughts, were found hidden in a plain wooden box on the highest bookshelf in the Lynde home. They had been left unopened for years, largely because they were exclusively directed to Abigail and may have caused his first born, the jewel-like Tiffany, to feel slighted. It wasn't until Abigail's mother presented them to her on her wedding day that she even knew of their existence, and she spent much of her wedding night studying them and staining page after page with her tears.

From the vantage point of a Brooklyn condominium, the Lyndes looked directly out at The Statue of Liberty, the distant shore of New Jersey and an endless parade of ferryboats crossing the harbor. Manhattan lay like a delicious smorgasbord to the north, Staten Island, a conundrum, to the south. This view was the focal point of their household, particularly during harbor events or electrical storms when lightning illuminated the waterfront and thunder shook the large panes of glass.

Involved and attractive, Cecily and Alex Lynde inhabited a political world that brought controversial people to their home. The children were never shielded from any of them. Their tender ears listened to fiery conversations about injustice, war and taxes, and the absolutes of change. The White House was not revered, but the nation was, along with an absolute belief in democracy's call.

Alex Lynde saw parenting and teaching as one. He used every opportunity to teach his girls as their lives unfolded. He also made a point of spending "special" times with them as individuals, like a morning with Tiffany or a luncheon with Abigail. Both girls were able to choose from a list of adventures he constantly updated, and they loved these exclusive, one-on-one times with their father.

On one of those days, an April day, the kind that opens forsythia and turns pale grass green, Abigail and her father took a trip to the famous cherry tree orchard in Brooklyn's botanical garden. Families all about them were spreading blankets and opening picnic baskets, but they had no basket and no blanket. They just let the pink wings of cherry blossoms fly about their heads and soaked up the sun's warming rays from where they stood. Despite the magic, Abigail was anxious to get to their next stop, the zoo.

At the zoo, they went to the large animal areas first, visiting the camels and the gnus, then the zebras. With the exuberance of spring, one zebra mounted another, its penis like a great gray tail. Abigail stopped short, fascinated, but embarrassed, too. She soon tugged on her father's hand to leave. But he didn't budge. Instead, he said, "This is the way zebras make babies, Abby. Just as all mammals do."

She wondered how a sweet little baby anything could actually be made out of such a strange and ugly tube. She also noticed that other families were veering away from the zebra sex, all but a group of rowdy teenage boys, who stayed to witness the activity. "Fuckin' awesome," they said. "Whaddabone!"

Her father stiffened. "Watch your language," he scolded, before stepping away and moving her down the familiar path to the less licentious elephant area. "We should respect all wild things," he said. "We're responsible for them. We mustn't take anything we have on this earth for granted. Its creatures teach us everything we need to know." He pointed to a mother elephant.

"Just look at how that mother turns her nose into a hose in order to bathe her calf," he said, as the elephant squirted water on her four-hundred-pound baby.

Abigail was about to ask him to pick her up so she could see the little elephant better, when a boy about her age dressed in a blue jacket and matching cap climbed up onto the same rail fence her hands were touching, and slipped over the top. He dropped like a bird to the cement basin below, his small blue cap taken by the wind and left floating in the watery trough. The calf ran to play with the cap, but the mother elephant, reacting to the invasion of her territory, immediately pressed the child to the ground with her huge flat foot.

Abigail was stricken, first by the boy's mother's wail, then by the cry of the beast, louder than the bleat of an Easter trumpet. She leaned forward, hoping to see the elephant's foot lift and the little boy climb out from under it, however, before she could focus, her father's hands reached about her waist and pulled her up and away.

"Let's go see your cousins at the monkey house," he said. "I hear them talking about you right now."

"But what happened to the little boy?" she asked. "Is he all right?"

Her father didn't answer; instead, his deft fingers tickled her ribs and caused her to squeal in misery and glee. Instinctively, she knew he did not want her to think about the child, and she tried to forget, because they were having one of their perfect days. But then the ambulance's siren filled the air, making the new leaves shiver and clouds cover the sun.

Later that night, she was unable to stop the horror from reappearing in a dream when an enormous gray elephant trunk reached up, grabbed her and sent her hurtling to the earth. She screamed as its gray foot, the size of the sky, came down to crush her into a paper doll.

Her father woke her from the nightmare and switched on the light. He asked about the dream. She told him what she could, and then he reminded her of the funny monkeys, the beautiful zebras' stripes and the pussy willows they had seen. He counted her toes, recited the silly story about this little piggy going to market and this little piggy staying home until the smallest little piggy who ran all the way home—and she had giggled as his trusted fingers scurried up her leg to her belly. Before she fell asleep, he described a rainbow and had her name all its colors, which she did. "Whenever you're afraid, think of the rainbow," he had said softly into her hair as she cuddled beside him. "That's where the angels play."

She saw the angels clearly. They had golden curls, wings of soft white feathers and haloes made of tiny stars above their heads. They flew about in little gowns, slid down multicolored slides and landed in cotton candy clouds. She fell asleep playing with them and woke in the morning to the familiar smells of coffee and toast in the kitchen. No one spoke about the elephant or the little boy again.

Abigail stared at her painting, and recognized the woman with the rolling pin. When will I stop being angry at my poor father, she thought. So what if I loved him too much, felt abandoned and lonely when he left? So what if the world was never the same afterwards? He wasn't a bad person just because he taught us we could ward off danger and cruelty with positive thinking and denial, and then left us to deal with life's hardships without him.

"Do you know what your painting is going to look like before you begin?" Max asked.

"Almost never. I didn't know what this painting would look like, that's for sure."

She doubted she could articulate her process. Did she see pictures inside her head waiting to come out? Was she channeling, doodling, taking a trip into her psyche? She had not asked herself such questions before.

"In this case, I drew a line that became a wall, and then a rectangle that became a window. From there, I let the painting happen. When I was done, I knew it. That's all I can say."

Two smiling women approached her as they moved from the hors d'oeuvres to the main gallery. She nodded and they looked right past her at something of greater interest on the far wall. She wanted to become a shadow at their heels as they talked.

The room continued to fill. The pleasant buzz of conversation created a surround sound and Abigail was grateful again for the canapés, the endless wine and crowded rooms. She sensed people were really looking at her work. It was like watching a movie and experiencing fear and joy simultaneously.

"Abigail. I am always interested in what motivates artists. Tell me, why do you paint?" Max persisted.

She assumed he wanted material for the article he was putting together, and the possibility of being quoted interrupted her mental circuitry. A pundit would want details about an artist's twists and pitfalls. It would probably read better if she described the takeover of her mind, the disappearance of time and anxiety. Surely, it would not do to confess that painting simply helped her escape the boredom of her household, a dead marriage, and a community designed to homogenize those who lived there. That would be far too mundane for his audience.

She turned the question back on him. "Why do you write? Why does a dancer dance?"

He merely smiled.

She continued, "I don't write and I don't dance, so I use what I have to work with—paints and brushes. I think that about sums it up."

"Your paintings have humor."

"I imagine most of us need humor to survive. Don't you, Mr. Lewis?"

"I try to laugh things off," he countered, "but too often the joke is on me."

"Yes," she nodded knowingly, "it's hard to laugh when the joke's on you."

That was the moment she saw the man enter the room. He was a stranger, she was sure, but something about him wanted her attention.

4

The Swing

"It's about joy," she said finally, going to the side of the person she was drawn to despite herself. He turned his face and rearranged his ruffled eyebrows. She almost sang, "How would you like to go up in a swing, up in the sky so blue?"

His face softened in an easy smile. The lines on either side of his mouth were deeply carved by former smiles, and he was game to chime in, "I imagine it's the best damn thing ever a child could do!"

"Up in the air and over the wall, 'til I can see so wide..." she prodded, her fingers leading like a choir director's.

"Birds and bees and herds of nerds over the countryside," he rhymed. "How'd I do?"

"No nerds," she laughed. "No birds or bees either, but close. Robert Louis Stevenson would not be offended, I'm sure."

"You're Abigail MacKenzie, I gather."

"I used to be. I am using Abigail Lynde, now," she corrected, liking the sound of her maiden name.

"You say your painting is about joy. Why not call it, *Joy*? Why, *The Swing*?"

"Because joy isn't the whole story. The child went too far, too high, and fell off the swing. End of joy." She stopped herself, trying to resist explaining away her art.

"I see. So it's not really about joy."

"Maybe it's about the danger of joy. Too much joy, and misery follows, something like that."

"Why not change it to, *Before the Fall*?"

The painting was not about the fall, it was about a point in time, the high point of magical thinking, of hopes and possibilities, but she mustn't explain. It was his to interpret.

"I'll work on something more original," she said, smiling, and stepped backwards, edging away from him into the crowd. She was going to resist the instant connection she felt with this man no matter how attractive he was. He was probably going to ask her next if she was the little girl in the swing, the one trying to hit the sky, the one who thought she could sprout wings if necessary.

The memory of Tommy Shortsleeves appeared from out of the ether. What were they—five, maybe, when Tommy Shortsleeves and she showed each other their bodies? They were best friends, imitators of life. Their land of make-believe included formal weddings, stocking stores, playing house and caring for doll babies.

It was a relationship that had been forged by both their mothers. Grace Shortsleeves was concerned that her little Tommy had no one his age in the neighborhood to play with, and when Cecily Lynde mentioned her weekly excursions to the Shortsleeves' neighborhood to study French, Mrs. Shortsleeves jumped at the chance to babysit. Tommy and Abigail bonded immediately, but, unfortunately, they became better acquainted than anyone anticipated.

Their sexual encounters were revealed one day when Grace found them playing doctor. The two children were down to their birthday suits with a lollipop stick stuck between Abigail's rosy buns. This medically-inspired achievement elicited screams from the child not unlike a pierced pig's, and Grace came running. Finding them stark naked, trying to beat each other to oblivion, she forgot any psychology she had learned at Mount Holyoke and started to berate them in a clearly hysterical voice.

"What are you doing? Get your clothes on immediately! This is a disgrace, Thomas Howard! What have you been up to?"

"I'm taking Abby's tempsure with the mometer," he answered honestly.

"You should know better Abby Lynde, taking off your clothes and letting Thomas do such a thing! I am going to call your mother and see to it she knows exactly what went on here this afternoon. You should be ashamed of yourselves."

Cecily arrived with her cheeks sucked in and her nose in the air and told Mrs. Shortsleeves that she was not at all surprised or amazed at what their children had done. "Haven't you ever played hospital, Grace?"

"I should say not!" she said, "I've always known how to protect myself. It is an instinctual thing a girl knows from the beginning."

Abigail didn't see Tommy for months, not until one day at the playground, when there he was. He sat next to her on the swingset and didn't say a word. Not even a hello. They started to swing side by side, going higher and higher until they made the chains of their swings scrunch at the top. They were like birds soaring above the park, above the heads below, reaching for the sun, for the thrill of height and daring. She imagined herself aloft when suddenly she was flying from the swing to the earth, just missing the chain-link fence before crashing to the asphalt where she lay flat as a puddle. The puddle soon became a bloody pond with lots of people, including Mrs. Shortsleeves and a park guard, hovering over her stunned wisp of a body. "Call an ambulance," someone yelled, and another commanded, "Don't touch her!"

She never opened her eyes to see Tommy Shortsleeves' tears or his mother shake her head. "That child is a wild one, she will be learning the hard way," she announced to no one in particular. A jet roared overhead, car keys clattered, and the child felt herself rising onto a stretcher. She saw her nanny's brown hands clasped in prayer and lost consciousness.

By the time she came to, emergency surgery had been performed and her jaw was rebuilt, leaving only a fine scar across its edge. It was no one she knew who saved her chin, a young resident at the hospital, a man who just happened to be there at the moment. He earned kudos among the staff for his work and many thought Abigail a lucky girl, but she did not. She couldn't chew or speak.

Even though she hurt and was sad, her father told her she was blessed. He told her the doctor was her special angel, a man who appeared when she needed him most, and she should be grateful. Being six she believed every word he said, but she could see the pain in his eyes and feel the worry that his long conversations with the nurses proved.

It was weeks before the feeding tubes were removed and her mouth slowly began to work again. Piles of books lay on her bed. Crayons and coloring books, a magic slate, and paper dolls, too, but she was lonely much of the time. She waited and waited for Tommy to come to visit. He never did.

When she told her mother she missed him, her mother said, "Hmm," and no more.

"Mom, if Tommy and I don't play doctor anymore, can he come over to play?" she asked one day while they were playing Go Fish.

"I don't think Mrs. Shortsleeves would go along with that. Really, Abby, can't you find some nice little girl to play with?"

She supposed she could. She would when one came along.

Looking back to the painting, Abigail saw the metaphor of freedom she had created using a child suspended above the world, above ripe red apples on trees, corn high as an elephant's eye and a swing extended to its full potential. Although she had unconsciously chosen this image of one in command of the earth and the sky to reflect joy, she also knew how such an ineffable moment led to danger.

She looked again at the amused man who had questioned her, who was at least interested enough to challenge her about her work. His type always had attracted her, the thick dark curls that went their own way, the tension in his square jaw. He caught her staring and came to her side.

"You know, we could get to know one another, if you wouldn't keep running away from me," he teased.

"I have to keep moving, its part of my job, meeting the patrons and schmoozing. No offense." Inadvertently, her hand checked her hair. She found it in place.

"Your work has me curious."

"Yes? And I am curious about your curiosity," she laughed.

"I wonder if you always limit yourself to half the story. There are only few dark colors here. Hardly any shadows."

"I prefer bright color. I like to see things in… in full light. Shadows aren't as predictable as we like to think. I only use them to connect the parts."

"In my line of work it's in the shadows that things get interesting. I have to study the shadows because that's where the real story is found."

She felt a wave of disappointment. He's a critic, and he hates my work, she thought. "Who do you write for?" she asked.

"No one. Can't get an audience to save me."

"You're not a critic?"

"Ha!" The big smile lit his face again. "That's a good one. I'm a wannabe mystery writer, sometimes a poet, as you must realize. But, I know nothing about art. Name's Barney. I'm a friend of Kendra's."

She was relieved and gushed a little too much. "You do know about art. You're reacting and responding. That's what it's all about. Everyone's an artist; it's part of being human. Why did you come here tonight if you're not interested in art?"

"I just needed something to do. A warm place to go after work. Besides I was… I wanted to meet you."

"Why?"

"Male instinct, I guess."

"Barney. Barney? You don't look like a Barney, it doesn't suit you."

She was being coy and knew it, so unlike her.

"Why? What does a Barney look like?" he grinned.

"He's overweight, has a six-pack in the back seat of his Chevy, maybe a little too much color in his face." She blushed at her meager attempts to be clever.

"It's a hangover from childhood. Only my old friends use the name. I thought we might become old friends, so I offered it up."

Abigail decided he was being as flirtatious as she. His dark eyes climbed into hers. She could almost see her own reflection in their deep brown hue. They said he liked her. It felt good to be liked. She wanted to encourage him, but knew she should move on. Warning signals were sounding. *Too soon, too soon*, they said.

"I think you know more about art than you realize. About these paintings, anyway. You've seen right through them, found aspects I'm just noticing myself," she said.

"The dark side?" he asked.

He had it right. There was dark side to each one of the images, one only she could know. Every painting was a cover-up. All the brightly painted stories lined up in a row masked what she really had to say. "Its absence, yes."

He nodded.

"Do you frequent gallery openings?" she asked.

"No," he answered. "I'm not sure I even like art."

His answer was too enigmatic for her to pursue. Perhaps it was just a come on, but she was not sure she wanted him to elaborate. She saw his left hand lift the wineglass to his lips and his eyes travel over her shoulder at someone or something else. It was time to leave while she could, and she headed once more toward the canapés.

5

The Aftermath

With death as its theme, Abigail shouldn't have been surprised at the attention *The Aftermath* was getting. More than one viewer saw it is a tribute to the Princess of Wales, ignoring the gender of the figure lying peacefully in the casket.

In August, when they took Princess Di from the Pont de l'Alma tunnel in Paris and sped her away with her heart pushed from the left side to the right, the officials waited as long as they could before they pronounced her dead. Even then, the bells did not toll their farewell. Rather, the news came in the harsh light of day, when the world would weep at yet another lesson of human frailty, and prove again that no one is above tragedy.

City newspapers and national magazines could not put her to rest. They continued to fill their pages with her photographs. Insinuations of murder not only kept her alive, but turned Dodi Al-Fayed, her lover, into a shady Romeo, and slandered his father, Mohmed. Even the beloved Queen of England was made suspect. Abigail supposed the function of gossip was to give distance to grief, to find cause for the unexplainable and lay to waste the folly of fate.

She felt a kinship for the young Diana who had married her prince, was forced to share him, and suffered in the limelight of his vain-glorious throne. A part of her understood how much the princess must have wanted something real, something with meaning, a love and a family that were truly bonded and functional. Diana had spent most of her adulthood posing and now the opportunity to embrace the real world was lost, forever.

The people who didn't know how to take the painting of grief were intriguing. Not only did they put Diana in the coffin, some saw it as a mockery of death and two women believed it was a feminist statement depicting four women crying over yet another. Some laughed and some whispered and moved quickly away. She noticed the man named Barney looking at it quizzically. He was not laughing, nor was he moving on. She was glad, because *The Aftermath* was dead serious to her.

It was about the sudden demise of her father. Jagged lines described the fractures of pain. Strong jewel-like colors emphasized death's glaring reality. The cluster of women grieving alongside the corpse could have been her mother, Tiffany, Grandma and herself, or any bundle of women who loved and lost someone.

Her father had died a month after the Easter Offensive in Vietnam, the largest bombing of Hanoi. As an anti-war activist and lawyer, he had taken on suits against the government and lobbied companies to join forces with the peace movement. Most of his time was spent writing speeches, marching, organizing and finding compatriots around the world. He had believed his work was making a difference until these attacks crystallized the government's real intentions. At this point he became so incensed he stood in front of the White House on Pennsylvania Avenue, gathering reporters and other dissidents who would listen to his words.

The Lynde's phones rang day in and day out with ardent followers and like-minded journalists. Ultimately, he had his entire family in the streets, his mother included, marching down Fifth Avenue holding placards that read, War Is Not the Answer and Arms are for Hugging, or singing the civil rights anthem adopted by all protestors, "We Shall Overcome".

Six days before his death, another death occurred, someone Alex worshipped, his boyhood hero, baseball player, Gil Hodges. An avid Dodger fan throughout his youth, Alex decided to pay his hero his respects by taking the family on a field trip to Ebbets' Field where he tried to infuse them with baseball lore outside the old stadium's locked doors. The three Lynde women only feigned interest as they heard about Hodges' famous grand slams and his illustrious career. "Hodges was Brooklyn's son! I am sure he will be buried here, in Greenwood Cemetery."

With this thought in mind, he decided they should go to the cemetery to see if Hodges was on his way home yet. He insisted all of Brooklyn's greatest heroes were laid to rest on the huge glacial hill at the high point of Brooklyn. No one was available at the gate to prove him right or wrong, but the family spent hours poking around the graveyard while Alex took pictures of them near notable tombstones that bore names like Horace Greeley, Ward McAllister and Henry Ward Beecher. He introduced the girls to the Lynde family gravesite where they read the name and date on the simple plaque under which their Grandpa Oscar was buried. But they didn't linger long because Alex spied Charles Ebbets' marker.

"Ebbets helped make Brooklyn, Brooklyn!" he explained to them. "Everyone in Brooklyn loved the Dodgers at one time. Back then, no one could imagine Brooklyn without the bums," he said, "except dah bums demselves. I'll never understand how they could have left."

In the early morning hours on the first Thursday after that prescient trip to the graveyard, Alex Lynde kissed his girls goodbye. He was headed for the Capitol again.

"Alex, you have to slow down. You're gone more than you're home. All these trips are going to take a toll somewhere down the line," Cecily warned as he left.

"It's only a short trip this time, we're building the coalition, my love." He swung his briefcase with one hand and knocked his knuckles on the dining room table with the other.

"I'll see you in a few days, princess," he said to Abigail, "And you too, little lady," to Tiffany.

"I want today, thank you," their mother said.

Abigail knew that his departures meant returns and always looked forward to the peppermints and the exotic gifts that they promised. Tiffany would get tiny dolls in native costumes and Abigail could count on another crystal swan.

No one was prepared for a visitor the following morning, when they heard a knock at the front door. Knocking was a rare occurrence, because their apartment occupied the entire fifth floor of the building, and a doorman, as well as a coded private elevator, denied strangers access to their door. Normally, the only sound they would hear was a key in the lock inserted by a family member.

"The door," Cecily called from her room. "Tiffany, will you answer it?"

"I'm late!" Tiffany called. "Abby, you answer it."

Something in the little girl didn't want to go to the door, but the next knock sounded urgent so she decided to do her sister's bidding. She pulled back the bolt and opened the door as far as the short chain-lock would allow. On the other side, filling the three-inch crack, stood a tall man in a blue uniform holding his hat in his hands. His shoes were black and shiny.

"Is your mother here, miss?" he asked. She knew he had bad news.

"Mommy, it's for you," Abigail called. "It's a policeman," she added, as she unhooked the lock's chain and tucked herself out of sight between the wall and the door.

Her mother appeared in the hallway clutching her satin robe close to her chest.

"Are you Cecily Lynde?" the man asked.

"I am. What's the matter, officer?"

"Maybe you should sit down," he suggested.

"What is it?"

She waved him in, but he stayed on the threshold, awkwardly twisting his cap.

"Are you the wife of Alexander Lynde?"

"I am. What is the matter?" she asked, impatiently.

"I am here to inform you that we have a gentleman at the city morgue who bears that name. He was examined by a coroner from New York Hospital at one this morning at The Plaza Hotel and then removed to the city morgue. They need an official identification. You, or a close relative are requested to come to the morgue."

"My God!"

"I'm sorry, Ma'am," the policeman said, holding his hat like a Frisbee.

"But, it can't be. My husband is out of town," Cecily argued.

"This report says: *An unknown party at The Park Plaza informed the service desk at 12:10 a.m. that a man was gravely ill in room 304 and asked that someone call an ambulance immediately. The manager, William Quigley, went to the aforesaid room and found an unconscious man with a receiver in hand lying on the bed. His identification read Alexander Lynde. Police were called immediately to the scene. Upon arrival, ambulance drivers found he had expired and called for the coroner from New York Hospital. At 1:00 a.m. on April 20th 1973, his remains were taken to Mid-Town City Morgue for further examination.* The identification and hotel registration referred us to this address and that's all I know."

"He was gone when they found him?" Cecily asked.

"Yes, Ma'am. It may help you to know it must have been fast. It says in this here report that the telephone receiver was dangling in his hand."

Abigail remembered the time that she had been knocked out cold and woke up in a hospital. She was afraid for her father. Afraid he would have to stay away as long as she had.

The policeman tried to hand Cecily the report, but she pushed it away.

"It's not possible," she said.

"Appears to be natural causes, Ma'am. I'm sorry, Ma'am."

Abigail stood, balanced on her toes, quiet and stiff as a board. She wished she could disappear, and the policeman with her.

"What's a morgue?" she wanted to ask.

"Do you have any relatives nearby who could help you with the identification?"

"I don't . . . I don't know . . . I can't think. Where must we go?"

"Downtown, at 33rd and 2nd."

It couldn't be too bad, the child thought, they wouldn't let her mother go alone if it was.

"I . . . we . . . what happened?"

"I don't have a medical report, Ma'am. You will get one at the morgue. I believe the coroner wants permission to perform an autopsy."

Just then, Tiffany emerged from her room looking like she was made up for a prom. "What is it? Mother?"

"It's your father. I have to go to the morgue. It seems they have someone there named Alexander Lynde."

Tiffany's mouth fell open. She covered it with one hand and grabbed her stomach with the other.

Abigail held onto the doorknob. It felt shiny and smooth, the oak door smelled like lemon oil. The black shoes of the policeman still glistened on the sill.

"I think you better call someone in the family, Miss," the policeman told Tiffany, as if she were a grown-up. Then he tucked his hat in his armpit and took out a pad and pencil and scratched the address of the morgue on a little piece of paper, the way you might write a friend's telephone number, and handed it to her. He turned and left, closing the door behind him.

The three left behind stood frozen in place

"What's a morgue?" Abigail finally asked.

Tiffany said, "Shut up."

The little girl started to cry and Tiffany yanked her out of the hallway. "Now you stop. Just stop right now. That crybaby stuff will only upset mom. We don't need any more upset around here. We don't know who this man is. It's a big city; there are probably ten Alexander Lyndes."

"No there aren't!" Abigail cried. "There's only one. I looked us up in the dictionary."

"The phone book, stupid. Go get dressed." Tiffany turned to her mother and put her hands on her mother's arms.

"Mom, what should we do?" she asked.

"Call Uncle Lyman," Cecily said. "Give him the address of the morgue and tell him I will meet him there."

"I want to go, too!" Abigail cried.

"Go on, Abby, get dressed. You have to go to school. I have to call Uncle Lyman." Tiffany ordered.

"But, I don't want to go to school," she cried. "I want to stay here until Mommy brings Daddy home."

"Go to school," Cecily commanded. She wasn't crying. She was standing extremely still, like a clock that had stopped ticking.

Tiffany went into the room and watched as her sister buckled her shoes. "Don't say anything and don't cry in front of mom. Think about her, you hear?"

"But when is Daddy coming home?"

"I don't know. Go to school."

Abigail put on her Norwegian sweater and ski cap and wondered why she was going anywhere. She walked down streets under little city trees that wore a hint of chartreuse at the ends of their red twigs, bravely announcing spring would come. At Sterling Place, she saw her classmate, Emily, and matched her friend's wave with one of her own. When they reached each another she smiled, just as she had been taught.

Emily challenged her to run, "Race you to the corner!" she cried.

Not wanting to disappoint, Abigail nodded. But something big and mysterious held down her feet and she found she couldn't run at all.

"Abby," Emily called as she circled back. "What's the matter?"

She couldn't explain. She dared not admit her darkest thoughts, that the world had gone topsy-turvy and there would be no more stars at night, no sun in the morning. But she knew it was wrong to act upset, knew it would be stupid to be sad or afraid when the man at the morgue might not be her father after all—that a morgue might be a garage or a hospital. So, as lightly as she could, she told Emily that her father had gone away and she didn't know where he'd gone or when he would be back.

"Huh?" was all the little girl could reply.

"He's locked in a hospital or something like that."

Emily skewed her mouth and shrugged her shoulders in a lack of understanding before she skipped away.

When Abigail arrived in her classroom, she asked Mrs. Barnes if she could go to the library because there was something important she had to look up.

"What is it, pet?" Mrs. Barnes asked with a patronizing smile.

"I need to look up the meaning of morgue."

"Why is that, Abigail?"

"Can't tell," was all she said.

"All right then. Take a pencil and paper with you and write it down."

In the library, her favorite room in the school, she went to the reference section. Opening the huge dictionary on the old oak stand, the one with the little box in front of it for short people, she put her finger in the "M" section and found the word with little trouble.

Morgue

'morg

noun

French

1821

1. A place where the bodies of persons found dead are kept until identified by relatives or are released for burial.

The weeks that followed hung like thick winter fog. Voices faded in and out, and time barely moved. Nights were the worst. Even though Uncle Lyman came and stayed, he paid the girls little attention because their mother was hurting so much. She obviously needed her brother more than anyone else.

In Abigail's room, surrounded by her father's gifts—the heart-shaped red satin purse, a herd of swans, her earliest pop-up books and myriad teddy bears—she prayed for a miracle. She waited and waited for her father to call and explain the mistake. To say the man who died was not Alexander Lynde after all. But the truth lay on her heart and made her eyes water, and fear grew into a heavy lump, growing greater and greater each day.

The funeral was held at the Old Dutch Reformed Church on 7th Avenue where the girls had gone to Sunday School, and where their father used to give talks now and then about making the world a better place.

The big gray church did not look friendly to Abigail on that gloomy Saturday. She was separated from her family at the door and handed off to Mr. Vanderpool, a church elder who had a hearing aid in his pocket that beeped. They sat in the back of the sanctuary, where Abigail stared at her family from afar.

Tiffany sat down in the first row with her mother and looked very serious and shy. They were right in front of the casket and both kept their heads bowed. More and more people arrived and spoke in whispers. Abigail had to strain to hear what those closest to her were saying because she wanted to understand. Why? Why had this happened and what would happen next? She wanted her father back more than she ever wanted anything or anyone in the world. If she could have screamed at God, she would have.

Two folk singers led the congregation in singing "We Shall Overcome," and the visiting minister, Reverend William Sloane Coffin, said a few words. People were crying openly and blowing their noses, but Abigail didn't. After the eulogies and prayers, a parade of mourners formed a long black line to walk down to the altar to look at the yellowy waxen figure laid out on purple velvet. Abigail studied the church's old mural of *The Empty Tomb*. She was more curious about its meaning now. She wanted answers to where a person goes after death.

At the very end of the viewing procession, Cecily and Tiffany, Grandma Lynde and Uncle Lyman got up to look in the coffin one more time. Tiffany kept her eyes down. Abigail knew she wouldn't have looked, either. Then, two men began to close the casket and, in a burst of emotion, Cecily stopped them by throwing herself across the dead man crying, "No! No! Alex, Alex! Don't leave. Don't leave us."

Abigail sank into the pew and buried her face in Mr. Vanderpool's sleeve. She was so embarrassed, so afraid. It was terrible to see her mother behave like that and even worse to know, once and for all, that the man locked in the fancy box under the American flag really was her father.

Uncle Lyman and three other men helped Cecily back to her seat. Tiffany was hiding her face. The men turned and closed the lid of the casket, put a big spray of red white and blue flowers on top and then rolled it from the front of the sanctuary to the back. Up the wine colored carpet it went, past the pews with their little bronze plaques commemorating all the other dead people who had been rolled out of that place, past old friends and new, and a little girl who had never had a chance to say goodbye. Family followed family in silence and they all went out the door toward the stretch limousines waiting at the curb.

Abigail remained pressed into Mr. Vanderpool's side until she overheard a lady in a brown coat ask him, "How could he have done it?"

"Do what, Mrs. Robley?" he asked distractedly.

"I understand it was . . ." she said in a whisper that made the little girl listen.

"Who in the world . . .? It was nothing of the sort, probably just one martini too many."

"But why didn't he call for help? Why no call? I mean in this day and age..." the woman insisted.

Abigail's ears grew red from trying to hear. She stepped a little closer.

"It appears he tried to call. They said the phone was dangling in his hand," he whispered. "It must have happened very fast."

He looked down at Abigail as if he'd just remembered she was there and gently led her away from the woman. "Such nonsense," he grumbled to himself.

They stood on the cold street where a group of people were deciding who was to ride in the limos, who would follow and in what order. Abigail realized she was not going to the cemetery, as no one seemed to notice she was there, except for Mr. Vanderpool. He kindly introduced her to his sister, an old woman who accompanied him to church now and then.

"Abigail, I am lucky enough to have you come to visit me this afternoon. Would you like that?" she asked.

"I think I should be with my family," Abigail answered, hoping the woman would understand.

"Well, children aren't allowed in the cemetery. So, while they are going up to the cemetery, you and I are going home to my house for some nice warm cocoa and homemade brownies. Won't that taste good on such a cold, sad day?"

The child knew where they were taking her father, and suspected the rules excluding children were made by the family, not the grave keepers; at least, no one had seemed to care when they walked around the cemetery only weeks before. She knew her father would be laid next to his father, Oscar, near Mr. Ebbets who was lying on the same historic ridge.

Beneath the soaring steeple and tall stone walls of the church, Abigail was lost in the confusion of black and gray that covered the sidewalks, the black umbrellas, overcoats and galoshes crowding the wet macadam. She felt more alone than she had ever felt before, in the rain, near the curb, along with winter's refuse caught in its crude seams.

No one in the family said a word to her. When the cars took off, Mr. Vanderpool's sister took her home to a strange house to stay overnight. She ended up spending three nights at the lady's house, sleeping in a four-poster bed with a canopy overhead, surrounded by walls covered with yellow roses. It may have been the prettiest room she had ever seen, but these were the longest nights of her short life.

Miss Vanderpool would sit on the bed and pat her hand, trying to be nice. Abigail wanted to help, so she pretended to enjoy the Pooh stories meant for two-year-olds, and tried to forget the worst prayer ever invented that was recited each night—"Now I lay me down to sleep I pray the Lord my soul to keep. If I should die before I wake, I pray the Lord my soul to take."

Despite all that ensued during the weeks after her father's death— the tears, the cards, the burial, the strangers caring for her, the child couldn't get the picture of the dangling receiver out of her head. Who was her father trying to call? Why did he drink one martini too many? Was his death the toll her mother had talked about? She couldn't ask, of course. Her mother wouldn't speak, couldn't speak, and if it weren't for Uncle Lyman the family may not have eaten either.

Abigail went from sad to mad. Mad that her father hadn't come back; mad at him for dying; mad that she couldn't be his special girl any longer; mad because he was careless with his life and hers; mad that God would take a person's father away.

Cecily was just as angry. She vowed never to go in a church again or trust another man. The girls soon learned not to talk about their father or anything that happened before he died. Bit by bit they saw his books and papers loaded onto the dumbwaiter, his clothes sent to the Salvation Army and his pictures buried in places unknown. They were condemned to live in a house filled with memories that weren't allowed to be spoken.

Abigail had a dream in which her father reminded her she could erase bad thoughts. So she began erasing him, just as her mother seemed to be doing. He usually appeared to her at night and tended to hover, until she developed a technique that pushed him away. This was done by literally turning her back on him and counting backwards. Another trick she invented was to design coloring book pages. First, she would draw the imaginary lines in her head and then fill them in with the colors of the rainbow. But, even with these devices at her disposal, it took about four years before her father's face, his crinkling blue eyes and easy laughter became fuzzy, at least blurred enough not to hurt.

Abigail thought she may have shared something special with the woman who opened her purse, dabbed her eyes and backed away. Had the painting also spoken to that Barney man with his arms folded and jaw set, standing very still, his gaze steady and inscrutable?

Of herself she asked, Can I make the demise of my marriage as clear as *The Aftermath*? Can I erase Hank? Divorce is so inconclusive compared to death. Better to be the widow, to see a casket slowly lowered into the dark earth, buried, forever. Kaput. Final. Fini. Done. I'd like bowers of flowers, notes of condolence, shoulders to cry on. She felt tears welling up and told herself, not to cry, not here, not now, how absurd!

6

The Promenade

"So much vitality here," Fred Barber said thoughtfully, as much to himself as to Kendra. "She's placed an equal amount of importance in the foreground as the background. The diffusion of color is reminiscent of Manet, don't you think?"

"It's her tribute to Brooklyn," Kendra answered, privately amazed at his reference to Manet.

"Have you a slide of *The Promenade*? Maybe we can find a place for it in *The New Yorker*."

"Is tomorrow too soon?"

"I imagine I can wait until then. It's a cityscape that has the spirit of a woman who knows and loves the city."

Kendra waved Abigail over to join the conversation. "Fred says you paint like a woman who loves the city. Is that true?"

Abigail gave him the easy answer, "I do."

She asked herself, is it true? Do I love the city? I loved Brooklyn, but Brooklyn isn't quite the city. It's more of a hometown, with its old churches, ghettos, row houses, friendly grocers and quirky compassion. Brooklyn promises a certain familiarity; even with its rough edges, it's forgiving; the people easy going. The pulse and competition of Manhattan is far beyond its neighboring boroughs.

She had to admit that now she questioned leaving Brooklyn's messiness to raise her babies elsewhere. Was it frustration and small mindedness that made her think her children needed well-groomed streets more than diversity? She wanted them to grow up away from the masses yearning to breathe free, away from the pitfalls of Brooklyn's crowded, testy sidewalks. She wasn't the only one. Almost everyone she had ever known had run off to the suburbs, or headed west.

Montmarte had been her choice for the very reasons she came to dislike the place. It was mired in a composed and proposed predictability. Although once a working port on the Hudson, it had morphed into preciousness. The clumsy barges that originally gave the town its life were replaced with sleek water toys honoring money rather than function. Boutiques and restaurants lined the river's pricey shore.

Abigail had observed her neighbor Trish Mulhane for the past six years. The two women were the same age, at least in the same generation, but that was where their similarity ended. Trish Mulhane took pride in the small things. Her garbage pails were always neatly arranged on a palette at the curb, the lids on straight and the garbage completely contained. Her wooden mailbox was decorated with pastel flowers and at its feet was a little metal heart stuck in the ground that read, The Mulhanes. In her windows, the blinds were opened at identical angles each morning, letting in identical stripes of light. The three conical bushes that stood along her driveway seemed to grow at exactly the same speed and remain perfectly symmetrical. The wood chips beneath them were freshened regularly, lest a weed below found air.

Trish's smiling face and a tray of butter cookies appeared at the door one morning shortly after the MacKenzies moved into the neighborhood. It was through her that Abigail learned dandelions were considered viral, and the color of house paint had to be ordained by committee. She also informed Abigail of at least one tidbit about every family on the street. Each of her little sketches closed with, "...but they are very nice people."

On her second visit, Trish let it be known that the former owners of the MacKenzies' house had failed to weed the dandelions. She offered, in a most gracious attitude of neighborly caring, to help Abigail clear them out whenever the time was right. "Oh, and don't forget about the paint committee!" she warned, sure they would freshen their little house soon.

They never did weed together. And when the MacKenzies painted their house they chose white rather than ask anyone for permission.

The Promenade, the neighborhood boulevard of her youth, had come to conjure up the time of her life when abundance was the norm. Not only had it provided a wide open lens of the city for everyone who walked its walk, it was her first bike path, first scooter route, the place where she learned to skateboard.

How she loved speed! Whatever the vehicle, she would race back and forth over the pavement, assailing the peace of sparrows and pigeons and the ever present benchsitters—the old folks who baked themselves in collars of aluminum foil to preserve their summer tans.

Her neighbors used the esplanade regularly, too, some to walk their purebred dogs or parade their expensive baby carriages; others to feed the squirrels and gulls, or to gossip. She became familiar with many of these characters. How could she ever forget Mrs. Friedman whose favorite expression was, "It could be worse."

"It's a nice day, isn't it, Mrs. Friedman?"

"It could be woyse."

"How are you feeling, Mrs. Friedman?"

"It could be woyse."

"Your dress is very pretty, Mrs. Friedman."

"It could be woyse."

Oh, and the button man! He wore sandwich boards over his shoulders displaying his wares front and back. His antique buttons were filled with messages like, Eat my Shorts, Truman does Bess, Smile–you loser, Mom upside-down is Wow, Ima Ova Acheeva, Take a Hike Ike. He was Dr. Lister to some, Les to others. Abigail didn't speak to him because he had dirty teeth where there were any teeth at all, and his eyes had big rings around them like a man who didn't sleep.

But, one day, he helped her up when she tripped on a crack in the pavement. Her wheels were still whirring in space when she felt his big bony hands lift her from a crumpled heap on the ground and place her on a bench. Some of his buttons spilled from his display as he put it aside, but he paid no attention. He shook his head sadly at the bloody mess of the child's scraped knees. "You let Papa fix this." He reached for a rag in his back pocket.

Abigail did not think she wanted the man to touch her, but she didn't know what else to do. He held her leg and dabbed at the wounds. "You are a brave goil, a very brave little goil." Big tears were coming down his cheeks, and as he wiped them away with his sleeve, she saw what looked like numbers tattooed on his wrist. She was wondering what they meant when her mother called. "Abigail, you come here. Come on. We have to go home. Now."

"Not to worry, Mrs.," he called, "I'm a doctor. Dr. Lister. I will take care of her." His eyes kept watering.

"Don't cry, Dr. Lister," Abigail said. "I'll be all right."

Then he took back the bloodied rag and wiped his nose with it. "You go along now, Sarah," he said.

"My name is Abigail," she said.

Cecily was upon them, snatching her daughter's gravel-stung hand and ignoring the man who had touched her child without permission. She saw only the ghost of the man.

As soon as they were out of hearing distance, Cecily said, "You must be very careful of strangers, Abby. There are sick people in the world. That man is a strange one. You must have noticed that much."

"But people call him doctor, Dr. Lister. He was nice to me. He cried when he saw my knee."

"Nevermind. He's peculiar."

But she did mind. And the next day she said, "Hello, Dr. Lister," just to prove she could think for herself. He nodded distractedly, but she suspected he had already forgotten her.

It was months after Alex Lynde's death before Cecily began to talk again, to cry or smile, and all three happened at once. It happened the day Monsieur Arsignol came to visit.

When he arrived, Abigail was sent outside to play in the first snow. She stomped her red galoshes through the sidewalk slush and managed to find two other girls to play with. They made snow angels and started to build a snow fort, but the girls grew cold and cranky and started arguing with each other. Abigail realized she was cold and uncomfortable, too. So, they split up, and Abigail went back in the building and rode the elevator up to the fifth floor. In the foyer of the apartment, she sat down on the hard marble floor to remove her wet boots. Laughter and talk were audible from the living room. One of the voices was her mother's.

Sitting in a puddle of melted snow, she listened to the lilt of her mother's voice and realized how much she had missed it. She couldn't wait to be inside, to see her face, alive again, but when she tried to open the door it was fastened hard. A few raps and the talking stopped.

"Who is it?" Cecily called from the other side.

"It's me, Abigail."

"You are not to come in just yet, Abigail. Now you go back outside and build yourself a snowman."

"But I don't want to build a snowman. My mittens are wet and I'm cold," she sniffed, the mucous from her nose mixing with the ice on her mitten.

"Make a snowgirl then. You have dry mittens in the drawer. Now go on!" There was happiness in her voice, an energy that Abigail had thought might never come back.

It was so good to hear her mother sound like herself again, Abigail decided to do what she was told, even if she wasn't allowed inside. She was only eight, but she understood more than most people realized.

A snowgirl took a very long time. It was tricky to roll up the balls for the bottom part but fun to pack the soft snow, especially when Paul the Pigeon Man forgot selling his peanuts long enough to help her. He found sticks for the mouth and arms, and then a triple peanut for her nose. Together, at the curb, they dug until they found two black rocks for eyes. Paul the Pigeon Man watched and nodded his approval as she put on the final touches, some dead leaves for hair, a newspaper cape.

"She's very pretty," the old man said. "What's her name?

"The Snow Queen," Abigail said, proudly.

Dr. Lister came along, and said, "Good afternoon, Miss. What's this? A snow girl?"

"No, Dr. Lister, this is the snow queen," she said proudly.

"Would you like a button for the queen?" he asked. He showed her one that read, Queen's Have More Fun!

"Oh! Thank you!" she exclaimed. "I'm Abigail, do you remember me?"

"Lester," the man said as he shuffled down the street. "I'm Lester."

She turned to the pigeon man, "His name is Dr. Lister, not Lester."

"Lester, Lister?" the pigeon man said. "Lister Lester, Lester Lister, no matter how you say it, it's one of dem names doen' woik."

A thought struck, and Abigail went home a second time. This time she got out of the elevator very quietly so as not to be heard. In the vestibule, she headed for the Chinese chest placed beneath the gilded mirror half again as tall as she. Each drawer in the chest held scarves and gloves. The top drawer had been her father's. She could almost feel him smiling down on her as she eased it open and took out his thickest pair of leather gloves, the ones with the rabbit fur lining. She also found a soft blue-and-black wool scarf.

The elevator was still open and she got back in and returned to the lobby. Alfred the doorman smiled at her. "Lots of coming and going today, Abigail."

"Yes, sir," she said, hugging the gloves and scarf close to her chest.

She ran and ran through the sloppy snow until she found Dr. Lister. He was sitting huddled next to a heat vent on some stairs that led to a basement entry. She handed him her father's things.

"Sarah?" he asked. "Is that you Sarah?"

"These are to keep you warm," she said, thinking it made no difference if he remembered her name.

Only two months later, in late February, Dr. Lister was found dead. He was frozen in a seated position on the stairs of an old brownstone on Henry Street. Cecily read the brief obituary in *The Times* at the table. "Listen to this." She read, "*Lester Listerwitz, Auschwitz survivor, and respected German surgeon, was found dead on a stairwell in an affluent Brooklyn neighborhood on February 11th. Dr. Listerwitz was noted for research leading to the control of epileptic brain seizures. An autopsy reveals malnutrition as cause of death.*

"Can you imagine such a thing happening here on our very own streets? It's appalling," she said.

"I think that was Dr. Lister," Abigail said. "The man who fixed my knee."

Cecily turned to her now frequent visitor, Monsieur Arsignol. "Why, I think I knew the man. How tragic! Imagine that, he starved to death! Ironic, isn't it? To think he survived the holocaust and died, here, in the land of plenty. You would have thought there was some organization, something or someone to save him."

Fred Barber asked, "In what part of New York were you brought up, Abigail?"

"Brooklyn," she answered.

"Your painting is full of smiles. I can see you were a happy child. City children were exotic to those of us growing up on a farm outside Polaris, Ohio. I, for one, felt sorry for the likes of you. Of course, I see things very differently, now."

"I'd never have believed you were a farm boy," she said.

"A miserable anomaly, my dear. Too queer for the farm."

She doesn't tell him she considers it remarkable that anyone outside the inner circle of New York could end up as the art critic for *The New Yorker.*

Then she looked for the smiles he saw in her painting. Perhaps they were the same smiles she was taught to show the world.

The Barney person was watching her. She knew he couldn't begin to know her thoughts, but she thought he was still trying. Involuntarily, she shook her head no to a question he hadn't asked.

7

The Man and His Little Women

"*The Man and His Little Women*. It has to be a family portrait," the lady in red postulated to Barney. Her skin-tight faux leather pants and blousy poppy patterned silk shirt competed with the room, but it wasn't just her outfit that grabbed Abigail's attention or her animated intercourse with Barney. What stung was that the interpretation of *The Man and His Little Women* was so utterly wrong.

Family Feud would have been a more appropriate title. Why in the world did I give this piece that name? We were not M. Arsignol's little women, no matter what he may have thought. He belonged strictly to Cecily, and even that was questionable, Abigail thought.

After school on Thursday afternoons, Abigail used to carry her pink plastic Barbie satchel to a ballet class one block from the Promenade. She had little doubt that her toes were meant for the stage, but loved just as much the independence she felt as she said goodbye to Albert the Doorman and headed down the street.

Occasionally, she ran into M. Arsignol arriving for a visit. When he first began to stop by, he would arrive like Santa, arms filled with gifts: flowers, cheeses and dark chocolates. Soon he started coming later in the evenings and only brought wine. If he was very late (as he often was) Abigail would go to bed, leaving her mother tapping her feet and her cigarette in a nervous rhythm. She knew his visits were important to her mother. It was pretty evident a romance was in the works.

Tiffany saw it too. She and Cecily had it out one night with words like, "Daddy's fingerprints are still all over the house. He hasn't even been gone a year! How can you be so mean to Daddy? How can you just forget him like that? I don't want Monsieur Arsignol for a father!"

"Well, that hardly seems to be something to worry your pretty head about Miss Teenage Queen. I think what I do or don't do should be of little or no concern to you," Cecily retaliated hotly.

"Why shouldn't it be of concern for me? My life is ruined and nobody cares. Nobody!" Tiffany screamed. "I can't do anything anymore. I can't go anywhere!"

"You might try to find a job. How about asking around and baby sitting evenings? Maybe you can get a stock girl's job at May's. They hire fifteen–year-olds."

"See? You don't care! You don't even hear what I feel. What do you want? Do you want me out of here? Am I supposed to go find myself an apartment?"

"I never said such a thing."

"No. But I bet you wish I would, so you could have Mr. Asshole around!"

"Arsignol. For heaven's sake Tiffany, I want to live. Please, grant me that, will you?"

"And I want to live too! You've taken away the things I loved most."

"I didn't take anything away from you. Your father is dead. He left us in terrible debt. There's no money. I am having trouble making ends meet. It's as simple as that."

"It's not simple. Why does Daddy dying have to be the end of everything," Tiffany cried. "I notice you still manage to have your hair frosted and you have enough money for fancy pedicures and new dresses. What about me?"

"If you want something enough you will find a way to get it. Your father left us nothing. Only an endless stream of bills."

Tiffany's hands flew into the air. "Sure. Blame Daddy. He's not even here to defend himself!"

"Oh, you are a wicked, wicked girl," Cecily said, before they both ran to separate rooms the way that widows and angry teenagers do.

In the months ahead, Cecily canceled Tiffany's horseback riding lessons at the Kensington Stables and her singing lessons with Herr Bruner. Out went Abigail's Jazz Ballet dance class which her mother called "superfluous". The florist's weekly deliveries stopped and so were Cecily's regular appointments at the St. George Spa. Soon, the new BMW was sold, and they were traveling by bus and subway.

Louie called one afternoon and asked Tiffany if Cecily was at home.

"She's grocery shopping. But she should be back soon," Tiffany said, looking at Abigail, rolling her eyes and sticking her index finger in her open mouth to show her disgust.

"Ah, I see. I must see her. Would it be all right if I came by in an hour, chéri?"

"I think so," Tiffany said, nonchalantly.

An hour went by and no mother appeared, but Louie did.

Tiffany went to the door to greet him.

"Bon soir, Mademoiselle," he bowed. "You are looking very beautiful tonight, chéri."

"Thanks," Tiffany said, taking the bottle of wine from his hand and bringing it into the kitchen to rest on the counter. "My mother's not here yet, Mr. Arsignol."

"You may call me Louie. What age are you now?"

"I'm sixteen," she fibbed.

"Ah, sixteen. In France that is when a girl becomes a woman." He looked around the kitchen as if in search of something. "Do you have an opennaire, Tiffany?"

Tiffany retrieved the silver plated corkscrew from the utensil drawer. "I can do it," she bragged.

With more difficulty than she would have preferred, the corkscrew finally penetrated the cork, but try as she did, she couldn't pull it out.

"With vintage wine, the cork is quite tight. Voici, let me do it, s'il vous plait," Louie said. It popped out easily and he passed the wine under his nose, then Tiffany's. "The aroma it eez quite nice, don't you think?

Tiffany said, "Very nice."

"We must let it breathe awhile, then we shall decide if it tastes az good az it promises."

She went to the china cabinet and took out two crystal wineglasses.

"The aroma is a very enticing quality. It is why a French woman spends so much on her perfume. Do you want to be remembered as a lovely rose, a wild flower or a cucumber, chèri?"

"I'd like to be remembered for my own smell. Not sweat, I mean, but, like, natural, you know."

"Ah, I see. You are très charmant, a very lovely young woman, Tiffany. Have you yet a boy friend?"

"No. I like someone, but I haven't gone out with him yet." She crossed her arms, leaned her back into the counter and looked out the window as if hoping her mother might skydive to the windowsill.

Monsieur Arsignol, put his hand on her shoulder and gently pulled her around, then towards him.

"You are an ingenue? An innocent. No?"

"I guess," Tiffany said, hating herself for blushing. She let her thick brown hair fall over her face.

"This is zee best time of all! When the illusions are still in place!" He smiled and put his middle finger under her chin. Forcing her to look into his eyes. She found them smiling at her.

"You have so much to look forward to," he said. "You must find a man to teach you."

He carefully poured a small amount of wine into a glass and handed it to her. "Now, chèri, you tell me if this is worth the exorbitant prize I paid for it."

Tiffany sipped the wine.

"It's delicious," she said.

"Ah, then you must have some more." He filled her glass and one for himself. "Quite nice," he observed. "Wine is the elixir of the gods." He drank quietly and watched her try to keep up.

"Here, let me wipe that drop from your lips," he said, moving close to her with his handkerchief in hand. Then, as if it was perfectly normal, he put his lips on hers.

Tiffany jerked away and clumsily backed out of the room. "My mother will be home any minute. I have to do my homework," she said.

Abigail heard her calling her friend Madeline on the phone. "... and then he stuck his tongue in my mouth, wriggling it all the way down my throat. It was gross!" There was a pause and then her sister said, "They do? Everybody?"

Late that night, Cecily was up and down, up and down. Abigail listened as doors opened and shut and the telephone wires crackled. Her mother was obviously having a terrible time sleeping. She knew what that was like. For two months after her father died, she had trouble closing her eyes at night. Then, after she got the flu and a fever, she slept for weeks on end tortured by monsters spiraling out of collapsing clouds and crowding her brain with ghoulish faces. One night she lay still and faced them. Strangely enough, they stared back and then melted into puddles of orange and red. Surviving that illness and facing the night visitors had helped her be less afraid, at least for awhile.

Abigail was worried about her mother. Maybe she, too, was afraid to sleep or having nightmares of her own. Maybe she wasn't able to look at her monsters. A chair scraped in the kitchen, and Abigail threw back her comforter to go and see if Cecily needed company. From the hallway she saw only her hand, a cigarette between two shaky fingers, resting on an ashtray, a thin trail of smoke curling above. It was quiet and eerie, the way the hand appeared detached from its source. The kitchen light haloed the edges of things like the grandfather clock, great grandfather Lynde's portrait, and the pewter pitchers on the breakfront. Abigail hid until it came to her that if she was up at night and all alone, she would want someone to give her a hug. So, she went to her mother's side.

"Abby? What in the world are you doing up at this hour?" her mother asked.

"I'm thirsty. I want a drink of water."

"Well, you can have some water and then you march yourself right up those stairs and go to sleep."

Her mother's eyes were swollen and her nose red.

Abigail went to her instead of the sink. "I love you, Mommy. It's going to be all right," She put her arms around her mother's long slim neck.

"I know, I know, and you love ice cream, too," Cecily said, without returning the hug.

Stung by her words, the child decided her mother didn't care very much about what she had to say and knew she was not going to be her source of comfort.

"Now, you go on," her mother said. "No more excuses."

By the end of the year, M. Arsignol was coming to visit twice a week. One Sunday he and Cecily were having an argument about where the family should live. They were sitting on the green silk damask sofa in front of the window that framed the city. Paperwork was spread on the glass coffee table next to their wine glasses. According to Louie, it was apparent that the condominium overlooking the harbor was too expensive for Cecily to maintain. Monsieur Arsignol suggested the family move to Avignon, assuring the girls and their mother that they would love southern France and grow brown as berries in its soft sunlight.

Cecily asked, "Why Avignon? Why not Paris?"

"Because, my love, I must not let one family intrude on another. You do understand? We must be discreet. I will see to it that you are comfortable."

He turned to Abigail. "Come here, little duck. Wouldn't you love to live in a beautiful old city near the sea?"

"But I already do!" she said.

"Ah, but in the south of France, it is warm all year round, and you shall learn the language and become very chic. Here, come here, sit on Louie's lap."

Docilely, she sat on her mother's friend's lap.

"This little ducky is about to become a swan," he said to Cecily. At the same time his hand reached under Abigail's skirt and wrapped itself around her upper thigh. His thumb moved back and forth on her most private place.

Abigail wondered at the tickle and thought it was wrong for

him to touch her, and yet her mother was standing right there, not concerned or saying anything. A mound rose beneath her bottom, hard and hot. She suspected what it was and began to lift herself off and away, but he pulled her back and held her more tightly.

"Swan?" Cecily asked, "as in an Anderson tale?"

"Swan as in long-necked, long-legged and beautiful. She will be very dangerous."

Abigail was insulted that he would say such a thing about her and mortified by his touch. She wrestled her way off Louie's lap and left the room.

"She's hardly begun," she heard her mother say. "Still a baby, thank God. Right now, it's the other one I am worried about. She's very different from Abigail. Of course, she should be. They're from different gene pools."

"Non? N'est pas."

"Oui. Long ago and insignificant at this point."

"Perhaps a new place, a new beginning would be good for them both."

The next morning Cecily tried to broach the idea with the girls.

Tiffany erupted. "He's a creep, Mom, a lecher, a pig! How can you go out with him?" she screamed.

"You stop that, right now. He's simply a Frenchman. All Frenchmen have mistresses. Just because we're Americans doesn't mean it wouldn't work for me. My values can tolerate the idea of his maintaining two households. The way he thinks doesn't make him a bad person."

"Mom, he kissed me! He stuck his fat tongue in my mouth. Is that bad enough for you?"

"Oh, such nonsense. Really, Tiffany, you don't have to lie in order to keep us here. I have no intention of going to France. It's just fun to play with such an idea. There's no money left and I am not sure which way to turn."

"Mom! How can you say that? You think I would make up a story about Louie just to change your mind? Mom, he's a dirty old man!"

"Well, I probably won't be seeing him anymore. Does that make you feel any better?"

"What would make me feel better is a mother who believed what I said. A mother who cared more about me than herself!" Tiffany cried.

As Abigail listened she decided not to tell her mother how M. Arsignol touched her between the legs. She didn't want to make her any angrier than she already was.

She wanted to tell Tiffany that she understood, and that Mr. Arsignol had acted like a dirty old man with her, too. But Tiffany's door was locked, and Abigail's knock was answered with, "Go away!"

The Man and his Little Women? What made me paint such a thing? The very thought of that man makes my skin crawl. My first abuser. I have tucked that memory away all these years. What did mother really think of him? Was she thinking at all? Did she really want to settle for Mr. Arsignol? She seemed only to see what she wanted to see. Did Tiffany and I make any difference at all?

Am I just like my mother, caught in my own blind struggle? I haven't got a clue about the children. My God, I was Stephanie's age when I sat on Mr. Arsignol's lap, and I remember every detail, including the secret shame and the fear of talking to anyone about it. Stephanie must be recording each step of her life right now, interpreting everything being said and not being said about her father's leaving. What have I offered her? What have I offered Joshua?

A few weeks earlier, Joshua had come home from school sniveling. After slamming the front door, he proceeded to throw his bookbag on the floor and run upstairs.

"Hold on, young man. That wasn't a very nice way to say hello," Abigail said.

"He's real mad," Stephanie explained. Tray Grossman told him Daddy went off with Mrs. Browne and took Max Browne with him. You know Max is on the Bullets. Their Little League team beat the Jets to the championship games last year. Joshie gave Max the finger when they won, and Max kicked him you know where. I guess Max hates him, too."

"What did you say?" Abigail's head swum in the onslaught of Stephanie's words.

"Max and Joshua, they hate each other."

"About Mrs. Browne?"

"I told him it wasn't true. Daddy was away on business. I told him he'll probably be home in a couple of days. That's right, isn't it Mom?"

"Not quite, Stephanie."

"What's not right?"

How could she say it? What was not right? She couldn't think it out when she tried to explain it to herself. What if he came home? What if he realized his craziness and came back and asked to start over? It would be important for the children to go on with their lives believing in him, having trust.

"Well, your father's job has been transferred to Tucson, and he won't be home for, well, quite a long time."

"How long?"

"I'm not sure."

"Where's Tucson? Are we going, too?"

It was then she decided the truth had to be more direct than she had thought was wise. It was no longer best to let it out slowly, one step at a time. She silently cursed the Grossmans for having had nothing better to do than gossip in front of their kids. She would let Irva know the collateral damage of her loose talk as soon as she was up to it.

"Stephanie, I think we better have a family conference. What do you say?"

"I don't care," Stephanie said in a voice much smaller than her usual.

"I mean, you don't believe that Daddy loves Max Browne more than Joshua?" Abigail asked. "Your father loves you, even if he has to be away right now."

"I don't know. Carlene's mother went to San Francisco with Tommy's father and never came back."

"Well, bad things do happen. But look at Carlene. Her life is just fine, isn't it?"

"I don't know."

"There are plenty of people who grow up in one parent families. I did!"

"But it made you very sad, when your father died. You said so."

"Yes, yes it did. But that was because I never saw him again."

"I want Daddy to come home now."

"Of course you do. I think you should come upstairs with me

while I talk to Joshua."

Climbing the stairs, Abigail thought how she wasn't ready for the truth herself. Even as she remembered her father's words, secrets are like rocks under tide, and believed the unknown could be more dangerous than the known, she couldn't invoke words that would make things less hurtful. How could she protect a little boy who believed his father left him for another little boy? How could she soften this cruel blindness of Hank's? Help her son understand what she could not?

Daddy is away was simply not enough. Daddy is coming home was not true either. Daddy is in a mid-life crisis? That would mean nothing to his children. They saw their own lives in crisis every day. That very day, the principal, Mrs. De Marco had called Abigail to say Joshua was in her office because he had refused to eat the school lunch. She was admonished for not providing her son with lunch for three days in a row. They had offered him school lunches to compensate, but he refused to eat. Worse, when Mrs. De Marco approached him in the cafeteria to coax him to at least try the cafeteria's food, he wouldn't. "I can't eat this shit," he said, instead.

"He seems not to be himself, Mrs. MacKenzie," the principal said. "Is there something we should know?"

Abigail assumed the nosey, righteous woman had probably heard what the rest of the town did.

She chose not to give her any satisfaction.

"Joshua," she called to the closed door.

"I don't want to talk," Joshua answered in a muffled voice.

"Well, I do." she said. "We need to have a family conference, okay?"

She opened the door a crack. Joshua's face was buried in his pillow. She went over to the side of his bed and Stephanie followed.

"I am sorry I forgot your lunch today," she began, leaning over to stroke his hair. It was a tangled mess, filled with the bits of dead grass. His denim comforter had little clogs of mud from his sneakers. She swept them to the floor.

"I'll try harder to remember from now on," she promised.

"I hate school lunches," he growled. "I hate school."

"No, you don't," she said, relieved because anger was easier for her to handle than grief.

"I hate school food, it tastes like cardboard."

"Joshua! You should try to appreciate the food you get. There are plenty of children who have nothing to eat."

"I'd rather not eat."

"Nevertheless, Joshua..." Now, she was reprimanding, not what she wanted to do.

"Joshua? I heard Tray Grossman said something about your father and Mrs. Browne?"

"No, he didn't."

"About Max then?"

Silence. He opened his eyes and glared at Stephanie.

"I didn't tell her!" Stephanie blurted.

"Well, it doesn't matter who told me does it? What you need to know is that Daddy has to work in Tucson, Arizona, for a while and if he ran into Mrs. Browne out there, it is nothing for you to worry about."

"When is Daddy coming home?" he sniffed.

"When he can," she said. Her stomach rose like a fist in her throat, her ears felt hot. This should not be her job, she thought. Hank was responsible and he should be facing the kids.

"See? I told you so," Stephanie said.

"How about we all go to the supermarket and buy only the foods we love most? Come on Joshua, then you can be the happiest boy in the lunchroom."

He rose slowly, and Abigail walked him to the bathroom to wash his face and run a brush gently through his hair.

At the Grand Union, not only did she fill the grocery cart with candies and cakes, but curly plastic straws, dinosaur patterned plastic sandwich bags and a bright red lunchbox shaped like a tool kit. She swore with each step that she wouldn't miss his lunch again. Stephanie was given free reign to shop, too. She put six-packs of macaroni and cheese in the basket, twelve-packs of kiddy juices, snack-sized potato chips and family wraps of Ballpark frankfurters. All that leafy produce, yogurt and tofu Abigail had fed them from the time they started to eat was obviously for naught.

How many other efforts will I discover meant little or nothing? What should I do? Stephanie is pretending not to know her father has left, is counting on his coming back, and poor Joshua is hurting all over.

She retreated to Kendra's storeroom, and called the children to make sure all was well at home, wanting to tell them she loved them first, last and always. As usual her picture didn't match reality.

8

Maternal Instinct

"When are you coming home, Mommy?" Joshua whined. "I want to watch "The Dinosaur Caper," and Stephanie went and told Mrs. Greenwald that I have to watch "The Little Mermaid." I hate "The Little Mermaid.""

"Put Stephanie on the phone, Joshua, I will talk to her." Abigail knew she should be there to take care of things.

"Mommy, you said...." Stephanie began before her mother could speak.

Stephanie had a history of manipulating babysitters. "I said no such thing. Now here's the deal. You let Joshua watch his movie. It's short. Then you can watch yours. Fair enough?"

"No. Mine is halfway done."

"Give your brother a break, Stephanie. He'll love you for it."

"I don't care if he loves me, I hate him."

"Put Mrs. Greenwald on." She could visualize Marlene's square figure on the other end of the phone. She was as solid as she looked.

"Yes? Is everything all right?" she asked.

"It is, Marlene, but I would like you to referee this battle of who watches what. Would you interrupt "Little Mermaid" and play "The Dinosaur Caper"? Stephanie can be bullish sometimes. Take the popcorn from the cabinet over the stove. Stick it in the microwave, won't you, and make a party of the change of venue. That should help."

"I will. Have a good time and don't you worry, Abigail. Are there lots and lots of people there?"

"More than I ever anticipated."

"Well, good for you. Snow is coming down here. Not too bad, but steady. Be sure to call before you leave."

She felt better having heard the children's voices, even with their complaints. But she wished for a way to settle the tension that persisted between them. She didn't want them to go the way she and Tiffany had, ending up hurt and apart.

Kendra smoothly worked the crowd, extolling the paintings. Abigail overheard her using words like primal, divine, essence, comedic. It was almost embarrassing.

"A few strokes and she creates a busy highway or establishes the depth of a ravine. Notice the teetering shapes of the city. And the details, look at the details in the laundry room, how she pulls us in. These paintings are replete with metaphors—the essence of story. She designs space with a knowing that can't be taught," she said.

Mostly, I have tried to find a space of my own, Abigail thought. Being mother and father to my children is going to be the hardest challenge of my life. Since they were toddlers, I've wanted to run from their noisy rivalry and the drudgery of housework. The sounds of engines running—washers, dryers, even the telephone's ring grated on my nerves. But, I knew I was lucky to have the best of the modern conveniences, not to mention the whole package—a husband, children, a house in the country. How could I possibly have wanted more, something selfishly my own?

The six and a half rooms on Apple Blossom Lane were quite adequate at first. Abigail did her best—scrubbed the sinks each morning, polished the wood, puffed pillows here and there and asked the children, "How was school?" when they got home. Their answers were routine.

"Okay."

"Well, good. What did you learn today?"

"Nothing."

"Did you eat all of your sandwich, Joshua?"

"Yes. Can I go to Cara's house?"

"May I."

"May I?

"Where's my soccer ball?"

And so on. She had wanted these children and loved them for their very existence. They were pretty and smart. Joshua looked like Hank, had his wavy brown hair and straight full lips. Stephanie looked like her, long and skinny from birth, with curlier lips, but with the same pale straight lashes and relentlessly stubborn, strawberry blonde hair. It now bothered her that, beyond the children's comings and goings, their food, their clothes and homework, she felt she hardly knew them.

The distance was not new. It started shortly after Stephanie arrived, when they were living in a tiny apartment on Hicks Street in Brooklyn Heights. She was born perfect, with ten fingers and ten toes, a sturdy pair of lungs and a dusting of yellow hair on her very round, beautifully shaped head. All life became centered on that tiny package of humanity—a rosebud, with eyes the color of heaven. Each breath and wriggle, a frown, a twisted smile, a wet burp, all of it, was evidence of life's miracles. Abigail could not have anticipated that six weeks later, she wouldn't want to touch her baby or that she'd be mired in a sinkhole of despair.

Night after terrible night, she lay in bed anxiously listening to the baby's breathing patterns. In the mornings, she couldn't find the energy to rise and do the wash, wrestle with food or the house. Her breasts swelled, purple as the Grand Tetons, and leaked milk onto her clothes from dawn 'til dusk. Feeding the baby seemed to bring little relief; the poor little thing cried for more and more. She was obviously starving.

Abigail went to the pediatrician, but he didn't help. When she saw him write down *failure to thrive* on the baby's record, she lost it. Little Stephanie's weight had gone down after six weeks of painful nursing, and how could any mother see it as anything other than a sign of her inadequacy? She abruptly stopped breast feeding in favor of formula, wrapped her tender breasts in towels and waited for the worthless milk they produced to dry up.

Hank, who was bleary-eyed and nervous enough himself, was unaware. She dared not tell him that she was a hollow shell, bereft of the child that had abandoned her womb and unable to give nurture at her breast. She didn't know how to warn him their baby would soon be leaving the earth. He seemed not to notice the dark rings around her eyes. Actually, he seemed not to see her at all. It was all about survival for both of them.

Their bedroom was reduced to a nursery. The layette, the diapers, wipes, lotions, intercom, bouncing fish, leaping lizards, cushy blocks and colorful balls, stuffed mice and kittens, even a singing mobile. Eight pounds of frail humanity had taken over.

"I am thinking you should be on your feet by now," Hank complained when she asked him to warm a bottle one morning.

She snapped back. "Do you think I like being half dead? The next baby can be all yours. The next baby can tear at your breasts, stretch your body and turn you inside out. You can feed it all night and find out it is losing weight. You can sit in the doctor's office and blame yourself for not being a milking cow!"

The energy she spent spitting out these words left her limp. And she hadn't begun to say it all. She didn't tell him her own death was imminent, that she was sure the kink in her neck was cancer and the pulsating headaches a sign of a tumor between her eyes. He couldn't know her fears, that cars on the road looked like weapons of mass destruction, danger lurked on every corner, beaches were contaminated with plastics and hypodermic needles. She thought the next generation of children might be the last, lost to a pandemic or war or the earth's self-destruction. Tragedy loomed everywhere, not just in her baby's probable demise, but in mirrors, at the table, in the skies and on the highways.

"Abby, all I said was that I am worried that you aren't up and around yet. Look at Paula, next door. Paula was up the day after Melinda was born, and look at Jennifer with three kids hanging on her, carting around her baby like a sac of groceries. Is there something wrong, something I don't know about? I'm thinking maybe it's more than the baby, that's all."

She couldn't argue. He was only saying what she knew to be true. Something was horribly wrong with her. She wasn't fit to be a mother.

Cecily arrived the next afternoon, and Abigail declared exhaustion, but out of disgrace began to put things in order in the overlooked apartment.

"You know I hate this place," she said. It's too small and too noisy."

"You're looking pale," Cecily said, her eyes taking inventory of her daughter's face. "Are you going to talk about it?"

"It is too terrible."

"What is so terrible?"

"Stephanie is dying."

Cecily dropped the towel and the dish she was drying. "Dear God! What in the world is wrong?"

"She's failing to thrive. That's when babies die. It's because I don't know how to love her. Remember the babies in the London orphanage who died from lack of love? All the babies who weren't held and loved, died."

"But you hold her all the time!"

"But not the right way. She knows, Stephanie knows I am not a good mother. She doesn't want to be here. If I could send her back, I would. She cries for hours, throws up her milk and fights me when I hold her. She's losing weight instead of growing!"

"That's not a death sentence. You're giving her formula now, and it looks to me like she's happy enough. Many babies lose weight after they're born. As for the crying, babies cry to test their lungs, not because they are miserable. It's their first accomplishment. All babies cry; they like to hear themselves. She's a feisty little thing, that's all."

"No. No, that's not all, Mom. I can't do it. I can't love her."

"Of course you can. You do."

"I don't. I mean, I don't want to love her too much."

"That's ridiculous! You can't love your baby too much. Where do you get these thoughts? I think your hormones are running amuck. You need to talk to your doctor."

Abigail didn't know where her thoughts came from. She only knew she had a terrible knowledge that God was not on her side, and she couldn't fight fate.

In three months the tide began to turn. Stephanie gained weight and started to respond happily to the stimuli around her. She slept for longer stretches and ate rice cereal like it was a whipped cream. She smiled at wind, at neighbors, at her dimpled hand in front of her face.

Summer hung on and Stephanie and Abigail got out of the house more often. One day she pushed the pram to the Promenade and sat on one of the benches. She watched the children playing in the sunshine, remembering her own limbs leaping on the same pavement. She wasn't afraid back then, but she was so small. So innocent.

Suddenly, points of color swirled and danced around her pulling her into the landscape. She watched, fascinated by the dappled pink hands throwing colorful disks under speckled skies. She heard laughter and saw mothers fused like bouquets with yellow spots floating over their heads like haloes. Dots of color danced at her feet. She lifted Stephanie from the carriage and bounced her on her lap. "Baby girl, baby girl, who are you?" she cooed.

The baby's fingers spread out and touched the air, she chirped and giggled.

"Momma's girl, Momma's girl, where are you?" Abigail asked.

"Momma," Stephanie answered. There was no mistaking it.

"Momma?" Abigail needed to hear it again, thinking it was not possible.

"Momma," Stephanie said again, as clear as a church bell.

A cloudburst of joy swept over Abigail. She had been named. Her daughter had claimed her.

"Stephanie, Stephanie, my bay-bee," she said, pulling her to her breast.

From that moment, life took on a daily rhythm and she was better able to accept herself as a mother and housewife. But things in her marriage bed were not so good. She knew she was less desirable, her body changed, and what had been a limited sexual energy was running even lower.

When Hank returned to her, five months later, it was in the middle of the night and she was barely conscious. She felt his touch, allowed him to turn her over and separate her legs, to sleepily make room for him and make possible his penetration as if she wasn't quite conscious, as if she didn't notice. Afterwards, she stroked his arms and laid her leg over his. "I love you," she said. But he said nothing back, just closed his eyes and went to that other world where anything is possible. It was not the way she wanted it to be, but hope sufficed.

For her twenty-fifth birthday, Hank planned a trip to the Grand Canyon in Arizona. The three of them boarded the plane, loaded down with a car seat, bottle bag, diaper bag, book bag, backpack, briefcase and an assortment of rattles and furry creatures, right along with their doubts that a baby and a trip out west would work. But it did.

They stayed at El Tovar, the famous hotel, once staffed by the legendary Harvey Girls whose feminine charms helped civilize the West. The hotel was as foreign to the two New Yorkers as a gassho in Shira kawa-cho. Its thick log walls and plain furniture spoke less of beauty and more about its ability to survive fire and time. The sole purpose of the place was that its guests step outside and face nature as it carved its way through history.

They arrived at night, tired and blind to what morning would bring. But they set the alarms so that they could rise before the sun and witness the canyon waking up.

Stephanie slept between them, snug as a peanut in its shell. When they awoke, the room was lit by moonlight and stars. Abigail had never seen so many stars. She didn't need to step outside to be awestruck. But then they ventured forth, and silently stood at the edge of a blackened cliff, waiting for dawn. A mule deer quietly approached and stood, a sentinel, beside them. Abigail couldn't breathe. Stephanie saw the creature and simply smiled, not recognizing the gift.

The sun began its ascent. Like a paintbrush loaded with gold, it streaked the canyon's face adding layer upon layer on its deep sides. No photograph, no retelling could have prepared them for the beauty, nor could they have anticipated the perspective that the grandness would place on their little threesome standing together in the early light.

It was that weekend that Hank and Abigail began to feel like a couple again, and it didn't take long before she was pregnant.

Joshua was born in 1990, a watershed year if there ever was one. The Berlin Wall came down when Soviet Union collapsed, and the Hubble Telescope rose above the earth's atmosphere. Abigail thought her father had to be singing, "We have overcome" from his sky watch and blessing the beautiful boy who arrived to square his family's table.

While nineties women competed for better jobs, ran for political office and discussed sex like it was sport, Abigail remained a mere observer. She didn't want a big job or free sex or particularly care about multiple orgasms either. Her aspirations were simple—a little house in the country with two kids and a picket fence. She believed the second baby would be the key that turned them into a real family, and she worked overtime to become the perfect mother. Her life cup overran with purpose.

From this sense of bounty, she talked Hank into looking outside the city for a better place to raise the children. When he found the cottage on Apple Blossom Lane, she eagerly said goodbye to the Heights and Brooklyn's expensive garages and noisy traffic. There would be no more worries about limited space, the inconveniences of stairs and elevators, garbage trucks breaking down regularly or police sirens waking them up at all hours. They were on their way north, north to Nirvana.

Their new house was surrounded by a white fence with rambling roses cascading down its sides. It sat on a side street at the edge of quaint Montmarte. Before long they were the textbook version of suburban life, with two children, a station wagon, a Porsche and pleasant enough neighbors. From this perch, Hank comfortably continued his climb up the corporate ladder, leaving the family firm for a multi-national bank with any number of opportunities for advancement.

It took years before Abigail began to resent the reiterations of daily routines and long for the pulse of the city. Her chores were redundant, unnoticed and insipid. She felt trapped, irrelevant and suspected she was the victim of a plot, a scheme handed down for generations of women in fairy tales, churches and school primers. Dick and Jane and their little dog Spot. They may not have adopted a dog named Spot, but they did have a boy and a girl, a cat, shutters on their windows and an apple tree with a swing in the front yard.

A new lease on life occurred when Abigail drew upon her years in art school and rediscovered the joy of the brush. Her painting became obsessive after the removal of an ancient oil heater from the cellar. With the unit gone, along with its maze of thick pipes, a space of about 10' x 10' appeared. She saw in it the potential of a studio, and eagerly set out to make it her own.

To begin, thirty years of mud and dead insects were scraped off a newly accessible window, one that allowed a token of natural light into the darkness, even a breath of fresh air. This sacred corner soon held an easel, a table, shelves, a high stool and a flood light. In no time at all, her muse appeared.

In this private space where ancient earth cooled sturdy granite walls, she would squeeze tubes of paint onto her palette, mix them with a flat knife and grow nearly drunk from the joy of it. She loved combining colors, the alchemy when they became something else, and the smell of the glistening oils and turpentine. Her canvas was a world she climbed into, where she was delivered from the ordinary, the very ordinariness she had believed she wanted, an ordinariness that had left her behind when she was only seven. She allowed herself to paint from the inside out.

Observing the observers, Abigail resisted an impulse to order everyone to stand back, to leave her alone. The paintings were speaking to her and she needed time to listen. An unremitting theme was coming into focus.

"Abigail, you are looking far too serious. Come with me," Kendra said, as she approached, her bangled hand reaching for Abigail's. "I have someone you must meet."

"These paintings are memories, Kendra. They can't have meaning to anyone else. I feel so exposed."

"Nonsense, darling. Every painting is personal at its inception, but once it's completed, it has its own destiny. No one sees the same painting you do."

"But, here's the rub, I feel like I am seeing them for the first time tonight."

9

Tenement Lace

A red dot appeared on *Tenement Lace*. It should have been an affirmation, but Abigail felt a pang of loss. It was one of her earliest paintings, drawn from the clotheslines and fire escapes of Brooklyn's backyards. The two who bought it were archetypal Manhattanites, Charles D. Henry, the Broadway producer, and Maynard Darling, his partner of long standing. Their faces weren't familiar, but their affect was.

"We love the nostalgia of this painting. It reminds us of our roots," Maynard explained.

"Yes, it mirrors my roots, too," Abigail said.

"Brooklyn?"

"Yes."

"Really? Where?"

"The Promenade." Abigail said, admitting to only the best of her addresses.

"Bed-Stuy, here," Maynard replied. Both of them knew what that meant. Bedford-Stuyvesant was one of the neighborhoods whites deserted when blacks moved in. The transition was neither sweet nor smooth. Of course, like so much of the city, it would probably wear another face soon enough.

Two years after the death of her husband and a brief affair with Louis Arsignol, Cecily moved the girls into an old Brooklyn brownstone in a volatile part of town; another Brooklyn than the one they had known. Some said it was the true Brooklyn. In the new neighborhood, kids played stickball in the street, stole hubcaps from strange cars parked in front of their houses, and spoke in languages both exotic and common. It was a place where Jews ruled one side of the street and Catholics the other, connected only by the clothes line lace strung across their backyards attaching one back wall with another.

Abigail had recreated the colorful canyons of stone houses with Mandarin orange, sienna and alizarin, interrupted with the patterns of blue-black fire escapes and suspensions of laundry. It was in the laundry that the story was told, hung by Old World women, who chose sunshine over dryers and optimistically fought the battle of New York weather and polluted skies.

Adjusting to a new neighborhood did not come easily to the girls. They were largely ignored because the Jewish kids stuck together like gummy bears and the Latinos operated in gangs where you were welcome or not. They were not.

Cecily tried to help them love their new, old house. "It was once handsome," she said. "Look at the herring bone patterns in the floor and the plaster roses strung from corner to corner on the ceilings! Did you ever see a grander chandelier? Fifty years ago ball gowns and petticoats swept these stairwells." Her allusions to former grandeur helped the rooms of crumbling flowers and worn dark wood look less abandoned.

Abigail could imagine the place in better days. The last owners were leftovers from the Irish wave of immigration. The Hallidays had five children and an extended family of a grandmother and aunt. The great herd of Hallidays had migrated to a big track house in Amityville, one of Long Island's burgeoning communities. The neglect they had perpetrated on the old place was the Lynde's to remedy, but Cecily didn't have a clue where to begin, or the money to do it. Instead, they rattled around in the aching, peeling rooms like squatters. No window opened or closed properly, their voices echoed off the cracked walls, water marks signaled problems in the roof and the radiators hissed and spat and contributed to mysterious creaks during the night.

Cecily's diminishing economic security caused her to come up with a survival plan. In short order, she gave up any ideas of restoring elegance to their home. She decided to divide the house into three apartments, two rooms on the third floor, a studio on the second and the remainder of the house to be theirs. She said the rentals would help make ends meet.

Tiffany and Abigail were allowed to choose separate bedrooms. Tiffany opted for a large bedroom behind the kitchen, one that had originally been used by the Halliday's aunt, and Cecily took a small space for herself toward the front, of the house, a room that had originally been the library. Abigail's bedroom was large and sunny and next to the second-floor stairwell. The other bedroom on the second floor was preserved for a roomer. Whoever he or she was, they would have to share the bathroom with Abigail.

She was thrilled to get the upstairs bedroom. Not only did it feel exclusive, but it had windows filled with branches that reflected the seasons—a small compensation for losing the views from the Promenade. She missed her old neighborhood and the familiar faces on the street, the heady smell of salt, the parade of boats and the jeweled city at night.

Anna Mae, their housekeeper and second mother, was gone, too. Anna Mae had always been there. She had taken care of the closets, washed the bathrooms and scrubbed the floors. She had changed the beds and straightened dresser drawers. It was Anna Mae who made sure their lives had a semblance of order and yet, it wasn't something any of them had appreciated until she was gone. In her absence, every day seemed to be filled with chores and arguments over who was responsible for what. Abigail would have given anything to see Anna Mae shake her head and say one more time, "My, my, how do you do?" Feel the comfort she'd known in the mahogany warmth of her arms. But she had to let Anna Mae go the way of so many other things.

At that time both Tiffany and Abigail were transferred from the tender hands of the Ethical Culture School, where a child's curiosity and proclivities were honored, to huge public schools composed mostly of new immigrants. Their schools were within walking distance of their house, however, so they could walk home for lunch.

Abigail needed the break from the tedious school days in which she had little to learn and much to escape. Her classmates were still learning to speak English while she could read and write everything and anything placed in front of her. Miss Cuminsky and she had English in common, and consequently Abigail was established as the teacher's right-hand girl.

"Abigail, will you run to the office with this message? Abigail, would you pass out the test papers? Why don't you help Theresa with her math work?"

Sometimes she was asked to read to the first graders. Some days she was asked to mark spelling tests. Always, she was in charge of the bulletin board. This was so, because when Miss Cuminsky asked her what made her happiest in school, the only thing she could think of was the time she had cut out ducks for the October bulletin board. It was then that Miss Cuminsky asked her to do December's, then January's and so on. It was an overwhelmed teacher's way of providing for a child who simply did not fit in. But, regardless of Miss Cuminsky's efforts, school was just a place for Abigail to go every day. It held few mysteries, no challenges and only a little pleasure; it neither persuaded nor repulsed the child as she waited out the days.

The Lynde's brownstone was only a block from Prospect Park's five hundred eighty five-acre playland. Anna Mae had taken Abigail there once or twice a week when the Lyndes lived on the Promenade. But back then they had to travel by taxi. Now the soft hills were there for the asking. The girls went sledding in the winter, and in the spring, when the meadows were mowed, sprinklers fixed and the dark green park benches painted, Abigail would climb to the top of Long Meadow and somersault down.

The paved pedestrian paths became new highways for Tiffany and Abigail. Their favorite path led to the opposite side of the park and its well-known zoo, where a vague memory of a child being crushed was supplanted by the ever-present illusion of festivity, the happy sounds of the merry-go-round, the colorful cotton candy vendors and purple wigged balloon man. Who could resist the elongated beauty of the giraffe and the folds of a hippo's skin?

Abigail was not old enough to object to cages that showed no consideration for a creature's natural habitats. When neurotic apes pounded their chests and leapt at wired glass screens, spitting and trying to express their frustration, the child thought it was normal ape behavior. She was drawn to the thirty-by-twenty-foot cages, where a Bengal tiger couldn't hide and an angry lion couldn't sprint, and their long days were reduced to glaring at one another and sounding an occasional roar.

Abigail's favorite pastime was to sit with a pad of paper, usually her father's old legal pads, and draw the animals in places she imagined were their homes. She tried talking to them when no one else was around, and that was often, because Tiffany was happy to extricate herself from her sister whenever she could. At sixteen, Tiffany preferred to sit in the sun or sip a soda at the concession stand out of her sister's sight.

Tiffany's new high school was a huge institution with thousands of kids. The prep school she had left behind had just twenty-one girls at each grade level. But she seemed happy with the change of venue. Her poise and beauty were attracting glances everywhere she went; even Abigail worshipped the sight of her. So did the neighborhood boys who would leave gifts on the stoop, sometimes ring the bell and run to a car parked down the street. Boys turned around and walked past her twice just to get a better look. She pretended to be bored by such antics.

Her first boyfriend, Bo, joined the school chorus that spring. They would meet after school and take the long way home. Tiffany was encumbered by Abigail and made her swear to stay away, to disappear herself, when Bo was around, so that he would be more apt to hangout at their house after school. She said a nine-year-old girl was not someone an eighteen-year-old man found particularly interesting.

But slowly, Bo acknowledged her presence, and Abigail saw in him a friend. She even met his family. They were just as nice as he was.

When Bo brought Tiffany and Abigail to his house after school one afternoon his mother, Mrs. Lupton, was nice enough to ask, "How is your mother, dear? She must be suffering with two girls to raise and the loss of that fine father of yours. He was a remarkable man. Always on the right side of things."

"She's okay, I guess, Mrs. Lupton. She's just having trouble making ends meet," Tiffany replied.

"It's more than a year now since he died, isn't it? And I imagine it is still hard for her?"

"I think so. I guess she will be getting a job soon. At least she talks about it."

"Well, this must have been a difficult time for you, too, dear. So tragic."

"Yes, pretty much."

When Tiffany was leaving, Mrs. Lupton handed her an envelope with her mother's name on it.

Cecily was fuming at the door when the girls arrived home. "Where have you been, Tiffany? I asked you to come home right after school. I need to trust you. I can't have you traipsing your sister all over the place."

"Mom, I have a life, too, you know. I told you I was going to Bo's house this afternoon."

It was the tone, the absence of apology that made Cecily explode.

"You most certainly did not. What were you doing there? Were his parents home?"

"His mother was there. I think she knows you. Hannah Lupton?"

"Hannah Lupton? I've never heard of her. Hannah Lupton? How would I know her?" She turned from Tiffany and made a fist of her hand to keep from slapping Tiffany's petulant face.

"I don't know. She seemed to know Daddy, that's all. She gave me this envelope to give to you."

Cecily reached for the envelope and tore it open. "For Heaven's sake! Why would Mrs. Lupton send me two hundred dollars? Does she think we are on the street? I will send this right back and tell her we do not need charity." The envelope was smacked back into Tiffany's hand.

"She was just trying to help you make ends meet," Tiffany said.

"Make ends meet! And where would she get that idea? Don't you ever, ever talk about our financial situation to any one outside this family again! Do you hear me?" Her face was twisted. "We are doing fine, just fine. We are going to keep this family together. I don't need the sympathy of strangers, especially from some woman I've never met. I don't suppose she told you how well she knew your father, did she? Well, did she?"

Tiffany threw the envelope at her mother's feet and left the room.

Abigail was alarmed by her mother's outburst. It had never occurred to her that there was even the remotest possibility of their family not staying together. When she went to bed that night she prayed, with as much earnestness as a nine-year-old could muster and implored her father to take care of them.

Shortly thereafter, Cecily's job search took on a whole new impetus.

She was given tests upon tests at the Everyman's Employment Agency. The girls listened as she told them about the personality tests she was taking, where cards were passed out and each applicant had to choose the color they believed represented them. "We want to help you discover the real you," the leader had explained. After each person decided on a color, they had to join ranks with the others that had chosen the same color. Cecily said she found herself sitting at a table with all the most uptight people in the room. "I really have to do something to change," she said. "The oranges go dancing, and the blues believe in Apple Pie. Smart people are green and I got stuck with the Golds, the organizers. The take care-of-business-people."

But she met a man that day who was looking for gold.

"Name's Allen," he said. "You a true Gold? You like schedules? Organizing other people your schtick? "

"I'm afraid so," Cecily said. "But it's recent. I used to be a romantic."

"No more romance inside you? Such a pretty woman, like you?"

"Only in the past tense."

"Yeah? Where did she go?"

"Buried. Life pushes you, and you become what you have to become."

"Yeah. But it's hard to push the Golds around. They keep the reins close to their chests. What's your name, anyway?"

Cecily wondered what he was doing there. "Are you here to find a job?" she asked.

"No. I'm here to meet the people who are looking for one."

That was clever of him, she thought, devious too. He wouldn't have to pay a finder's fee.

"I need someone at the Connor's Real Estate Office; a self-starter, organized, attractive, intelligent and hungry. You hungry?"

"I'm afraid so," Cecily answered.

"Married?"

"Widowed."

"Kids?"

"Two."

"That's pretty tough. When are you available?"

"Tomorrow," Cecily said. She hadn't even thought about a babysitter yet.

"Come to the office around ten. We'll talk." He handed her his business card.

When the noon break came he disappeared and Cecily asked herself if he could have been legitimate. She looked at the business card he'd handed her and noticed his office was walking distance from their house. Accessibility and need inspired her to check out the office the following morning.

Connor's Real Estate was less than a fifteen-minute walk from her front door. It sat on 7th Avenue, near 5th Street, squeezed between an appliance store whose windows screamed EVERYTHING MUST GO!!! and an indoor/outdoor mom and pop grocery store called Chico's. At Allen Connor's office, Mom looked at the faded photographs stuck to the picture windows and the curling letters above them. Large and black, they said confidently, YOU'LL FIND IT HERE.

She doubted it.

He saw her and jumped up from his desk, shirttails almost out of his belt line. She watched as he pulled a handkerchief from his back pocket and wiped his forehead. It was hot out with humidity to match. But that was to be expected in July. His neck needed a wipe, too. His armpits needed something more.

"Allen?" she said. "Were you serious yesterday?"

"Hey. You made it. I don't remember your name, but I knew you were my girl!"

"Cecily Lynde."

"Hello, Cecily Lynde. Well, well, well. So you took a chance. That's a plus. A real plus. Name's Jake. Jacob Polinsky. Have a seat."

She sat on the tired leather office chair. "I thought you said your name was Allen Connors?"

"Well. That's the name of the agency. It sounds less ethnic, dontcha think?"

He had wide eyes on a wide face. An afternoon shadow covered his chin although it was morning. Dark curly hair stuck out of his shiny shirt. A gold chain rested on his thick neck. On his wrist was a diamond-studded gold watch. His fingers were wrapped in gold, too. She doubted the gold or the diamonds were real.

"You educated?" he asked.

"Vassar."

"Class."

"'55."

"No. I meant class. You've got class. That's what we need around here, a little class."

She thought he had that right.

His desk was a chaotic spill of newspaper, cups, take-out food wrappers and photos. Beneath it, black-and-white squares of scuffed linoleum evidenced what had fallen or accumulated over time. Aside from two chairs, there were exactly no amenities that might have entertained clients if they had to wait. No magazines, no coffee, no music, no brochures. Not even a couch. The place was a dismal aesthetic failure.

"We? Who is the we you are referring to?" Cecily asked.

"Allen Connor."

"Oh. So there really is an Allen Connor?"

"Only up heah, Doll." He pointed to his head.

She knew she should leave. Why she sat there with this distasteful man in his dirty office, she could not guess. There were beads of perspiration on his upper lip and on the plank of his brow. She could almost smell his greasy hair. It was just three small words that hooked her.

"I need you," he said. "I need you to clean this place up, be my front office. Answer my phones. I know that's beneath a Vassar girl, but maybe there's a future here for you—one that goes beyond office management. There are apartments to rent. You could study and get a license for selling commercial real estate. A smart girl like you—it'd be a piece of cake. You make two thousand a month extra if you bust your ass—excuse me—butt. You see what I mean?"

"I don't know."

"Not good enough for ya', huh?"

"It's not that. The truth is I've never worked. I don't even know what I want to do."

"Listen. Come on board. I'll pay you good to turn this place around and give me what money can't buy. If you hate it—so, you move on. Okay?"

And that was how Cecily Lynde, Vassar girl, society hostess and former wife of the late, great Alexander Lynde, was introduced to the world of realty. She took the job and became Jacob Polinsky's fixer.

Abigail remembered the new woman that emerged when her mother went to work. She was determined and proud. Nothing could quash her spirit, even the unimaginable. She thought, some of my mother's pride must somewhere in my genes. But what have I done with it?

Tootsie was licking her leg. Someone must have let her escape from the storeroom. Abigail tried to connect with the silly little creature. She lifted her to her cheek. The dog nuzzled her face, then swiped her lips with a tiny coarse tongue. She had room for this furry love object of Kendra's at the moment, and that was good, because not to love Tootsie was beyond consideration. It was required.

"Oh, my little Poopsie," Kendra cried, her red trimmed fingers retrieving her baby. "Mommy's itsy bitsy darling, girl! Come, let's find you a treat, my sweet."

Abigail smiled as she relinquished the dog, hoping her relief was masked with tenderness.

She knew Kendra's love object was no more than a furry substitute for a relationship, a hopeless solution for love, always destined to end in loss. To love a cat or a dog, a horse or a gerbil almost guaranteed grief. Of course, a box turtle or a parrot could outlive you but they weren't exactly cuddly. Abigail would always prefer wild creatures;

never fail to thrill catching them in nature, a badger on the side of the road, a hawk in flight, a fish breaking the water's surface.

"Wade, Wade, darling, come here!" Kendra beckoned the man Abigail thought was Barney.

Wade? Barney is also Wade? Strange how much more appropriate Wade seems, Abigail thought. He waved at Kendra and disengaged himself from the lady in red and the corner where she had penned him. His approaching face was no less than a beacon. She saw in it something alarmingly… alarmingly what?

"Darling, you must meet my friend, Wade," Kendra said as he entered their space.

"We have already met," Abigail said. "But I'm afraid I was introduced to a Barney, not a Wade." She looked toward the door. "Oh, please excuse me," she said, "I must see the person who just arrived!" Abruptly, she turned away from them and negotiated her way to the foyer.

10

The Park

In the painting, *The Park*, two translucent girls survey a park which was meant to be Prospect Park, the stanchion of Abigail's early happy childhood. The place where brass rings were won at the carousel, her family took yearly pilgrimages to the lily cross, and Tiffany rode Flash, a horse from Kensington Stables. Abigail was the playground princess, hula hoop expert and recorder of babies at the zoo—good things, all, except...

Cecily was throwing herself at work, Tiffany was throwing herself at Bo, and Abigail was waiting for something good to come her way. Grandma Lynde was the only person who seemed to notice she was left alone much of the time. But Grandma Lynde had moved "away." She had vacated Brooklyn's Bay Ridge, overlooking the Sheepshead Bay, for a small apartment in Manhattan on West 63rd Street. It was her statement of independence and, more importantly, put her a short distance from Bloomingdales, which she described as her favorite New York restaurant, where everything was good enough to eat. Not only that, she was near New York Hospital, the Metropolitan and a short bus ride to the theater of her choice.

Despite her new forms of accessible entertainment, Grandma Lynde did not abandon Abigail. She routinely rode the subway for thirty five minutes and walked eight city blocks, just to pay her a visit. It may have been something as simple as going for an ice cream cone or taking a walk along the park, but Grandma would show up.

Abigail had been told she looked like her grandmother. It was obvious she had inherited the fine blonde hair and fair skin. But Grandma was growing shorter while Abigail was growing like bamboo. With Grandma Lynde's face usually hidden under unusual hats, it was hard for the child to see exactly what else they had in common. Nevertheless, she adored her Grandma Lynde, who was making a point of doing the things she liked best with the time she had left. Her religion was Life, so she said, and she lived that without complaint.

She was visiting the day Abigail found a tiny kitten hiding under a car parked in front of the house. It was a mangy, little beast with nails as big as its teeth and eyes like blue sapphires. She fell in love with it immediately, wrapped it in a dish towel and brought it in the house. She took a tiny doll's bottle and filled it with milk, then let the kitten suck to its heart's content.

Cecily came home that evening and saw the kitten. "We don't need any animals around this house," she said, before her coat was in the closet. Grandmother Lynde pouted, her freckled arms crossed and silver bracelets clanged while she picked at her skin in a nervous way. She said, "Now, Cecily."

"Mother Lynde, you know we are having enough trouble taking care of ourselves without adding animals to our worries," Cecily scolded.

Abigail began to sob, but her Grandma took Cecily aside and talked her into letting the child keep it. She said that animals were healing for children who spend a lot of the time alone. She said more, but Abigail didn't hear it.

Cecily capitulated. "All right, Abby, but you are entirely responsible for it. Now you can begin by putting it in the sink and washing the filth off the poor creature."

The sickly little kitten died two days later, but at least Abigail knew she had tried. She wrapped its stiff carcass in an old linen cloth, laid it in a shoebox and gave it a good funeral. Then with prayers and rose petals, she planted it in the ground under a rose bush, the only flowering plant in the yard. The rock she decorated with a red heart may still rest on that grave.

Grandma Lynde was not one to talk down to children. Often she would carry on a conversation with Abigail as if she was with a friend, and sometimes she would say nothing at all; whatever Grandma's mood, it suited her granddaughter just fine.

They were sipping an egg cream at Carlton's one afternoon, sitting at the counter on stools before a tarnished mirror, looking at one another in their reflections instead of face to face.

"You miss your father, don't you Abby?" Grandma Lynde asked.

"Sometimes," Abigail said, aware that Grandma didn't need to know how hard she was trying to forget him.

"You're a lot like him, I think," she added. "You look like him, and you care for creatures that can't care for themselves. I think he is very proud, up there in Heaven."

Abigail supposed she looked like her father, but she wished she looked more like her mother. Tiffany looked more like Cecily, except for her dark hair, which set her apart from the whole family. Abigail's compensation was that Grandma Lynde loved her best.

Sometimes Grandma Lynde was upset with Cecily. "Doesn't your mother iron your clothes, Abby?" Or, "I have brought my little manicure set. You let Grandma cut your nails, precious child. It's a shame your mother expects you to do so much for yourself." Or, "How could she have sold those books of Alex's? He loved them so. I would have been happy to take them off her hands."

Sometimes she made excuses for Cecily, too. "Your mother is working late at night because she has to. I just hope neither of you girls has to deal with what your mother has gone through."

It was the summer of '72. Two things marked summer that year. President Nixon went to China and the Lynde sisters saw the Carol Burnett Show in living color because summer vacation brought with it a new 24" Zenith color TV. Grandma Lynde said she was sick of the rolling images the family had learned to accept, and she didn't care if she was corrupting the girls or not. She thought it was a wonderful form of entertainment and could be very educational. Plus it would keep them off the streets.

Abigail still preferred books. Most of her summer was spent reading Laura Ingalls Wilder's books, with the intention of reading all eight novels. She also became increasingly interested in movie stars and put together scrapbooks of her favorites. She looked for one more beautiful than Tiffany, but found none.

While Cecily was buying awnings and rugs for Connor's Real Estate Office, Tiffany was supposed to be looking after Abigail. They would listen to Simon and Garfunkel or the Beatles and dance with abandon. Abigail decided ballet was boring compared to rock and roll.

Tiffany was more interested in Bo than news or stars or music. If it wasn't Bo on the phone or Bo at the door, it was Bo bumping into them at the library or the park, and occasionally joining them for bus rides to the beach. Cecily didn't mind Bo's presence, as long as it was a threesome. Unfortunately, Tiffany didn't quite see it that way. Abigail became more and more of an unwanted weight around her neck.

Bo and Tiffany were listening to some new albums one hot Tuesday, and Abigail started to dance as if she was auditioning for a Broadway show. Bo started to egg her on and Tiffany had had enough. She groaned and said, "You know, you could go out and play with those kids on the street, Abby. Why don't you make some friends your own age?"

Abigail thought that was a good idea and stepped outside where four boys were playing stickball. The summer macadam was hot, but the streets were pretty empty so the kids could play between occasional cars. She stood with one foot crossed over the other and her arms folded, trying to look as casual as she could, waiting and watching in hopes that they'd take on a fifth player. The ball came her way. "Hey, stupido, watch out," one of the boys yelled, running right over her feet, causing her to lose her balance. The rest of the boys laughed when she fell and didn't care if she was hurt or humiliated. She pulled herself up and wiped the gravel out of her palms. She wouldn't show them it hurt. Not for all the world.

Boys were weird. It would probably be better if they didn't even exist, she thought, as she shook herself out and moved on. She didn't need them. She would go to the park, across Boulevard West, along the high stone wall to the entrance which she knew so well. Again she thought how glad she was to live near the playground.

Inside the park, strollers and mothers, little kids, sweethearts and old folks moved in slow motion. The heavy heat may have explained why. She went to her old playground, the same place where she'd been reckless on the swings. It consisted of a circular, fenced in section where once she had run while Anna Mae knit—clucking and shaking her head from left to right at other children's misbehavior. "Mercy me," she would say. "Mercy me."

Both of them were always in sight of the guards assigned to the park. The guards were distinguished by their green uniforms and names like poems, Guiseppe Marconi, Antonio Rossuto, Paco Ramirez, Boris Butaruga. Abigail loved the foreignness of them. She was at home there with her nanny who would make sure no child would hurt her, and the grandfatherly men who made sure the park was clean and safe.

She showed off for the guards whenever she could, brought them to see her sandcastles and begged them to watch her cross the monkey bars. Sometimes Anna Mae would share their morning snacks with whomever was on duty. On Abigail's sixth birthday, she got the little roller skates that made her mobile. As soon as she had them figured out, she begged the park men to sit on the bench while she performed on the smooth asphalt around the sleeping sprinkler. That was before her father died, before she moved and the whole park became her neighborhood.

Even though it was a little less than two years since she had visited the playground, it looked different. Someone had shrunk everything down to a tiny replica of what it had once been. It was now so small she didn't fit into its landscape anymore. She decided not to go through the gate.

It wasn't hard for her to make her way to the zoo. She was sure of herself, sure of the familiar paths, knew each curve and marker—the water fountain, the rhododendrons behind the white arrows pointing left to the Japanese Garden. Before she reached the zoo's gate, mouth-watering smells of hot dogs grilling and freshly popped corn greeted her, but the tinkling tunes of the merry-go-round were absent. She headed in that direction, anyway, to check-up on the painted horses with legs frozen in mid-gallop and gilded manes forever flying. She saw the sign: Out of Order. It didn't matter; she had no money for a ride.

At the seal pool she wished she could join them in their cool green water. At the picnic area she envied the kids who were splashing under the sprinkler, but sprinklers were beneath her now. None of the kids looked older than six and she was headed for the double digits soon.

Clouds started to cover the sun and the heat grew worse, so she decided to go home. At the bridle path, four Arabian horses ridden by two men and two women came cantering around the bend. The riders' jodhpurs and high boots were too hot for the day and yet, she would have given away all her belongings to be on the back of the horse with the white mane and coal black eyes, wearing her old riding boots and the velvet helmet now in a box in her closet.

A man walking behind her caught up to her and said, "Fine looking specimens aren't they?"

"They're Arabian stallions," she answered.

"So you know horses, eh?" the man asked. He was old, a tall, thin, gray-haired man with eyes like blue ice.

"Yes sir, a little. I used to ride."

"No more?"

"Nope. My father died."

"And you don't ride because of that?"

The horses broke into a gallop and went around the bend; myrtle and ash leaves shivered in their wake.

"Well, my mom's having a hard time making ends meet, and we all have to give up stuff in order to get along. I don't mind as long as we can stay together."

He scanned the path, looking forward and back. No one was in sight.

"Where is your mother?" he asked.

"Oh, she's at work."

"And you are here all alone?" his eyes showed surprise.

She figured he was impressed. "Oh sure. I go to the park all the time. I know it better than anyone here. This is one of my favorite spots." She couldn't count how many times she and Tiffany had sat in that very spot, on the large flat stone under the oak tree, waiting for the sound of hoofbeats.

The horses were long gone when a drop hit her cheek, then another, and then bigger raindrops started to fall. "Yikes! I better get going," she said.

The man asked, "Where do you live?"

He looked concerned. She didn't want him to worry, because she was perfectly capable of finding her way.

"Just at the edge of the park," on Fifth Street, she answered.

"Well, I bet I know a shortcut that you never heard about. Trust me?"

"Okay!"

"My name is Gustav, but you can call me Gus," he said. "What's yours?"

"My name is Abigail, but you can call me Abby."

"That's a very pretty name," he said. "I will call you Abigail."

He took her hand. He had a big warm hand, and she remembered how it had felt walking through the park with her father.

They walked up one hill and down another, going well off the paved paths toward the duck pond where idle paddleboats sat waiting for sunshine. Her legs had powered those boats on occasion, but she had never seen it so quiet or been on this side of the water.

"I don't think this is a shortcut for me, I live over there," she said, pointing to the right, to the other side of the lake. She did not want to make the man wrong, but felt very sure he was not going to get her home any faster if they kept going in the same direction; and the rain was picking up. "I think I better go now."

"Trust me," he said again. "I have a special way over that hill and out." His grip tightened, and his voice sounded more insistent. She knew one thing was true, he knew a part of the park she had never seen before.

Now, the rain became a steady downpour, veiling the landscape. Her orientation was off because she was avoiding puddles and mud. Water stuck to her eyelids and dribbled off her nose. She clung to the man's hand hoping he was right, trying to remember which way was home. When they stopped under a weighted tree to take a respite from the rain, she saw a graveyard sitting on the other side of the old iron fence. She wondered who was buried in the park. The sign read "Private" even though the park was public.

"I never knew this was here," she admitted.

He waved his free hand toward the headstones. "Everyone in there has something in common," he said.

"They do?" she asked.

"Yes. They're all dead," he chuckled.

"I d...d...don't like it here, it's sp...spooky," she shivered. She was wet and uncomfortable. She had to go to the bathroom.

Abigail hardly knew what happened next. It was like a bad dream. The old man pulled her toward him and grabbed her hands, holding them behind her back. He became hard and mean. He started kissing her and no matter how she turned her head, she felt his yellow teeth and grizzly chin. He pushed his face into hers and then he let go of her hands to tear at her shorts.

"No!" she cried, "Stop it!" With her hands loosed, she pushed at his shoulders until he grabbed her arms to stop her. She squirmed and tried to kick, but she tripped and fell over backwards with her underwear, like ropes, tying her ankles. His muddied paws ripped at them as he lowered himself over her body. Although she couldn't scream, her feet flailed about. She smelled tobacco and something sickly sweet on his breath, felt the firmness under his pants and kicked as hard as she could.

"You do that again and you won't like what comes next," he said, his cold eyes boring her into the ground. "Lie still and you won't get hurt."

Terror told her to do what he said.

"That's a girl. That's a good little girl," he said.

The arms of the maple tree reached toward her, a bird watched safely on a high bough. They were the only witnesses to the disgrace.

For seconds she stayed still as stone, wondering what was coming next—wondering if she was going to die, asking herself why he would do such an awful thing. Then she instinctively lifted her knee and caught him in the crotch, colliding with that red wrinkled part of him. He grunted, grabbed himself and fell over as she rolled away. Clambering to her feet, she aimed at the spot that caused him pain, and kicked him over and over again. After she stamped on one of his hands with all the force she could, she grabbed her panties and started to run. Raindrops spread the dirt from her head and blinded her eyes, but her legs had Herculean strength as they found their way over the hills hoping to reach something familiar. She was terrified he was chasing her, afraid she was lost until she saw the path leading to the playground and the green suit of a park guard taking garbage out of the big pail by the gate. She ran right into him, it was Guiseppe Marconi.

She started to cry so hard she couldn't form words.

He put his arms around her. "What is it, fanciulla?"

"A man...a man..." she said.

The guard took her into the stone building she used to think was home to the park guards. It was a practical room with lockers and benches and a table covered with newspapers and magazines. The desk had a phone on it. His thick crooked fingers shakily dialed the police.

She knew water and mud were caked on her face, her arms and legs and clothes. Despite the heat, she began to shiver. Guiseppe went to a closet, retrieved an Army blanket and wrapped her in it, all the time repeating, "Sonofabeetch, the sonofabeetch." It was only minutes before the police arrived.

"Can you describe the man, Miss?"

"Did he put anything inside you?"

"Did he have a weapon?"

She watched as one of the policemen scribbled down her answers. Her teacher would have given him a D in penmanship.

"Have you ever seen this man before, Miss?"

"Why did you speak to him?"

"Where was your mother?"

"Did you know his name?"

"Didn't your mother tell you not to talk to strangers?"

Did Cecily tell her not to talk to strangers? She thought. Sometimes she wanted her to talk to strangers. Say hello to the Jeffersons. Go say hi to Lily's mother. Then again, her mother didn't like the button man, Dr. Lister. But he wasn't a stranger, just strange.

She answered the policeman's question with, "I don't know."

"Where were you exactly, when you were attacked, Miss?"

"Did he take off his pants?"

"How did you get away?

"Which way did he run?

"Did you come right here after this happened?

"How old do you think he was?

"Did he speak English?

"How come you went off with this man?

"Do you think you could identify him if you saw him again?

"Were there any witnesses?

"Did anyone see the two of you together?"

She did the best she could. Then one policeman left and another man came in. This one wore a brown suit and was very fatherly. It didn't take long before she realized he was repeating all the questions she had already answered.

She wondered if they thought she had imagined the whole thing.

She felt dirty and ashamed, like she was to blame.

Outside, the rain kept coming down making streaks on the grimy window of the office. She asked if she could go home.

After another half-hour of questioning, they put her in the backseat of a police car. To be in a police car and go down the street with its red light flashing and stop in front of her house was another embarrassment. She didn't want to get out of the car, thought the neighbors would be looking out their windows or worse than that, the dumb neighborhood boys might see her.

Tiffany was at the door, her face flushed with anger. "Where were you? Do you know we've been worried sick?"

"Your mother at home, Miss?" the policeman asked Tiffany.

"She will be any minute," answered Tiffany, ignoring the man. "Abby, what happened?"

Abigail wasn't going to tell her in front of Bo.

"Can you reach your mother by phone?" the policeman asked.

"Why? What happened?" Tiffany asked again.

"We need to get this young lady to a hospital and checked out. Would you try to reach your mother or a relative or some other responsible adult?"

Abigail just wanted to be alone. "I have to go up to my room and change," she said.

"Sorry, Missy, you can't do that. You have to sit here and wait until we get someone to take you to the hospital."

"But, I'm all right."

Bo asked if Tiffany wanted him to stay, and she said she thought he had better be going. He didn't even say good-bye. As he was leaving, a taxi pulled up in front of the house where the police car was still running; its light going around and around. Cecily climbed out and ran up the front stairs leaving the cab's door ajar.

"Tiffany?" Cecily cried, dashing up the steps, the cab driver following.

"Your daughter has had a run in with a man in the park," the policeman said. "I assume you're her mother?"

"I am. What happened?"

"Let's all sit down and let her tell us," he suggested.

"Ma'am," said the driver, "hate to bother ya' but that'll be $5.00."

Cecily reached in her purse to find money. The driver got a ten dollar bill and left without offering change.

"Are you hurt?" Cecily asked, her eyes looking at Abigail's soiled blouse and muddy shorts.

Her daughter couldn't talk without crying, so the police took over.

"Perhaps you'd like the sister to leave the room, while I relay what your daughter has told us so far."

Tiffany acted insulted and said she would like to stay.

"Go," Mom said and Tiffany retreated to the kitchen.

Abigail sat curled in a tight ball as the policeman read his report, which was mostly the very words she had used. When he was done he said, "Best you get her over to Kings County Hospital and let them examine her. If there's any sperm, we can preserve it as evidence. Don't know how much damage the sicko did."

"Dear God. This is just terrible." Cecily's arms went around herself.

"We'll give you a ride, Ma'am, if you'd like. "

"I'd appreciate it, but I'd prefer to go to the Methodist Hospital. Her doctor is there and I want her to be examined by someone she knows. She's been through enough. My poor baby!"

Then, as if led by some force within her that couldn't help itself, Cecily turned to the weeping child and asked, "What were you doing in the park alone, Abby?"

"I always go there," she said. "I go there all the time."

"What? What are you saying? That's not true!"

Mortified, Cecily turned to the police. "I've never in my life left my child in that park alone, officers."

Abigail was too tired to explain that when she was with her sister she might just as well have been alone.

Cecily called Tiffany. "Tiffany Marie, would you come in here please?" It was the voice that made a person want to do anything but. "Where were you this afternoon, Tiffany? Why weren't you with your sister?"

Tiffany's white face turned crimson. "I thought she was playing with the kids out front. When it started raining and she didn't come in, I figured she went to someone's house."

"Ma'am, I think we need to get this little lady to the hospital and then home so she can wash up and start feeling better. Why don't you go get her some clean clothes so she can change at the hospital?"

Cecily nodded, pulling herself together as she corrected her tone and suggested in her best mother voice, that Abigail come with her to pick out something to wear after the exam.

They arrived at the hospital and were ushered into a private space surrounded by heavy curtains and bright lights. After they asked Cecily and the policeman some questions, more police arrived. Abigail was asked to look at some pictures they brought from the station house. "We've been looking for this guy," they said. "Your cooperation could spare another kid."

"She will not be any part of any investigation," Cecily said. "It's over and it is going to stay over."

"You may feel differently tomorrow. We will be in touch."

A smiling nurse helped Abigail take off her clothes and put them on a chair. Then she gave her a little printed robe that didn't fasten. After her temperature was taken and pulse read; Abigail tried to explain that she wasn't sick, and that she knew she didn't have a fever; she was so cold her teeth rattled.

"Don't be afraid. You will be fine," the nurse said. "No one here is going to hurt you."

Then the unbelievable happened. A doctor came in that she had never met before and asked her to place her feet in stirrups, to make sure she wasn't hurt between her legs. From this bizarre position, with the doctor's head between her knees, he asked her what grade she would be going into in the fall and what was her favorite subject. She began to cry again, and he told her to relax. "This little procedure is what all women do regularly. It is for your own good."

She could not imagine why.

"Well, there's no sperm and no external or internal bruising," he said to Cecily and the nurse who wrote down his words.

Abigail remained silent on the ride home. At bedtime, her mother said, "It's best not to think about what happened today. You never have to see that man again. You never will, I'm sure. Now, go to sleep and have sweet dreams, Pooh Bear."

For awhile she tried to remember the old man's face so she could identify him if the police called. His icy blue eyes were unforgettable. She pictured his neck, thin as a turkey's and his blue-gray, claw-like hands.

When the day finally came and the police called with a suspect, Cecily answered the phone. "Please, leave us alone. I have no intention of subjecting her to anymore questioning. No, I will not bring her in. Please, don't call here again," she said.

The police did not press the matter, and Abigail worried that the man might find her again. She had told him where she lived and knew she would have to watch for him all the time, coming and going from school, in the doorways of stores, in cars, on her street. But, after a while, she stopped worrying and almost forgot about the old man and the awful thing that happened in the park.

For Tiffany, the incident was just more evidence that her life was a mess. She believed things would never go right again; not only had her father died, and left them poor and unhappy, now, her sister had helped bring the house down around them. Mom blamed Tiffany for not taking her responsibilities seriously and cut off her allowance as punishment. Tiffany blamed Abigail, said she hated her and that she was going to leave home as soon as she could. Maybe she'd go to Hollywood or Las Vegas. Maybe she'd go to Mexico. She even threatened to go to Madagascar, wherever that was. Anywhere would be better than home as far as Tiffany was concerned.

Standing before *The Park*, and its innocent allure, Abigail was almost overcome. The two transparent girls in the painting had to be Tiffany and herself. She could have wept for them. They weren't even present in their own bodies.

She hadn't known what she was painting, but now she knew. The truth had outed itself, revealing a secret too painful to remember.

Are Stephanie and Joshua becoming engaged in the same kind of pretense and denial I've practiced all these years? Abigail asked herself. Am I forcing them to bury the truth? I have to get all of us to a therapist as soon as possible. Where have I been for the past year? This is their divorce as well as mine, and it is time to sit down with a counselor and talk. Maybe have a chance to listen to their thoughts. Hank's gone, with another woman—filing for divorce. What could be more final? It will never be the same for the kids again. I have to protect them and help them to trust me, start putting them first.

Max introduced Abigail to a woman named Felice Brenner, from Brooklyn. She wanted to say how much she wanted to own *The Park* and tell the artist that Prospect Park was hers, too.

Ironically, the painting was going back to its source. Felice Brenner never needed to know the dreadful story behind the happy colors. Children would still run happily in the park's meadows and mothers wheel carriages down its paths.

11

Woman With A Rose

As Abigail paused in front of the painting, *Woman with a Rose*, Barney or Wade, moved in from behind. "Are we having fun yet?" he whispered in her ear.

She blushed at his warm breath and audacity and regretted having encouraged the man with two names.

To her right, a pensive young woman dressed smartly in black stood beside her husband. His head was slightly pulled back from his shoulders, his expression skeptical. "But it's sad, Hon," he said. "I wouldn't want to look at that long face everyday."

Shades of Hank MacKenzie, Abigail thought.

Woman with a Rose used to hang in the foyer of their house on Apple Blossom Lane, but Hank didn't like it. He asked why it was there when it had gloom written all over it. She had taken it down shortly thereafter.

"Is there anything wrong with owning a painting that's sad?" his wife asked. "Maybe that's what I like about it."

The oil, done in warm colors, represented a downcast woman. The subject's loosely wrapped robe was a blend of alizarin and cobalt; ochre and raw umber washed the walls and warmed the space behind. Pale cadmium yellow lit a rose near her fingertips. Abigail was aware that mystery surrounded the figure—a definite departure from the other paintings, as it didn't fall into the "joyful" school of whimsy where the rest of her work had been cast.

The subject, obviously a lonely woman, was a woman she knew too well, a composite of her mother, sister, and herself, she being the loneliest of the three. Loneliness had pursued her since she knew the meaning of the word. Even when she was first married and mothering her children, at the happiest times, it would show up like an ache in her shoulders.

And she was struggling daily with the aching since Hank left. It was like a cannonball had ripped through her and left a hole too big to heal. She imagined people could see the gaping wound, even in this crowd of strangers.

She had dealt with her father's death, her sister's angry exodus and her mother's near abandonment. Now, the sanest thing she had ever done, marrying Hank, had turned into one more disaster to survive. It was just too much.

He didn't get it, she thought. Or am I the one? Am I the one who didn't get it? What did he let go of? Was I there? Was I ever truly present? Were we connected? Am I connected to anyone under the sun?

She thought of Jane Browne, always surrounded by people, and asked herself if that's what seduced Hank. Was it sociability she offered? Was she someone he felt he could play with, someone easy, someone he could hold onto without the tension he had to deal with in their relationship? Did he find a passion with Jane Browne that he hadn't known before? Did she appreciate things his wife had taken for granted?

Abigail stopped her thoughts. I must let go. I must let go and become my own person.

After Alex Lynde died, becoming independent was a major hurdle for Cecily, but she made it. Once lover Louie was out of the picture and real estate in, she went back to school and passed the real estate boards the first time around. At this time, Connor's Real Estate was grossing over two million a year and her earnings, though only a small percent, felt sufficient. It no longer mattered that Jake was uncouth, that he burped and slurped his meals or used language she found objectionable. He had made it possible for her to start marketing and selling houses and eventually take on the commercial market.

"You got class, Baby," he'd say to her again and again. "I love you, Doll."

"She would deflect his affections with gentle amusement, "Jake, you need a young woman, one without responsibilities," she'd say, putting herself in the position of being wrong for him, instead of his being wrong for her. It wasn't effective.

Abigail was in the office one day when she overheard Jake say, "I'm doing this for us, for the kids, 'cause someday you're going to want what I got."

"Do you honestly think I would be more interested in you if you were to become Mr. Universe?" her mother asked. "Please, Jake, let's be serious. What in the world does a man's beauty contest have to do with us?"

"If I win, I get a hundred thousand grand plus a lotta money for sponsoring products. That's what!"

"Oh my. That is impressive. What must you do to win?" she teased.

"First it's the state and then the nationals, you know, like Miss America."

"But, what do you do? Walk down a runway in an evening dress?" she joked.

He hadn't even smiled. "I lift weights and flex my muscles. That's about all there is to it."

Abigail realized Jake was proud of his physique. It interested her to think she had just thought he was fat.

"Well, I certainly wish you the best of luck. It should be quite an exciting event," Cecily said, smiling dismissively, as she returned to her listing sheets.

"You think so, Doll? Why don'cha come to it. I can get you a front row seat."

"Oh no! I couldn't. The children...."

"The children? They're just an excuse! Bring Abby, here, with ya!"

Abigail didn't want to go. She had no desire to see Jake Polinsky with his clothes mostly off, sweating in front of cameras and believing he could win a prize for it. Evidently, her mother was of the same opinion.

Late that night, there was a pounding on their front door. Cecily leapt from the chair where she'd dozed off. Her book fell to the floor, its back broken from the impact. Tiffany rose from her bed in the back room and appeared in the doorway, wrapped in her blanket, hair in a frenzy. "Who could that be?" she asked.

Her mother said, "Go back to bed, I'll handle this," and went to the door.

Abigail listened from stairwell at the top of the stairs.

"Jacob? What are you doing here in the middle of the night? You have scared us half to death! Is everything all right?"

"I won! I won! I am goddamned Mr. Manhattan! Can you beat that, Doll?" he boomed. "Now let's get married. Will you marry me?"

"Oh, for heaven's sake, come inside, you'll wake the neighbors."

The door slammed behind him.

"I think you've been drinking, Jake. Let me make you some coffee."

"I don't want any fucking coffee, I want you, Doll. I love you. Don't you want to marry Mr. Manhattan? Come on, get your coat. Come out with me. We'll go get a pizza and talk about it."

"Jake, you have to leave, really. The girls…"

"Girls schmirls! Fuck the girls. Come on, Doll. I'm good for you; you're good for me. How about it?"

"Jake, I want you to go now. No more talk like this. I can't marry you. I will never marry you, and you must stop this nonsense."

His color rose along with his voice. He staggered a little and his shoulders became bearlike.

"Bitch. You goddamned bitch. You think you're too good for me. That's it, isn't it? You think you are too high-class for Jake Polinsky. But I'll teach ya' whose got the class. You'll see."

Cecily remained calm and said, "Fine." She put one hand on his arm and the other on his back and turned him toward the door.

"Now, take yourself down the street and go get a cup of coffee and a donut. Move." She shoved him gently but he shoved her back, against the door, trying to kiss her.

As she twisted out of his arms, he took his big hand and pounded it in frustration on the door. "Damn it. Damn it," he said.

Tiffany ran into the vestibule screaming, "Stop! Stop, or I'll call the police!"

"Jesus Christ, go ahead," Jake said, dropping back, opening the door and almost falling down the ten stone stairs of the front stoop.

Cecily threw the deadbolt and stood in the hallway with her back against the door. She was shaking from head to toe.

"Mom!" Tiffany said. "Why did you let him in? He was drunk! What are you going to do now?

"I don't know, I don't know. You go to bed and don't worry. He's harmless, an oaf." Then she collapsed on the couch and wailed, "Alex, you bastard. See what you've done? How could you have done this to us?"

From the top of the stairs, Abigail asked her father much the same question.

Her mother didn't go to work the next day or the day after that. Jake Polinsky called time after time until they removed the phone from its cradle. These were dark days for all of them. Money was short because of Cecily's absence from work and they missed the funny stories she used to bring home with her. The three of them began to lose the feeling of terra firma. By day number six, they were eating breakfast all day long; the next day without the eggs and then without the toast. Cecily spent her last dollar on milk. At the end of the week the refrigerator was almost empty—just a few pieces of dry cheese, some old bologna and condiments left. When Abigail complained, saying there was nothing to eat, Tiffany told her, "Don't complain. Mom has it hard enough."

On day number nine, Cecily put on her tailored gray suit, her charmed silver earrings and necklace and high black Italian leather heels. Holding her back very straight, she went to face Jake.

She was gone for about two hours but returned with money, groceries and a newspaper.

"I've quit my job," she announced. "After I extracted my parting wages, I said goodbye. We may starve, but I cannot work under the same roof with that buffoon anymore."

The same day she called three real estate offices and on Friday went for an interview.

Abigail tried to convince Tiffany that they should help their mother get a job. She said her friend at school told her that you can buy a candle and pray to it and wishes will come true. It happened all the time at her church, she said.

"Don't be so gullible. Why doesn't everyone do it then?" Tiffany asked.

"You have to do it at my friend's church. That's why so many people go there. They can't even fit in the door. You know how crowded it is on Sundays—how people have to stand on the front steps in order to get in?" Abigail explained. "We could at least try. It's right around the corner and open all the time. You know, the one with two steeples? It's called Scared Heart."

"Sacred Heart," Tiffany corrected, and shook her head, no. "Don't be so superstitious."

But Abigail wouldn't give up. She continued to beg until Tiffany relented. Then the two of them went through every pocket in the three closets; searched catch-alls behind and beneath the couches and chair pillows, and all told, came up with one dollar and sixty-two cents, which they divided between them, figuring two offerings, two candles, two prayers equaled twice the chance for their prayers to be answered.

Armed with their change they made their way to the church. The magic candles were against the far wall tucked under a statue. The girls didn't recognize the saint but knew full well the meaning of the flames in the red glasses. Clinkity-clink went their coins into the collection box. It was like tapping on God's door. The sound itself made them tense with excitement. They found the can holding long matches to light their candles and imitated two other wishful people by kneeling on the cushions before the tiers of candles. While they knelt, Abigail saw unexplainable shadows cross the pretty face of the plaster lady in the niche in the wall, then she saw a slight smile appear on the lady's lips. She wanted to touch her white, outstretched hand, positioned like it was, to give a blessing or a pat on the head. A warm feeling ran from Abigail's head down to her toes.

Two hours later, curled up in front of the TV, they heard Cecily call. "Girls! I'm home!" She had that ringing voice that meant good tidings were at hand.

They rushed to greet her.

"Well, I found another job in another real estate firm, and it may not be as profitable as Connors' but it should be enough, at least there's more potential than Jake could offer. What do you think?"

"Wow! It worked!" they cried.

"What worked?" Cecily laughed.

They told her about the candle lighting, and the lady's smile, and all three of them agreed it was indeed a miracle. Afterwards, Tiffany put on her records and they danced like gypsies to Bolero. That was one night Abigail would always remember. It felt like they were a real family.

Before the month was out, the family was awakened by another pounding at the door. "It is probably that man again. I am not letting him in. Girls go to your rooms and put a pillow over your head. He's not coming in."

"Should we call the police, Mother?" Tiffany asked.

"Don't worry, I can handle this."

She went to the door and opened it a crack. Through the slim line of light she said, "Go away Jake. You frighten the girls. Go home. "

"Please, please, I'm sorry for what I did. Listen, I have to talk to you. I did something crazy. I ... I... I got married."

"Married?"

"Yeah. Please, Oh God, Doll, I gotta talk to you."

"Only for a minute, you understand?"

"I understand."

She undid the locks and let him in. He was a mess. His face covered with blotches and his eyes red with tears or exhaustion. He looked so strange sitting on the damask covered settee. Like a bear on a lily pad. He just didn't fit.

"Let me get you something to drink. Would you like a cup of coffee? Some tea?"

"Nah."

"Well, you sit down and pull yourself together."

She listened as he noisily blew into his handkerchief and folded his huge body into itself. He wrung his hands between his knees. Mr. Manhattan looked far from it.

"I did it because of you. I did it because I want to have sons and daughters and a life. She gave me two hundred thousand dollars to marry her."

"She did what?"

"She paid me to do it. I'm not gonna win the nationals, Doll. She's a sure thing. She wants what I got." The tea kettle started whistling.

"Well, then, that's good, isn't it?" Cecily tried to think what she should say as she walked toward the kitchen, leaving him to pull himself together. But he lifted his bulk from the comfort of the settee and followed her.

Abigail had run downstairs to stand beside Tiffany who quietly left the bedroom door slightly open.

"No, Doll. What's good is you. I want you." He sat down at the glass topped kitchen table, put his head in his hands and started crying, big honking sobs.

"Now stop. Drink this tea and get control of yourself. Really, Jake. You have made me up. I am not what you think. You must like this young woman?"

"I don't even know her. I went to a Lonely Hearts Club Dance down at the Jewish Center. She was staring at me every time I looked at her, like she needed me to talk to her, so I did. We went off and got married last night. Look. Look at this."

He reached in his pocket, pulled out his wallet and showed Cecily the check. "See? Two hundred thousand bucks."

Cecily didn't say she wondered if the check was good or question how any sum could justify such an act. Nor did she ask where the profits he should have reaped from his real estate business had gone?

"I love you, Doll. I'm sorry I botched things up. I'm gonna pay with my life. But someday, you'll see, it'll be you wanting me. You'll see."

Abigail was sure that day would never come.

After his tea, he went home like a sorry puppy. Tiffany, who was still holding the phone in her hand in the event she had to call for help, asked her mother what she was going to do.

"He's just sad because a romance he made up is not going to come true. I am never going to see him again," she said.

The new real estate job was based on commissions. It did not have the comfortable financial base pay provided by Connor's Real Estate, but it did have an energetic woman at its helm. Unfortunately, it didn't take long for Cecily to realize she was getting the sloughed-off customers, the ones none of the other brokers wanted. But she held on, believing that work in would soon produce profit out.

When Tiffany started working she became more and more independent. Her employer was Martin's Department Store in Brooklyn's retail district on Fulton Street across from Macy's and Mays and full of the things she loved most: Revlon, Calvin Klein, and Ralph Lauren. On good days, when she came home with armfuls of purchases and no paycheck, her mother simply remarked that if Tiffany died young, she hoped Heaven had a shopping mall. On bad days, she would say Tiffany was going to die young if she didn't relinquish her paycheck. A screaming match would ensue, neither of them willing to give in.

Abigail practiced becoming invisible during those bouts of trial and blame.

Once, Tiffany screamed in the heat of battle, "I want my father back! How could he go and die just when I needed him most."

Cecily called her a heartless girl who knew nothing about the world. She said, "If you had any idea, any idea at all of how selfish and cruel your words are, you wouldn't be able to hold your head up. So, I am not going to tell you. No, I'll leave you to your illusions; you have at least got that. It's more than I will ever have again. I can only hope you never have to face the truth."

But Tiffany was not worried about truth. She was riding high, still connected to her prep school friends and only marginally connected to Abigail and Cecily. She cared little about the huge public school from which she was about to graduate, either. She had even cooled her relationship with Bo. Poor Bo. He was kept dangling on the side, while she experimented with other boys, going on long weekends to Ithaca and Princeton, and spending time with friends she had made at work.

It wasn't enough that men ogled her on the street. She fueled their attentions, using tricks of clothing and make-up to make her appearance an event. Her carefully modulated, swaying walk asked to be noticed. It even helped her get minor modeling jobs in the department store where she worked. Her life really changed when they nominated her for the Miss Subway Contest. Tiffany claimed her happiness was due to the possibility of making money to pay for college, but her mother pointed out she hadn't applied to any school, anywhere, and her grades were not high enough to merit a scholarship. She slept through the SATs.

The winning nominees for the Miss Subway title had instant celebrity; their pictures were posted all over New York, a heady thing for any eighteen-year-old. The public was engaged by choosing the winner, entering their choices in ballot boxes placed strategically in subway stations and stores throughout the city. Tiffany's face, along with four others, was in every subway car, bus and store display in the five boroughs. It even made it to a few billboards on the highways. For the entire summer, Abigail ran from store to store filling out ballots and stuffing the ballot boxes with names of her own invention: Candy Stripe, Tex S. Burger, Phil Herrup, Red Pepper, Ben Taken, Moe Downe, Ima Queen and the like.

With the onset of fame, expensive clothes were forgiven, and Martin's facilitated her excesses with employee discounts and a credit line. Tiffany's closet was virtually bursting at the seams, a treasure chest of fashion.

With her mother and Tiffany so busy, Abigail was left more and more on her own, but she was almost eleven and could take care of herself. As always, books, dreams, albums and sketchpads occupied most of her time. She grew to like the new old house and the neighborhood's noisy energy. Although she didn't fit into the groups of kids on her street, she made friends with the adults around her.

Zena and Sergi, along with their little dog, Sasha, lived in the third floor apartment that Cecily had carved out of two bedrooms in order to help cover household expenses. Sergi was a bearded Russian Jew and Zena, Yugoslavian. He called her his little Slav, and she wondered if Slav meant slave, because Zena waited on Sergi hand and foot. She even cut his meat. Sergi was wide and short just like his fingers. He chewed with his mouth open and talked louder and louder during a meal. But there was a lot to like about Sergi. He was a kind, robust man who always seemed to want to help. He lifted Cecily's couches when she wanted to change a room around, and moved the garbage pails up and down the cellar stairs on collection days. He fixed doors that became unhinged and occasionally brought home an extra loaf of bread for the Lyndes from the bakery. Sergi was a good person.

Cecily rented the room on the second floor, adjoining Abigail's, to a boarder named Seymour Horstacht. He was peculiar and reclusive. If he said hello it was a surprise. Seymour wore brown everythings. Brown shoes, shirts, jackets, ties and a brown overcoat. His hair was almost brown, and his eyes were a washed out brown, too. He carried packages wrapped in brown paper in and out of the house all the time. His obscurity made Abigail all the more curious about him.

She decided to investigate his room, and filched the master key that hung on the wall in the kitchen pantry. Up the stairs she went, at the quietest time of the day in the empty house, the time right after school while her mother was still at the office, Tiffany at modeling school and the upstairs tenants still at work.

Fortunately, the lock on the door between her room and Seymour's was dead-bolted, but the lock from his room to the stairwell was of the old-fashioned variety. Like any good sleuth, she easily inserted the old skeleton key and opened the door. Inside Seymour's apartment, she discovered a somber decor. It was the stuff her mother had no use for, and nothing in the room was affected by Seymour's occupancy. A heavy dark wood table and chairs sat in front of the only window. A single naked light hung from the center of the ceiling without any purpose other than to illuminate. On the back of one of the chairs were two pairs of black socks drying; on another, Seymour's boxer shorts. On a far wall was an old chest of drawers, its top used to showcase framed sepia-tinted photographs of Franklin Delano Roosevelt. A framed letter from FDR to someone named Bertrand Russell sat in the middle. On the mantle of the dysfunctional fireplace were more framed examples of Roosevelt's autographs and memorabilia of speeches and buttons, book covers and coins and things related to the World War. Books of Roosevelt's life, both biographical and historical, were evenly stacked next to the bed. On top of them was a flashlight Seymour must have used when he read at night.

The room revealed nothing else. Not a sign of decorating, of family or comfort, just an overwhelming brown sadness. She wondered where his things were, the things that told a person about who he really was. She opened his top drawer. A spill of nudity presented itself. Breasts and labia, some wide rearends upended. Abigail knew it was filthy stuff and was ashamed for having looked in places where she shouldn't. It made her want to gag. She shut the drawer quickly and ran out of the room, forgetting to lock the door. For the next two hours she contemplated how she would tell her mother that a pervert lived in their house.

It was late September, and they were having an Indian summer. The night didn't offer any relief to the day and Abigail lay in bed, miserable in the weight of her pajamas and trying not to hear the shuffling of the man on the other side of the wall. He had come home late and was taking his time getting settled. She wondered if he could tell he had been trespassed.

When it was quiet, save for an occasional car going down the street, she opened her windows, and her door, hoping for a little cross breeze. Relief was not to be had. The heavy air stayed stale and still.

Then she heard Seymour's door open, and she figured he was just going to use the bathroom until a light shone on her from the hallway.

"Little girls who trespass sometimes get hurt," Seymour's voice said softly in the dark.

She pretended to toss in her sleep, turn over and at the same time pull a sheet up to her chin. For interminable minutes, she lay as still as possible. The sound of her heart thumping so loudly she was sure it was audible to the man in the hallway. Was he going to strangle her? What evidence had she left behind? How had he known she'd gone into his room? She should scream, but then her mother would find out she'd spied. The glare of the flashlight continued and she decided she would scream, regardless of the consequences, if it didn't go away by her internal count of three. Fortuitously, the darkness returned and she heard Seymour's door close and the lock click behind him.

On cat feet, she tiptoed downstairs to Tiffany's room. "Can I sleep with you tonight?" she asked. "I had a bad dream."

"Okay silly," Tiffany said. And Abigail tried to believe it was true, that what had occurred was just a bad dream. But in the days that followed she stayed as far away from Seymour as possible and never, ever left her door open again. From then on, she kept her bedroom door closed with a chair propped against it, and prayed Seymour would move away.

Tiffany turned into a celebrity. She didn't become Miss Subway, but by the time the contest was over, it hardly mattered whether she won or not. Stylists had changed her looks into something more sophisticated and The Panache Modeling School not only gave her a free scholarship, they introduced her to an agent. Any legitimate thoughts of college she once had, gave way to the opportunity to model.

Tiffany's first major television commercial was filmed in November. It made possible a Screen Actors Guild membership and ran for months. It may not have taken a lot of talent to hold a roll of toilet paper, fold a piece into a square and blot her lips, but Abigail put her sister in a class with Elizabeth Taylor. The camera focused on her eyes, her nose and her mouth, so that it looked like she was in love with the piece of tissue. As usual, Abigail basked in her sister's glory, forgetting that one person's success is not necessarily another's.

When Cecily explained how much she expected Tiffany to contribute to the family's budget, Tiffany balked. "Why don't you sell your fur coats if we're so poverty stricken?" she asked.

Her mother got red in the face. "The world of glamour is doing you no good," she warned.

"Ha! You're just jealous!" Tiffany retaliated.

Cecily's hand flew up and struck Tiffany across her face. The smack must have stung, but Tiffany didn't cry.

Soon after, Tiffany quit her job at the department store in favor of modeling school, and it all worked out because the store continued to call her regularly to walk the runway for their fashion shows—Miss Subway Contestant, Tiffany Lynde presents the latest fall fashions— and the modeling school gave her work as part of their training.

On weekends Cecily and Tiffany were dating men they only vaguely alluded to, while Abigail was left to wonder if anyone, anywhere, would ever notice her. She killed time by illustrating the novels she loved: *Little Women*, *Jane Eyre*, and *Rebecca of Sunnybrook Farm*. She was also gathering materials to record the story of her sister's rising stardom. She had enough photos, ads, notes and newspaper clippings to fill two scrapbooks. Someday, she knew, they would be in a biography, which, of course, she would write. Meanwhile, she faithfully tracked the television commercials featuring Tiffany. They ran continually, and Abigail kept a scoreboard between ABC, NBC, and CBS. Cecily and Tiffany loved her for this effort and glowed over the royalty checks that followed. Otherwise, each of them lived in a world of her own, and no one seemed to notice as the younger girl's body stretched into angles and string.

By the end of the seventh grade Abigail was as tall as Tiffany and by the following fall she was taller. Her nose sharpened along with her elbows, her freckles largely disappeared and her rib cage became a washboard. Only a hint of breasts sat upon the boney plain she called her chest.

"The woman with the rose, who is she waiting for?" the young woman beside her asked.

"You know, I'm not sure. Maybe it's a prince, or maybe it's herself. I think you should decide," Abigail suggested.

"I think it's the prince," she said. "I think that's what every woman wants."

Abigail thought, things don't change. It is still what every young woman dreams of, the knight in shining armor, the stuff of fairy tales. Obviously, this young woman doesn't know that yet. Should I mention to her how wise it would be to have a back up, a plan where she can be sure she can save herself?

Kendra's new friend was still behind her. She could feel his energy filling the space between them. He might be interesting but he wouldn't become her back up. She was going to stay free as a bird until she got her bearings. In case he was asking, she sent him a silent message. No way, no room, nobody wanted.

12

Curtains Up

Abigail's thirteenth year was like many other adolescents', replete with growing pains. The joints of her arms and legs ached throughout the night. A bone appeared in her nose where freckles once ruled. Poached egg breasts emerged on her chest which she hid modestly under huge sweatshirts and cast-off shirts from Uncle Lyman. One minute she was laughing at the sound of a clogged up ketchup bottle, the next, weeping over Bobby Goldsboro. Stable, she was not.

Meanwhile, her sister's world was opening like a beautiful flower. She watched Tiffany's comings and goings with awe and envy, feeling sad one day because she was losing her sister, and the next, content just to be in her wake.

In a rare act of altruism, Tiffany gave Abigail a ticket for a Broadway show on her fourteenth birthday. It might have been the nicest thing Tiffany had ever done for her sister or anyone else. She explained the gift away saying she thought they should see it together because it was a story about sisters.

Preparing for the big night became traumatic as Abigail realized she had nothing to wear that suited a Broadway theater. She told Tiffany about her dilemma and Tiffany rummaged through her closet until she found an outfit that almost fit. It was a stretchy two-piece hippie outfit with low-cut pants that began beneath her naval and flared at her feet. The tie-top blouse was meant to cling to her breasts like a bathing suit but sagged where it should have pointed. Abigail was mortified, but the outfit was the only thing Tiffany said would work. To compensate for her missing breasts Abigail folded white athletic socks and stuck them into her AA bra. Then she ironed an old London Fog raincoat to cover it all and prayed for rain.

The evening finally came, and she and Tiffany sat in the living room waiting for their escort, Trevor Williams, to arrive. Trevor was the new man in Tiffany's life. It was a beautiful spring night, and to Abigail's chagrin there was not so much as a threat of rain.

Tiffany had no problem looking her best in a low cut clingy blue dress that accented every beautiful curve she had on its way to her ankles. Abigail, meanwhile, was miserable about her straight bangs and clumsy French braid. She sat worrying, anxious that her stiff patent leather flats would squeak and the socks on her bosom might escape.

Suddenly, Tiffany burst out laughing. "Take the socks out, Abby, you don't need them," she said.

Abigail could have killed her, but she did as she was told before the walking, talking Marlboro man arrived.

Trevor and Tiffany glittered like superstars as they entered the golden doors of the Winter Garden Theater. All eyes turned in their direction with Abigail scurrying behind them, a willing shadow, her precious ticket in hand. Feeling invisible, she was free to gape at the theatergoers as she wound through the epitome of contemporary fashion and the traditionally elegant sipping wine in the lobby. Abigail headed toward the loge, her raincoat buttoned to her neck, and then waited at the door until an usher checked her seat number and guided the three of them to velvet seats only ten rows from the stage.

As the lights went down, excitement grew. She could hardly wait for the great curtain to rise, but the music came first, bursting forth from the orchestra pit beneath the proscenium, and then, magically, rising from the hole in the floor to prepare the audience for what lay ahead.

She could have had no idea then, that the songs in that overture were on their way to becoming part of the world's musical memory. "Tradition," "Sunrise Sunset," "If I were a Rich Man," "Do You Love Me?"—each one was better than the next. To say she was a happy witness would have been an understatement.

Her hands clapped spontaneously as the huge chandeliers lifted to the ceiling, and bit by bit, the curtain rose to expose the village of Anatevka where a fiddler sat on a rooftop playing his fiddle. Soon she met Tevye, his wife Golde and their daughters, and became one with their love and heartaches.

She couldn't wait to talk about the play, about the songs and the dancing, and where tradition began and ended in the story of the Russian Jews; but Abigail felt like she was talking to herself as they stood in the lobby during the intermission. Tiffany was busy gazing adoringly at Mr. Beautiful's face, hanging onto his arm like it was her lifeline. He behaved no differently than she, consumed entirely with himself.

It may have been Abigail's imagination, but she saw the crowd part as they left the theater. It felt like they were a charmed threesome as they passed through the throngs to one of the yellow checkered cabs in front.

In no time at all, Tiffany was moving out of the house. It happened when Cecily insisted she pay rent.

"Rent? You want me to pay to live here? Why would I want to live here?" Tiffany protested. "All you do is complain that I don't do enough. You stand by while Abby steals my clothes and makes a mess of my things; there's never any food in the fridge, we even run out of soap! I don't have a decent closet or any real privacy. You want a maid, not a daughter. I'm not going to wait on the two of you for the rest if my life. I'd rather live in a hovel in Manhattan than this pathetic place!" Her voice grew louder as she spoke. Her hands flailed. She was on fire.

"That's the thanks I get for keeping this family together? That's all you can say after I've fed and housed you and cared for you all these years?" Cecily yelled in return. "Well, you can go! Go with my blessing! You have a few things to learn, young lady."

And go she did, and learn she did—a very great deal in a very short time. She dined at Sartre's, took ski trips to Switzerland, partied at Studio 57, danced at the Top of the Sixes and laughed at Caroline's comedy club. The glamour wheel took her for a spin, and on the way, she became more sophisticated; knew where to find the concierge, how to order from a French menu, acquired a taste for bouillabaisse and escargots, and to say s'il vous plait when it mattered. She could tell Givenchy from Dior and Pucci from Gucci. The brownstone she had vacated in Brooklyn interested her almost not at all. When she did sweep in and out, she often left a trail of trouble behind.

Abigail was sure she was partly to blame for her sister's leaving and felt guilty for the times she had made her angry. It was true that she often went into her closet and borrowed a belt or a sweater, or one of her chain necklaces, and sometimes she did experiment with her makeup. Also, every time she opened her mouth she said something that annoyed Tiffany, and there could be no doubt that Tiffany particularly resented her presence when Trevor was around. But Abigail didn't care. She was so in love with love she wanted to see them together whenever possible.

Cecily blamed Trevor Williams for the change in Tiffany. From the time they started dating, Tiffany turned more and more into a stranger. But stranger or not, nasty or not, she was missed by her mother and sister. They didn't talk about it. It was too touchy. When Grandma Lynde probed, she was told only the good news.

Bo missed her, too. At the end of his first semester at law school, he stopped by and found a way to work her into the conversation within a few minutes. Abigail decided not to tell him about Trevor. She knew he knew he had been demoted from boyfriend to friend, but she also knew he was the best man her sister would ever find. She figured Tiffany would see the light someday.

It was May, and Abigail and Bo were sitting on the stone steps of the front stoop, sharing the fresh air. His long legs were covered in worn-out denim, his slim arms covered by blue Oxford cloth and a holey gray wool sweater that looked like he'd found it on the subway. The honey colored hair that used to be so well-groomed was now in a ratty ponytail down his back. He looked different, but all she needed to do was talk to him for five minutes and she knew he was the same old Bo. He had a kindness about him that stayed. It was real. He would hate the vain Trevor. When she grew up, if Tiffany hadn't seen the light, Abigail planned to make up for her sister's bad taste.

The very best thing that happened to Abigail that spring was that the boarder, Seymour Horstacht, was gone. He had moved away just a week before her sister left. It was a major relief to find his scratchy note on the kitchen table explaining he wanted to be closer to Hyde Park and his research. With him gone, the house once again felt safe.

"What a bizarre man," Cecily had said, as she read the note aloud. "Why Hyde Park, I wonder? What research?"

Abigail could have told her. She had been there on a school field trip and seen all the FDR memorabilia. Roosevelt's home would have been as interesting to Seymour as women's parts. He would probably have learned by now, that FDR was a momma's boy and that he married his own cousin. Even Abigail knew cousins don't marry cousins.

"I'm just as happy he moved on," Cecily said. "There was something dark about him. Depressed, I guess."

Evidently, Abigail had covered up her fears pretty well, at least enough to keep her mother from learning of her trespass. With Seymour gone, she could sleep through the night again.

But, without Tiffany, the big old house lost its juice. Often the refrigerator's only sign of life was the mold reinventing itself on dead bologna. The telephone rang only infrequently, and all the lovely lotions that once filled the shelves in the bathrooms were gone. The former forays into Tiffany's closets and bureau drawers were over. She almost missed their bitter fights and tears, and the lively tensions between them.

A fourteen-year-old and her distracted mother do not a family make. Abigail worked hard not to be in her mother's way, to do her own meals and clothes without complaint. She spent a lot of time at the library and went to the museum's art classes after school.

Her mother asked her to start calling her Cecily, because it sounded more grown up than Mom and Mommy. But the truth was Abigail didn't call her much of anything because she saw her so little. Her mother often worked late at the office and sometimes ate dinner with clients.

"I am going to be on the late side tonight, Abigail. You okay?"

"Sure, Cecily," she'd say.

Abigail guessed she was fine, no perverts hovering, and Sergi and Zena, her unwitting babysitters, upstairs. It was easy for her to join them on the third floor if they invited her and even when they didn't. The young couple would offer pretzels and root beer and she would entertain them with stories about the illustrious Tiffany. Most of her stories were made up on the spot.

One night Cecily brought a new man home with her. She was a little wobbly and he was red-faced and loud. Abigail disliked him, immediately. "Hey there girl, your momma said you was bee-u-ti-ful, but I didn't expect Grace Kelly."

The man was obviously a jerk.

"I was talking about my other daughter, Tiffany," her mother said.

"Well, this one is pretty special, too, I'd say. A bee-u-ty in the making."

"I'm going to bed, Cecily," Abigail announced.

"You see? You are too much. I warned you she is shy," Cecily laughed.

Abigail said, "Nite," and climbed the stairs. Before she reached the stairwell she heard her mother say, "You stop, now, Bobby. Honestly, you will never change!"

As Abigail brushed her teeth and washed her face in the bathroom next to Seymour's old room, she was grateful again that he was gone, and when her head hit the pillow she quickly fell asleep to the fuzzy sounds below.

In the morning, Cecily called from the front hall to announce she was leaving. "I'm going, Abby! It's 7:30 and you have exactly half an hour to wash, eat and get out of here!"

Abigail staggered out of bed, went to the bathroom in nothing but her panties and heard the guestroom door open. In a swift move, she shut the bathroom door and slipped the bolt neatly in place. Soon after, she heard feet negotiating the stairs. Clippity-clip, stop, clippity-clip, stop. She froze. Then she remembered the night before and figured her mother's friend Bobby Something must have stayed overnight.

She dashed into her room, pulled on a sweater and stepped into her jeans. Then she ran a brush through her tangled hair, checking herself in the mirror and saw a wrinkle neatly pressed into her face. She pinched her cheeks as hard as she could to make it go away, but that problem quickly became secondary to the sound of Bobby Something on his way back upstairs. Instinct told her to close the bedroom door and lock herself in. She pulled the dresser to the door, just in time for his knock.

"Hey, gorgeous, let me in. Why don't we get to know each other," he said.

"Sorry, I am getting ready for school. I don't have any time," she answered, at the same time she was pushing Grandma's heavy cherry hope chest against the dresser.

"Whatcha doin' in there?" he asked. "Come on out, and I'll give you a ride to school in my truck."

"Don't have time," she said, now yanking the bookcase in the same direction, to make a final wedge between the door and the wall.

"Hey, Honey, you'll save time if you ride with ol' Bobby here, come on. I'll give you a ride."

She grabbed the sharpest pencil from her desk and stood prepared to stab him in the eyes if she had to.

"You get out of the house or I am going to start screaming out my window."

"Why, you little baby bitch," he said.

She went to the window and rattled the sash as much as she could as she opened it, leaning out as far as she dared. "I am telling you, unless I see you on the way down the street, I am going to start screaming."

"Hell. I'm outta here," he said. The walls reverberated as he slammed the door.

She watched him stalk up the street and climb into his red truck and take off like he was going to a fire.

School was as ordinary as ever that day but leaving was different. The bravery Abigail had felt in the morning was missing by the time she approached her house. Bobby's truck was nowhere in sight, and yet she didn't want to go in. Instead, she went to visit the friendly Steinbergs a few houses down the street and said she was locked out.

"Come in, come in!" Mrs. Steinberg said. She was a large woman with a heavy German accent and doilies on her chairs.

With a smile she led her into her kitchen for some iced tea. "You must want to meet my granddaughter, she has just moved into the house across the street," she said. "Why don't I call her?" And that is how Abigail met Melissa, who was to become her very best friend.

By the time she left the Steinbergs' her mother was home from work. "I'm so tired," her mother said. "I thought you might have set the table, Abby."

Abigail went to the kitchen, folded two yellow cotton napkins with the corners placed toward the right and pulled two gold trimmed dinner plates from the shelves. She placed the silverware properly at their sides and went back into the living room. "Table's done," she announced.

She watched silently while Cecily took off her shoes and opened the mail. She was watching as Cecily threw the envelopes down on the cocktail table and collapsed into the sofa, rare tears running down her cheeks. She knew it wasn't the right moment to add anything to her mother's pain, so instead of telling her about Bobby Something, she went to the kitchen and made some instant coffee, adding two teaspoons of sugar and a bit of cream before placing it in her mother's hands.

A plane on its way to LaGuardia came low over their heads and shook the paintings on the wall. "Wow, that's a low one," she said.

"I wish it would just crash into us and end the whole miserable thing," Cecily groaned.

Abigail shuddered at the thought. She couldn't believe Cecily meant what she said. She couldn't really wish them both dead.

"What am I going to do with all these bills?" she asked an invisible someone on the ceiling.

"Mom?" Abigail tried.

"It's impossible. That's what it is, impossible."

"Cecily? Mom? You know that Bobby Something, the man who was here last night? Was he an old boyfriend of yours?"

"Oh, please. He is not an old friend. He was at a reception at the St. George for realtors. He isn't even in real estate. I knew him when I was your age, a no good then, and no good now. He is a bore. An unmitigated bore."

Did she mean boar or bore, Abigail wondered. "He was worse

than that, he…"

"Please, let's not talk about Bobby, I would rather forget the man."

And so they didn't. Abigail decided it was far more important that her mother wanted to go on living.

13

The Bookworm

The summer of '76 was one of unusual heat. Even the cicadas complained, noisily chewing leaves from trees already fighting for survival. Brooklyn's streets smelled of baked concrete and dry worms. During such a summer, with Tiffany long gone to Los Angeles, Melissa working for her father, and Cecily wrapped up in yet another man, Abigail was left to sweat out the days alone.

As usual, books were her escape hatch. Under the tutelage of Jane Austen, Gustave Flaubert and Sigrid Undstet her own little miseries looked petty. She devoured each author's words, reading sentences over and over again to put them to memory. Jane Austen was her soul sister in that they shared a love for the written word. *I declare, after all there is no enjoyment like reading. How much sooner one tires of anything than of a book.*

Madame Bovary and Kristin Lavransdatter were found on the family bookshelves. These women's lives revealed what it was to be human, to be sexual and flawed. At the same time they warned of the dangers of passion, a danger she had attributed solely to men.

The curse, her menses, began in June, a belated event that came three years after she first received a Kotex pad in health education class. The tired little packet was torn and filthy by this time, but still existed as a reminder that someday she would join the world of women who bled. She became a woman and yet she saw most men as foreign objects. Bo and Uncle Lyman were the exceptions, although they were mostly missing in action, living lives outside her fifteen-year-old world.

Bo called one slow day in late July to find out what was going on in Hollywood and to see how the other Lynde ladies were getting along. After Abigail had filled him in on some of Tiffany's news, he invited her to visit the campus at NYU and see his law school. He said he thought she might enjoy the exhibit of David Hockney who was being featured in the hottest gallery in Greenwich Village. "We can catch a lunch at the Corner Bistro, if you like."

If she liked? She didn't tell him she had never heard of Hockney, but she would die to go see his show. She was swept away that Bo would care enough about her to share his world.

Bo had a way of talking easily, making it fine for a person to be who she really was. For instance, he didn't tease her for confessing to have crushes on David Bowie and Billy Joel. Instead, he said he would kill to know Goldie Hawn. He made a point of discussing books, describing what he was reading and the books he would write someday. The last time he'd stopped by, he'd left a book at the house called *The Cosmic Connection* by one of Brooklyn's own, Carl Sagan. He asked her to read it so they could discuss it the next time he came for a visit. He said it had a way of putting all things in perspective.

If she could have designed a big brother it would have been Bo.

Abigail kept her date with Bo a secret; not because anyone would have thought it a big deal, but because she wanted the whole experience for herself. Going to the city to have lunch with Bo Lupton was simply too special for words.

She dressed carefully, choosing what she imagined looked appropriate for Greenwich Village. Melissa had given her a cute miniskirt her father had said was too short. She wore that, topped with a sleeveless tank shirt. The "Bare Trap" shoes she'd scrubbed floors for, cinched the look. She curled her hair in Meg Ryan ringlets, reviewed Sagan and was off.

The IRT express took her to the Atlantic Avenue station where she had to change subways for a local to Bleeker Street. As she tried to exit the train, a horde of people pushed her back into the car and crushed her against the opposite door. Before she knew it, she was reading Chamber Street on the tile walls of a station she had never seen before. Rather than go any further she got off the train, climbed the stairs and went through another turnstile to reverse her direction.

In only a minute or two the next train arrived. As she stepped from the platform into the car, a man came charging up behind her and stuck his finger up her skirt. It was a violation so bold that she felt blinded and could not turn to see the perpetrator. She covered her face and leaned into a stranger's shoulder.

The woman asked, "You all right, Honey?" as her friendly arms managed to keep Abigail erect.

"I'm all right," Abigail said, and then added. "Men are horrible."

"Men are good for one thing, and they ain't so good at that," the woman said, guiding the limp girl to a seat where she sat in a daze until she reached the Atlantic Avenue Station again. Too shaken to leave the train, she stayed in her seat until she was back to Grand Army Plaza.

At the plaza, she climbed the familiar stone steps, gulped the free air and began the long trek home, down Prospect Park West, beyond the Arch of Courage, past the Seafarer's House, her old Ethical Culture School, the park entrance, until she turned right at the corner of 5th Street and went up the steps to the house, pushing herself all the way. She took a shower right away and scrubbed herself everywhere, wishing all the while she had been born a boy, and wondering how she had brought so many cruelties on herself. Were all girls humiliated again and again?

When the phone rang, she didn't answer it, knowing it was Bo, knowing he was worried, but needing time to concoct an excuse. The next time he called, she told him she had become ill on the train and had to turn around. It was close enough to the truth. He accepted it as such, although he never asked her to join him again.

Summer stretched out in lizard time, long stupid days of waiting for signs of life. Her radio became her best friend, filling her head with new desires via the songs of Bowie and Hot Chocolate. When The Captain and Tennille sang "Love Will Keep us Together" she wondered, what love? Would love ever offer her that kind of tomorrow?

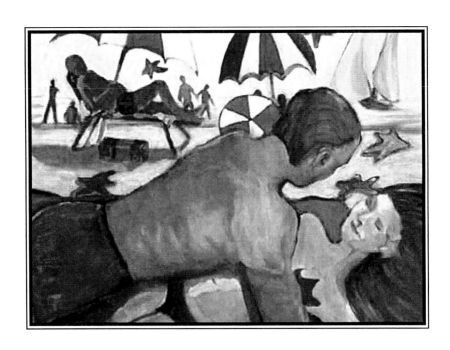

14

Starfish Rising

"This isn't just any beach. It's the artist's beach. What better way to describe its seduction than lovers?"

Kendra was speculating but effective.

"I want it for the house in the Hamptons," a determined voice said.

Abigail was amazed. An eighth painting sold?

"You'll have it by Christmas," Kendra promised.

Starfish Rising took a surreal look at life on a beach, where fiction and reality can become confused.

A beach or an air-conditioned movie were the only way to find relief during that Brooklyn summer. Abigail could have gone to Coney Island or Riis Park, but she needed a buddy to travel with. She wished she was old enough to go to the Poconos and see Simon &

Garfunkel, but that was the stuff of dreams.

The upside of her boredom was that when school started in September, she was grateful for its rigors and happier than ever to have Melissa as a friend. Despite the more than five thousand students who shared the high school's hallways and her friend's proximity, Abigail spent most days largely on her own. She and Melissa were on the same academic tracks, but other than a science class, they only had time to talk as they walked back and forth from school together. Salvation came in the form of a niche Abigail found in the art room.

Her art teacher, a nondescript middle-aged man named Dr. Andrews, encouraged her to use the art room to her heart's content. He gave her a free pass that allowed entry to the room at any time of the day, a privilege awarded only to an honored few. She had a shelf for her unfinished work and access to brushes and paints the teacher kept hidden in his private storage closet. The art room became her touchstone in the very large city school where she felt mostly out of place.

The lavatories housed smokers and users. Sections of the cafeteria were taken over by cliques of varied ethnicities. Abigail would have preferred soiling herself or starving than going to either place. If it wasn't for hours of exploration in the art room, with its plugged sinks and broken stools, its taped broken windows and marginal supplies, she might have left school that year. Instead, she was saved. Saved by art and Dr. Andrews.

Dr. Andrews related art to all other subjects: literature, physics, math, history, and philosophy. He blamed the volatile nature of American youth on history classes that meted out time and greatness according to wars, instead of the highest achievements of culture. He taught the Golden Mean as a philosophical truth and ruminated on the significance of its dynamic stability. If he had run the world of education, art would have been the sun at the center of all learning.

When Abigail's sixteenth spring arrived, she vowed she would not have a summer as dull as the last. A new energy was coursing through her veins. She was no longer growing upward, her feet had finally found their size, and a miracle had taken place on her chest, one she had not expected.

Each morning she would study her emerging self in the mirror and secretly admire her full-blown breasts and the small waist above hips now rounded beyond the comfort of old jeans. However, for the world she covered herself in baggy sweats and shirts, hoping no one else would notice her changes.

She wished she was as comfortable with her curves as Melissa. She and Melissa were locked in a two-step. Wherever Melissa went, Abigail went too; the grocery store, the post office, even dental visits. They saw the world through the same eyes, went to the same movies, read the same magazines and pretended to disdain most boys. They didn't drug, they didn't smoke, and they didn't drink. They imagined themselves above such things. But they both wanted more than they had: clothes, albums, lotions, potions and mad money. So they decided to find jobs for the summer.

Finding a full-time seasonal job was not easy, at least not listed in the classifieds. The city's parks department needed people, but Abigail nixed that idea. Local stores took their applications, but didn't respond. They had no skills to be office temps. So, the girls ultimately turned to the high school's Summer Work bulletin board. It was late May by the time an ad was posted that showed promise. It read:

MOTHER'S HELPERS WANTED.
DO YOU LIKE CHILDREN? ARE YOU A STRONG SWIMMER?
MOTHER'S HELPERS WANTED FOR LONG ISLAND BEACH HOUSE,
JULY AND AUGUST.

The vision of children and sand appealed to them. They had never had a life-saving course but both knew how to swim. Without a second thought, they checked in at the guidance office. Dr. Clark said, "So, you're sure you really want to help out two mothers for the summer?" The girls nodded eagerly.

"You will have to live on Long Island, stay for five days a week and be very responsible for the children on the beach. Think of yourselves as private lifeguards."

They knew they would like that sort of thing.

"You will have to do some housework, too. You two ladies up for that?"

"We do all the housework now, for our parents, what difference would someone else's house make?" Melissa said.

Dr. Clark smiled. "Not to mention they are offering $150.00 a week."

The money sounded like manna from heaven to the girls, the perfect answer to their need for excitement and cash.

Dr. Clark handed them questionnaires to fill out and informed them at the same time that he thought they were excellent candidates. He said he would call after he had reviewed their academic records. "Are you willing to take the life-saving classes at the Y?" he asked. They responded happily, "Sure!"

The following day he called the girls to his office. "I have spoken to the mothers, and the jobs are yours as long as you pass your life-saving course and have no objections to living in a conservative Jewish home."

They took the class, swam every day after school for the month of June and passed with flying colors. Not only that, they felt stronger and surer of themselves for the effort.

Melissa was crushed when her father refused to let her go. He said he needed her around the house more than some "Jews in the boonies."

Abigail thought Mr. Steiger sounded very prejudiced, but more than this, she was disappointed that Melissa couldn't leave town with her. She even reconsidered her determination to go away for the summer, until Cecily encouraged her, and the blankness of her slate for the weeks ahead convinced her to put aside anxieties and pack her bags.

On the first Monday in July, Abigail hung a backpack from her shoulders, hauled her old leather suitcase and rode a bus to the Long Island Railroad station. She bought a round trip ticket for Patchogue, Long Island, and took a seat by a window that sped by one pretty community after another. When she debarked onto the platform into the flat green landscape of Patchogue, she looked around for a big family waiting to greet her but saw only a foreign looking woman approaching. On this warm summer day, she was wearing heavy black clothes, a scarf and stockings.

"Abigail Lynde?" the woman asked.

"Mrs. Rose-in-sky?"

"I am Mrs. Rosinsky. You are Abigail?"

The woman could have played Tevye's wife, Golde, but she wasn't going to dance and sing, of that Abigail was sure.

"This way," she said, pointing to a long black car with a heavily bearded man in the driver's seat who didn't offer to take her bag or bother to open any doors. Abigail's suitcase was shoved in the backseat where her three wards awaited. They peered at her solemnly, through dark, impossibly thick, lashes.

She said, "Hello," and they looked down and remained silent. She directed her eyes to the driver's license attached to the rear of the driver's seat and saw his name was Cohen, not Rosinsky. It led her to believe he was not the father. The car was hot and the old velvet on the seats, threadbare. Someone in the car had an odor problem.

The kids were sad. She wondered if their father was dead, too. Mute, they drove by green-and-white signs bearing biblical names like Jericho, St. John, Bethany, St. James, until they turned into a new neighborhood of look-alike houses all sitting exactly the same distance from the street and from one another. Each house had a small tree in the front yard and a concrete path from the street to the door. The garages next to the houses were as large as the houses themselves. A variety of colors, but not much else, identified one house from the other.

They arrived at a square, gray-and-white two-story home with a two-car addition, and parked in the driveway. Mrs. Rosinsky led them to the front door, and the driver left without a word. Abigail carried her bag inside and looked around. The rooms were large and clean. However, color and warmth were as absent as a hi-fi or television. No art hung on the walls, no pillows softened the couches, no paper trail of newspapers and magazines or mail created the "normal" litter. She looked for toys, shelves for books and knick-knacks, mirrors or paintings on the wall.

The only books she saw were utilitarian. The *Webster's Unabridged Dictionary* was centered on the dining room table, and a Bible, along with a little paperback ABC book, rested on a tin tray table. A huge picture window exposed the backyard and revealed that it, too, was spare, at least in contrast to the neighbors' playlands of colorful plastics: swimming pools, swing sets and patio furniture. In the Rosinsky's yard, no shrub, no grass, not even a buttercup bloomed.

After she was shown the room adjacent to the utility room where she would sleep, she was given a brief tour of the rest of the house. The garage had been turned into bedrooms, making the house more spacious on the inside than it looked from the road. To her surprise, the Rosinsky's had two kitchens, one for dairy and one for meat, Mrs. Rosinsky explained. "The utensils, pots and dishes are never to touch one another. We keep a kosher kitchen," she said. "You may eat whatever you want from either room, but the dishes and silver must remain separate."

In the utility room Mrs. Rosinsky opened a cabinet door. "Here you will find dust cloths and detergents. You must wipe down the moldings and furniture every day, and wash the children's clothes at night. My little one, Miriam, is bathed before bed."

The baby, Miriam, responding to the sound of her name, buried her light brown curls in the folds of her mother's jersey skirt.

"How old is she?" Abigail asked.

"Just two."

She already knew that, but it was something to say. Miriam's tiny hand emerged from her mother's skirt with two fingers up in a victory sign. Abigail smiled.

"Little bird, you will let Abigail bathe and dress you," Mrs. Rosinsky said.

"The children can call me Abby."

"Abigail, it is from the Bible, no?"

She wasn't sure, but she thought it a good idea to nod in the affirmative.

"I have another son. His name is Abraham. He is yet again in Israel for summer studies. He is my oldest. Abigail is female for Abraham. Yes?"

"Yes," she said, happy for any connection, whatsoever.

Then she learned the older girl's name was Leah and the younger son was Jonah. Names seemed to help. She felt a little safer.

They sat down and broke bread together, at least she thought it was bread. It was drier and flatter than any bread she had ever eaten. The glass of water she was served helped it go down.

"So, you will take Abigail for a walk to the beach, eh?" Mrs. Rosinsky said to Leah when they were done with their snack of bread and figs. Without a word Leah led Abigail from the front door to the street with the other two children behind. Abigail took little Miriam's hand, and they paraded soberly along the sidewalk like a family of ducks, past houses with new trees and mowed patches of lawn, flowers and fences until the pavement turned to wooden planks. On either side, wild roses lay among the beach grass. The salty smell of sea drew them across the windswept dunes to an open stretch of sand and sea.

"I love the ocean!" Abigail said. "Come on, let's run to the water. First one to get their toes wet gets a lollipop. All of them ran like the wind, and Leah won the lollipop, but Abigail had little boxes of raisins in her backpack for the others, so they weren't disappointed. The sand at the beach was like sugar, fine and white. It wasn't easy to make firm, so she brought the children down to the water's edge and demonstrated the art of sand castles. They used discarded cups and large clamshells to dig and shape their masterpiece, scooping sand and water, dribbling turrets, forming moats and carving doorways. It was to be the first of many sand castles to be created by the Rosinsky children that summer.

The walk back from the beach was very different from their walk to it. Jonah jabbered away, insisting that they go back first thing in the morning and build a huge wall to protect the castle. Leah reminded him of the tides. A weary Miriam asked to be carried in Abigail's arms. As those brown chubby arms wrapped themselves around her neck, Abigail thought things might just work out.

After the children were bathed and put into clean clothes, Abigail helped Mrs. Rosinsky prepare the evening meal. "You must understand what it means to be kosher. We live as children of God, always aware that He is with us and making sure we practice His laws. There are disciplines you may not know, but I will teach you. Soon my husband, Dr. Rosinsky, will be home. He is a teacher, a professor at Yeshiva University," she said proudly.

Abigail was unpacking her bags as Dr. Rosinsky's car pulled into the driveway. She could see him emerge, burly and dark. He had a unibrow that made his face look sterner than most. Fear and disappointment filled her. He was nothing like Tevye. This house was not what she had expected at all. There was no music, no laughter, no joy. She wanted to go home.

A week passed before Mrs. Rosinsky gave up standing over Abigail's shoulder to point to the areas she should dust. She was growing familiar with the family's rhythms, though, and in between chores, able to escape to the books she had brought from home. It wasn't long before, at the children's cajoling, Dr. Rosinsky invited her to the table to join Leah and Jonah for studies. He was teaching his children the power of words. "One man will kill another over a word," he said. "Nations go to war and families divide because they don't have the words to make themselves understood. That is why God tells us the word is sacred." The children were taught phrases from the Torah and then a page from *Webster's Unabridged Dictionary*.

As she participated in their disciplines and tried to memorize new words along with them, the children were delighted. They shared the humor of their mistakes. When Abigail confused a dreidl with a sweet bun it became a part of the family humor. "Would you like a bite of my dreidl?" they teased. Or, "Do you like your dreidl hot or cold?"

The only time Leah and Jonah played outside was at the beach. Mrs. Rosinsky said the neighborhood was filled with goyim, and that their prejudices had already surfaced. She did not want her children corrupted or endangered in any way and saw the beach as the most neutral ground for her babies. But, she had a problem; she didn't like the beach. She would not disrobe, and the sun made her feel sick. Abigail better understood why a mother's helper was the answer to the woman's dilemma. It was at the beach that she was able to best connect with the children. In the fragrant air, they were the happiest; the sunlight their common denominator, the slow roll of surf a shared playmate.

Abigail had no idea what goyim were but imagined feral animals, some kind of infestation of bugs or poisonous bushes. She didn't ask. Conversation was not part of the equation with her employers. They made it very clear that she was help, and she was ordered around as such. "You will go to your room, now," Mrs. Rosinsky would say when she wanted her privacy. "Clean the baby's crib before you have your breakfast... do not sit in here to read... take those things into the kitchen." Communication came at her like demands instead of requests.

"You are to go home on Friday, before we begin Sabbat. Take your clothes home with you and the books you have brought."

She was to leave no traces of herself behind. Never once was there a thank you or a job well done. Mrs. Rosinsky merely withheld criticism and kept true to her financial agreement.

Dr. Rosinsky was slightly more verbal, but his eyes never met Abigail's. It was as if he couldn't look at her, as if it would be an intrusion or a sin. That was fine with her and remained true until the third week of July when Abraham called from Israel. After the call, Dr. Rosinsky knocked on her door, and she opened it to find him wringing his hands and wiping his eyes with a huge white handkerchief. This time he talked straight to her. "Abigail, our son, he has been injured. I do not want to upset the children, they love him very much. Will you take them outside and keep them busy? Mrs. Rosinsky and I must pray before we decide what to do next."

She walked the kids to the village and bought them ice cream cones. They wanted seconds, which she refused. She had to take them to the public water fountain to wash their faces and hoped they didn't run into any goyim. She couldn't get the chocolate off Miriam's blouse, but when they got home Mrs. Rosinsky was too upset to notice or hear about their sweet treat.

The next day Abigail heard that Abraham would be coming home without his right leg. A bomb had gone off in his classroom, killing three students and the rabbi.

In the following days, morning and night, Mr. Rosinsky would tie a black box, a tefillin, to his arm and another on his head. She would tiptoe past him while he chanted aloud before the candles on the sideboard. Over and over she heard, Sh'ema Yisreal adonai elohenu, adonai e chod. She figured it meant something like God is great and God can fix anything, but she dared not ask.

At the Rosinsky table, amidst tears and prayers, she heard pieces of Abraham's story. Other Jewish families came by, lit candles, drank wine and sat with the family, while Mr. Rosinsky read from the Holy Book. Again and again, they reiterated how blessed they were that Abraham was alive, and prayed for the families who were suffering. The most vehement of their prayers was for God's justice to be meted out to the brutes behind the bomb.

Abraham Rosinsky arrived a week later. Abigail was not prepared. He was taller and handsomer than his father, and he had a fierceness not normal for a boy his age. He was as different from the Lynde family as she was from his and seemed like an adult, even though he was only two years older than she. He didn't seem to care about sports or cars or girls. He was mostly interested in the country he just left, a country surrounded by enemies who wanted to erase it from the face of the earth. He said it was in a perpetual state of survival, fighting for its life. He told funny stories, too, about the Gaza Strip where he lived with other teenagers.

"We are all equal, all obliged to learn to shoot and tend the gardens. Only twenty percent of the land is arable, so our gardens are as important as our guns. I do not find it easy that my roommate is a sixteen-year-old girl who is half my size and a finer sharpshooter than I. But she does not appreciate that my potatoes are growing so big."

"And no one called us right after the bomb exploded. Why didn't you call?" Dr. Rosinsky admonished.

"Aaron..." his mother said, stopping her husband's reproach.

"Papa, you had your work to do, and Mama had the children. I was all right where I was. There was nothing more you could do. Anyway, I was unable to be moved. I did not want you to feel you had to join me," Abraham explained.

At first Abraham showed exactly no interest in Abigail. She remained quiet when he was around his brother and sisters, feeling naïve in his presence. Ignorant, too. So much so, she went to the library to learn about the places and people he represented, rather than ask him questions. She found *Exodus*, by Leon Uris, and was immediately caught up in the story, falling in love with the hero, Ari Ben Canaan and sympathizing with the displaced people wanting a land of their own, believing they had a homeland to reclaim.

One afternoon, she was sitting on the wooden steps of the back porch, reading, when Mrs. Rosinsky brought out a pot of green beans for her to trim. Abraham was nearby in a metal chair facing the sun and reading something Yiddish. Abigail set her book down.

"What are you reading, Abigail?" Mrs. Rosinsky asked.

She told her it was a book was about the birth of Israel. Mrs. Rosinsky looked at with one eyebrow raised, shook her head and went indoors. Abraham rose, balanced precariously on his crutch, and hopped over to see the title.

He laughed. "What is this, *The Birth of Israel?* The birth of Israel was 4,000 years ago."

The kids were playing with the jump rope that Abigail had brought from home and singing the song she had taught them, "A my name is Abby and my husband's name is Abe, we come from Armageddon, and we sell ankle bracelets."

She blushed.

He lifted the book so it covered most of his face. She watched his long fingers turn the pages of the book slowly, saw his index finger running through the paragraphs.

"It's a wonderful book!" she gushed. "About the new Israel."

"I am not supposed to talk to you," he answered. "It is forbidden."

"By your father?"

"Yes, as God is my Father." He closed the book and put it back on the step. "You cannot understand."

"But you are talking to me right now," she pointed out. He had to be joking.

"I cannot," he said, still not looking her way. "But I know you are as lovely as a rose."

A rose? Could he have said such a thing? Her face burned, even her throat felt hot. What could he mean? She called Jonah. "Jonah, come here!"

The spidery eight-year-old ran over to them eagerly.

"Jonah? How is it you are allowed to talk to me and your brother is not?" she asked.

"He is a man!" Jonah exclaimed, the whites of his eyes defining the dark browns of their centers.

"And what does that mean?" she asked dangerously.

"And you are a woman. He must not fall in love with you," Jonah laughed, and ran back to the anthill he had disrupted by his jumping.

Mrs. Rosinsky came to the door. "You have finished the beans? Come inside, Abigail. There is dust on the refrigerator."

She did as she was told, sponging off the enamel box, without a thought. Her insides were agitated and excited by his words. It may have been her first compliment, although it came at her from such an oblique angle she wasn't sure if it meant anything at all. She felt a pang, one she had never felt before. If they were to love one another, it would be a forbidden love, like the intoxicating love she had read about in her favorite novels and only understood from afar.

In the following weeks Abraham received his first prosthesis. It was made of a lightweight plastic but challenged his still sensitive stub. At first he became more like the leg than the leg became him. He would buckle it on and move tentatively about the house. Mrs. Rosinsky tried not to watch. The kids were fascinated, regarding it no differently than a toy. Abraham regarded it as an athlete would and was determined to become mobile, pushing himself daily. He went to the hospital in Mr. Cohen's black limo each morning for the first week, then three days the next, and the next. He never complained. Abigail saw him as nothing less than a hero, her very own Ari Ben Canaan.

Weekends home had been precious to Abigail. At first she couldn't wait to see her mother and leave the struggles of the Rosinsky household behind. Brooklyn's scruffy streets felt more familiar, more real than the newer streets of Long Island. She luxuriated in time, lying in bed fantasizing until eleven in the morning, taking long hot baths, eating junk food and watching TV. She and Melissa would take in a movie and go to clothing stores they couldn't afford.

Melissa wasn't always available, but Abigail was learning to be content without her. The most significant turnabout, however, was that it became easier each week to get on the train and make the return trip to Long Island. She noticed how her tummy fluttered as she got closer and closer to Patchogue.

On her fifth weekend home, Abigail found that Tiffany had arrived unannounced, her first visit in almost a year. Unfortunately, she had come to take everything she owned from the house. It was to be a purging.

Cecily didn't react to Tiffany's declaration that she was moving out for good. Her words could have been raindrops on glass. "It's about time we had access to those closets you left full to bursting," her mother said. A person who didn't know better would have thought her leaving was more of a gift than a loss.

Abigail offered to help in the exorcism of her sister's things. Together, she and Tiffany filled garbage bags with the stuff of time. Out went old shoes and school papers, as did the textbooks with Bo's name wrapped in hearts on their covers. So did school newspapers and movie magazines. Then they hit the mother lode of outgrown and forgotten clothes. If Abigail hadn't interceded they may have been tossed like so many rags. But Tiffany was quick to become her sister's benefactor. Frayed jeans, shorts, tie-dye T-shirts, tank tops and two-piece bathing suits were piled up on the bed. Jackets and blouses that Abigail couldn't imagine buying were plopped on her lap.

"These are meant to be yours," Tiffany said. "You may be taller and thinner than I, but they'll fit beautifully." She seemed genuinely thrilled as Abigail modeled the dresses and jeans and proved her right. It was a happy day, maybe their best. They were being what they both wanted to be, if only for a moment in time.

"I'm getting married," Tiffany said quietly.

Abigail almost fell over. "What? Who's the guy?"

"Troy!" Tiffany's voice was all smiles.

Abigail was obviously expected to know more than she did. "Troy who? First Trevor and now Troy? Are they brothers?"

"Troy Hildenbrand," she said, obviously thinking the entire world should recognize his name. "He's nothing like Trevor."

"But we don't even know him," Abigail protested. "That's not even a real name. Who names a kid Troy?"

"Mrs. Hildenbrand," Tiffany laughed. "Don't worry. You'll love him. I met him on the set of the Firestone commercial. You wouldn't believe it. I saw him lift the front end of a Jeep, right off the ground."

"Really? Is that why you're marrying him?"

"It doesn't hurt that he's drop dead gorgeous!"

"But when did you realize he was the one to marry?"

"Six months ago. But I just knew we were right together from the start. Now don't be a poop about this, Abby. You're going to be my maid of honor, and I need you to be happy for me. We are sisters, remember?"

"Right."

"I know you're smarter than I, and I know the whole family likes you better, but I love you anyway."

"Don't you ever think of Bo?"

"He's just a buddy. Really, Abby, I'm saving him for you."

Poor Bo, Abigail thought. She knew poor Bo was waiting all this time for Tiffany to come to her senses. "When will we be marching down the aisle together?" she asked.

"I think November would be nice. Not too hot and not too cold."

Abigail returned to Long Island on Monday, armed with a whole new summer wardrobe. It never occurred to her that it would not meet with Mrs. Rosinsky's approval; she hadn't seemed to notice what she wore in the past. But this was a summer for learning, and she had a long way to go.

She took to poetry. Not the dense kind, but the Edna St. Vincent Millay romantic kind.

O' summer you have come
And brought me
Newts and oyster shells
And little hands and
Big ideas and sands
And water swells
My head is in a dreidl spin with
Thoughts too new to grasp
But I reach and wait and
Dream love's here
To bloom me like a rose.

As Abigail remembered the richness of the beach she realized she had never taken her own children to a public beach. She thought, my own children have never known days stretched as far and as idle as a beach day, or the gentle sounds of water and gulls in collusion. I've never shared the joy of a sand castle or collected shells with them. Instead, they are products of the prized Pool Club of Montmarte, and know only about waterwings, swimming instructors, pool rules and competitions. They have been taught to stay in their own lanes, wear goggles to protect their eyes and play "Marco Polo" until their lungs give out. What have they missed? What have I?

15

Beachcombers

The second week in August, Abigail stepped onto the platform in Patchogue besieged by happy children. Miriam's sweet arms lassoed her leg; Jonah began chattering in her face about a seven-inch starfish; Leah locked arms with her and Mr. Cohen actually got out of the cab to carry her bag. Mrs. Rosinsky held back. She didn't scowl, but it was clear something was wrong.

When they reentered the house she followed Abigail into her room. "You are not to dress like that in this house," she ordered.

It must have been the v-neck sleeveless T-shirt that upset her. A little cleavage was showing, but the children had seen more than that at the beach since the beginning of the summer. Abigail thought her disapproval was ridiculous but said nothing. She knew the woman would not have relented.

Her brave new wardrobe was buried in the dresser drawers and Uncle Lyman's discarded shirts retrieved, their sleeves rolled and shirttails out, as Abigail conformed to the censorship. She guessed it was cover up or quit. Besides, the days were warm and the beach a place where Mrs. Rosinsky did not venture. She would not see the new suit, the one with the back cut down to the waist and the sides cut high above the hip. Of course, it was a modest suit compared to the teeny-weeny bikinis that were standard wear on Long Island beaches that year.

Yes, Mrs. Rosinsky would have been shocked to see how sexy the beach was that summer and yet, she had to have realized that her children were thriving in its sunshine. Jonah had turned dark bronze and looked wonderfully healthy. So did Leah, with her shiny dark braids tied up on her head exposing a neck as lithe as Nefertitti's. Miriam was happiest with her red pail and blue shovel and water tickling her toes.

They always went to the same part of the beach, at the far eastern end, right at the point where private homes and no trespassing signs ended public access. Just a stone's throw away, across swirls of beach grass, were low dunes and miles of white sand and ocean. Abigail liked to spread their blankets as close to the high tide mark as possible. Its demarcation defined by the flotsam of the Atlantic's undersea gardens had its advantages. She felt a great responsibility as the guardian of the children, and this rise in the sand offered her a constant view of the sand and sea. After Miriam was knocked down by a rogue wave and rescued by two people only feet from where she stood, she never allowed the children to wander from her side. Miriam and she became one fish in the water, and it didn't take long to teach the other two how to dive into the waves and belly surf to shore on the shallow rollers.

To make the hours pass between water play, they went beyond the art of sandcastles and built sand sculptures of fish and mermaids, camels, snakes and fat cats. Each day they would search for shells to sort and decide which of their finds was most perfect. They never left the beach without Miriam's pail filled with a stash. Abigail lectured to the children on the wonder of shells, the proof that every creature was awarded special gifts. "Isn't it amazing that such simple creatures have a way to survive?" she asked. "If mushy mussels can build purple houses with silver linings, and a spineless oyster can create scalloped arches with hinges, imagine what people can do!"

She was talking to herself, of course. Trying to be her own cheerleader.

They planted the shells nightly at the back end of the Rosinsky property. One row marched east and the other marched west. Leah's shells moved east, Jonah's west. Miriam and Abigail tucked in the spaces between the larger shells with tiny periwinkles. The goal was to have east meet west by summer's end.

Mrs. Rosinsky didn't seem to notice, but Abraham did. He said, "So what will Mama think when she finds this row of shells? Will she think it a miracle? That maybe the sea was once in her backyard?" They all laughed in anticipation.

"Maybe it will make up for the cross that burned in the front yard," he said.

A shadow fell across the children's faces.

Abigail had learned about cross burnings in the South and the activities of the KKK. She thought such things only happened in the South, certainly not in the North, not in New York.

"Who burned the cross?" she asked Jonah.

"Jew haters," Leah answered. "It happened right after we moved in."

One Wednesday night, Abigail found herself alone after dinner. Abraham was at the hospital doing his exercises, Dr. Rosinsky working late, and Mrs. Rosinsky limply stretched out on the couch, distracted by the heat. Leah and Jonah were concentrating on one of the Lynde family's jigsaw puzzles at the dining room table, and little Miriam lay fast asleep in her crib.

Instead of going to her room to read, Abigail decided to take a walk to the water. Sunlight still shone on the western horizon while the moon was morphing into a solid form in the east. Across the lavender waters, sailboats gracefully aimed for their moorings, and far out on the horizon, a bulky gray transport ship moved its cargo south. She sat away from the water, not wanting to disturb the pipers and gulls busily working its foamy edge. Softly undulating waves weaved silky patterns in the sand, each a little different from the last.

She imagined Abraham as a soldier. Saw him through Leon Uris' eyes, dressed in a beret, bullets strapped across his chest, fearless in the face of random danger. She wished they could have met when he was whole, that they could have walked the beach together in Haifa. He would be her teacher and she his accomplished spokeswoman. They would go to the tomb of Elijah, the Wailing Wall and explore the city of Acre. Together, they would stand up against outdated laws of religion with a love that would overcome ancient ways and free everyone who was held down by obsolete customs. They would bring the old people into the new world, the modern world of science and sense. Their children would drink milk with their hamburgers and play with the neighborhood children.

She saw the two of them, Abigail and Abraham, on a hill, arm and arm, the living evidence that the world is capable of change. She thought of her mother and sister. What a difference Abraham represented from Troy Hildenbrand or Davis Corwin! Tiffany might opt for muscles and beauty, and her mother for money and power, but it was strength of character that made her long for Abraham. He was a man. A leader of the people. A hero and a good son. He was the type of man she wanted. Her heart hurt just thinking about him.

She jumped at a strange sound from the walkway and didn't realize it was the sound of crutches striking wood until she saw Abraham's head appear through the tall beach grass. He looked for all the world like a man who had conquered adversity, his chin up and eyes looking ahead.

Suddenly, his crutch caught between two planks and threw him off balance, plunging him into the thorny rugosa rose bushes that lined the path. He went down silently, but she screamed as she ran toward him. "Abraham! Are you all right? Are you hurt? Oh my God, Abraham!"

"Go away," he said. "I can get up by myself."

But she could see how impossible that would be. His face was bleeding and his hands were shaking, scratched, too. He tried to lift himself up with one crutch, but the prosthesis made it more difficult.

"Please let me help," she begged, removing her shirt to wipe his face, letting the striped cotton absorb his blood.

He twisted away. "No! I said, no. Turn around."

She didn't argue but didn't obey either. Instead, she climbed into the bushes, took one of the crutches and leaned it into the wooden path, making a bridge on which he could brace himself. He struggled to get up and pulled himself into a position, high enough to stand. She wrapped her arm around his waist and placed his arm around her shoulder so they could walk through the nasty shrubs to the foot of the dune and the clear sands.

Like two herons they stood and watched the magic of the moonlit beach. A seagull with a broken wing startled their silence when it emerged from the grass behind them on a trek to the water. They watched the broken wing carve a parallel path beside its footprints.

"He hasn't got a chance," Abraham said. "Even if he gets to the water."

She knew that was how it was with him at that moment. He felt like the bird, broken, foolish and grasping at hope.

"If I had a gun I would shoot it and put it out of its misery," he said.

"Come on, sit down on the dune. You can rest," she said, wanting to believe they would rest together. She would nurse him back to his true self. A wind picked up and pushed the salty air through her hair, pushing it into her face, between her lips, across her eyes, stroking her with its sultry warmth."

Abraham took the bloodied shirt and put it next to him. "I'd do better if I could take the damn leg off," he said.

"Do it then," she said.

"I have to take off my pants."

"So? That's no big deal," she said, as if she was always around boys taking their pants off.

He unbuckled his belt and wriggled until his pants were around his ankles. She lifted the pants away from his feet, smelled the sweat of his efforts, saw the dark hair on his leg and quickly looked away.

When the prosthesis was undone, she took it from him and placed it carefully against some driftwood, where it stood like a pot marker on the sand.

She could not believe they were so close, that this near disaster had brought them to this moment and made him accessible. It was obviously their fate, maybe even the hand of God that brought them to this moment.

She hugged herself at the enormity of it and willed her body to grow calm as she waited to hear his breathing quiet down. A flirting cricket tried to compete with the sound of her heart. The moon's face smiled benevolently down on them, like some great goddess. She felt magnetized, drawn like electrons to his body. She didn't know who reached out first, she only knew they ignited. He pulled her to him, pushed her shoulders into the sand and started to kiss her, hard and hungrily. She hardly could catch her breath and still he pressed on. She felt the wetness of his face, tasted the saltiness of his tears washing her, and the fierceness of the stubble of his young beard. She probably could have said no. She was sure afterwards she could have found the breath, but she allowed him to bury her with his need. She was electrified, terrified and fascinated all at the same time, and she didn't struggle as he went inside her shorts and found her wetness. She didn't turn away as he lifted himself with a superhuman force, rising and falling until he exploded and collapsed on her, clumsy and crude, grunting and cursing, inundating her with his own primordial soup, then rolling over at the agony of his effort.

The sticky paste ran from her as she lay waiting. Waiting for him to turn and hold her face in his hands, to tell her she was a rose like no other.

She waited as sand and semen coagulated on her clothes and body like a creeping fungus, waited for words that would tell her everything would be all right. Waited for the gentlest expression of relief or gratitude or pleasure or love. But he was not thinking about her. He shook with anger and frustration instead. He reached for his leg but she had placed it too far away, looking as it was, like a dismembered body part.

Abigail started to cry.

"Shut up!" he said. "Shut up!"

She couldn't. Her romance had lasted, maybe two hundred and fifty seconds. It died in less.

In another instance, she might have run home and thrown herself across her bed to cry herself to sleep, but there she was on a sand dune with a boy with one leg, needing to get him on his feet again. She wiped her tears on her bloodied sleeve, tried to swipe the sandy semen off her pants and grabbed the prosthesis. Its straps were not too complicated, and she managed to help him buckle it. With strength and determination to match his intention, he made his way back through the cool sand to the path, navigating each step, carefully, until he was back on the macadam and on his way home.

They did not talk until they reached the house. "You must go in first," he directed.

She circled around the house to the back door and stole her way to her room.

No more than a minute later, she heard a rap at her door.

"Abigail?" Mrs. Rosinsky called.

"Yes?"

"You are home?"

"Yes."

"You must not go out at night without telling me."

"I'm sorry. I just went for a walk on the beach."

"It is not safe at the beach at night. You were alone?"

"Yes."

"Good night, then, Abigail."

Mrs. Rosinsky's feet padded down the hall just in time to catch her son walking in the front door. "You have fallen?" she asked. "Where were you?"

"I took a walk."

"Here, you come here. I will wash you face. You are scratched. Did you fall on broken glass?"

"No. I fell on a rosebush."

Sand was caught on his tear-stained face and in his tousled, damp hair.

"I see," she said.

The next morning Mr. and Mrs. Rosinsky took Abigail to the train station with her weathered suitcase, a spillage of books and a tote bag full of the forbidden clothes. They discussed nothing. She had been simply told she was no longer needed at the house. When the whistle sounded and the nose of the train appeared, Mrs. Rosinsky did a strange thing. She took Abigail's hand and looked her straight in the eye. "You will understand, someday," she said. "We love our son, too. But he is a child of God, and God comes first."

"Will you tell the children goodbye for me?"

Mrs. Rosinsky gave a nod, and Abigail turned to board the train.

She was relieved to see Melissa was not working the day she arrived home. It gave her a chance to test the excuse she had composed for losing her job. She explained that she quit because the Rosinsky's were weird and mean and only paid her to the minute. She said she had been bored and hungry most of the time.

"My father says all Jews are cheap and only out for themselves. He says you can't trust them. That's why he didn't let me go."

"Well, they don't trust us either," Abigail said. "I think they hated me because a cross was burned on their lawn when they moved into their house and they thought all Christians were the same."

"See?" she said. "Most people know about Jews."

"But burning crosses is against the law. It's an awful thing. How can you hate Jews? They are all around us and go to school with us," Abigail pointed out.

"Yeah, but do they talk to us or play with us in the street? No. Most of them think they're too good for us. They only play with each other."

A demon in Abigail made her agree. "Maybe that's it," she said. "Mrs. Rosinsky ordered me around like I was her servant and told me what to wear. Meanwhile, she dressed in clothes that should have been incinerated. I only went back there each week because of Abraham."

"Who's he?" she asked.

"I told you about him. He was their oldest son. I thought he was brave and interesting. I sort of fell in love with him. But it was a mess. We weren't allowed to talk because he was not allowed to fall in love with me. I thought it was pretty romantic at first until he almost raped me."

"He almost raped you? You were either raped or not. Like you are either pregnant, or not. It's not a little rape or a little bit pregnant."

"Well, he didn't go all the way, if you know what I mean?"

"I know he can't date you because you're a shiksa, Abby. Jews, real Jews can't mix with goyim," Melissa said.

"Am I goyim?"

"Sure!" she said.

"Well, why did they hire me then? If they don't like us why would they hire us?"

"See? That's why my father didn't let me take the job, dummy."

"I should have left sooner," Abigail said.

Then she began the practiced art of erasing the Rosinsky family from her mind. Abraham, Jonah and his sisters were history.

History? Abigail thought. There is no such thing as denying history. No such thing as obliterating pieces of the past. It's all important; each piece needed to complete another, if the puzzle is ever to become whole. If I am ever to become whole, I will have to admit that Abraham Rosinsky was my first love, even if I never got the chance to tell him so. Instead, I crushed another memory, contaminating what was good by turning it into something bad.

16

Altar Ego

The telephone rang. With a mother's instinct, Abigail knew it was Montmarte calling, even before Kendra flagged her down and mouthed, "It's for you."

She tried not to panic as she wove through the congested room.

Marlene, the babysitter, was calling with a weather update. "The snow's coming down quite heavily up here," she warned. "I think you should stay where you are. I will put up for the night."

"Oh, I would appreciate that one way or another, Marlene. There are fresh sheets and a pillow in the hall closet for the family room bed. Did the kids stop their bickering?"

"Yes. Yes, they're getting ready for bed now....Abigail?"

"Yes?"

"We need to talk about Stephanie one of these days."

"Oh, dear. Why? Is it something you can tell me now? I need a break from all this schmoozing. Is it serious?" She was ready for anything.

"Well it could be," Marlene said. "Did you know she thinks her father left because of something she did?"

"She told you that?"

"In so many words. Something about stains on the slipcovers?"

Abigail had dismissed Stephanie's litany about the Magic Marker stains on the Porsche's leather upholstery. For Stephanie to think that Hank left over something so flimsy was just too far-fetched to take seriously. She had told her his going away had nothing to do with Magic Markers, but Stephanie was obviously unconvinced and still trying to confess her guilt to someone who would listen, even Marlene, a babysitter.

"Marlene, this is one more of a hundred things I have to handle when I get back to the real world. Thanks so much for your concern."

She hung up the phone and tried to digest all that was coming at her. As if the canvas's secrets weren't enough, messages seemed to be coming from every other direction.

Kendra took her elbow and led her back into the gallery. "Darling, would you tell these people about *Altar Ego*?" she asked. Then whispered, "Everything all right?"

"Fine," Abigail said, as they headed toward the painting of the bride and groom. She faced the questioning faces, "And what is it you would like to know about *Altar Ego*?" she asked.

A gray-haired woman commented. "At first, I thought it was a misspelling. Then it struck me you were describing weddings with a touch of cynicism. Am I right?"

Abigail wasn't going to take the bait. She couldn't talk about the true source of this piece since she hadn't divined it yet. But cynicism wasn't too far off.

"It does suggest the veiled tensions behind a wedding," she admitted.

Was it the obscure faces and crooked candles, or the tipsy cross that gave it away? Abigail wondered. Maybe it was the bouquet of obviously fake flowers in the foreground. "I merely attempted to paint two people at the altar. The rest of the design was just that, design." Or was it?

"I see more in this painting," Kendra teased. "Whose wedding was your inspiration?"

"Don't most young women anticipate their wedding day will be the high point of the romance? They want the dress, the party, the ceremony, the whole package? And after the gown, the holy vows, the promises of eternal love, isn't that when reality strikes?"

"You've got that right," a man snickered.

Abigail's belief in romance was in full swing during that sixteenth summer when she met Abraham and discovered what falling in love with love meant. After returning from the Rosinsky household, flush with the money she saved and her grief and anger stuffed away like a broken necklace in a silver box, she was determined to take her summer back. Her cohort, Melissa, managed to abandon her job and join her for the last two weeks of summer.

The two joined the throngs of beachgoers at Riis Park. Every teenager in Brooklyn knew, as they would confirm, that a continual party goes on at Riis Park from June to September. The public beach stretches about a mile between Brooklyn and Queens, its wide white sands broken up into bays, with each bay having a reputation of its own. Such divisions may have disturbed Jacob Riis, the great egalitarian for whom the beach was named, but then in 1890 egalitarian had a different meaning. It meant accessible to all. And that much remained true.

At the far end of the thirteen bays was the gay bay where men openly held hands and ran into the water together. Straights went there to gawk; some to test their mettle, others to taunt. Moving south, young families and different ethnic groups found their territories. The young adults gathered on the three bays nearest the bus line.

Melissa and Abigail didn't belong to any of the tribes that gathered there, but they were happy enough to watch the overt flirting among the scores of ready bodies. Kegs of beer, joints, Frisbees, music boxes and suntan oils were the name of the game. Beach umbrellas were not. It was a blatant tan and scan meat market of givers and takers.

Melissa wore her polka-dot bikini as if she was born in it; her rich hair quickly grew blonder, and her body glistened with baby oil. Abigail was proud to walk beside her, proud she was her friend.

One day, when the waves were unpredictable and a person had to choose between frying or drowning, Abigail chose the latter. Despite the warning posted on sticks in the sand, the roiling waters were teeming with people. She was not the only one struggling against the powerful undertow that had lifeguards blowing their whistles every two seconds. When she realized the pull was taking her beyond safety, she dove deep into a breaker heading for shore. As she attempted to stand up, another body surfer crashed into her knees and sent her into the chaos of conflicted waters, some going in, some going out.

It was like being tossed in a washing machine, turning up, falling down, rolling over and over herself, no more than flotsam in the suds, as wave after wave knocked her about. When she met smooth water, sputtering and choking, out of breath and trying to manipulate the top of her suit which had moved down to her waist, she fought off someone trying to help, because she cared more about her exposure than breathing. She sank under the water again, just as two strong arms encircled her and pulled her to the surface. She didn't resist— couldn't by that time. Her lifesaver and she moved toward shore until they were able to connect their feet to the ocean's bottom and stumble out of the turbulence.

Once free of the water, both of them collapsed. Abigail struggled with the straps of her suit and secured her breasts where they were supposed to be. Weak from exhaustion she couldn't even bring herself to remove the strings of sandy hair stuck to her face.

"I am sorry," her hero said. "I am the one who hit you."

"It's okay," she said. "It was an accident, wasn't it?"

"Yes," he said, shaking his head. "I was in trouble. Strong waves."

They sat still for a moment while she caught her breath, and he caught his. She glimpsed his profile, the line of his cheekbone, his tangled dark hair, his body, browner than most. He looked a little like Abraham.

"You good?" he asked.

She nodded, noting the foreign accent and wondering what it was.

She couldn't speak, stared at her feet instead. Fragments of shells and sea grape were strewn about. A tiny hermit crab peeked out of its newly confiscated home.

"I go now?"

She nodded again. Of course he would. It was the story of her life. She turned and watched his square shoulders and strong legs as he walked away and hated herself for being dumber than dumb.

Melissa emerged from the water like the nymph she was.

"Who was that? Neptune? Did you find him in the water? Is he a god or does he just look like one?"

"I don't know him. We didn't really talk. He knocked me into the waves and then helped me get on my feet. He only hung around to make sure I was okay."

"What's his name?" Melissa asked.

"I have no idea," Abigail laughed.

"Come on. You found the most gorgeous fish in the ocean, and you didn't ask him his name?"

"I was too busy recovering."

"Let's go find him and tell him we want to learn to body surf."

"I am through with waves today."

"Well, I'm not," she pouted, her hands neatly planted on her hips.

They walked down the beach until they saw his beautiful back again, standing apart from the gaggles of teenage girls and beer drinking boys. He looked more interested in the waves than the parties.

Melissa walked up to his side and thanked him for rescuing her very best friend in the entire world. She used her hands and laughed with all her teeth showing, her body golden in the scant bikini and long fingers pulling her wet mane from her face. She did the talking for both of them, and Abigail wished she could be her, instead of feeling like a salted fish baking in the sun. By the time the two girls parted from their beautiful god of the sea, Melissa had made a date to see him again. And so it began.

For Abigail, the saga of Melissa and Ari was a vicarious thrill. It turned out that he was not a god as in Neptune, or an Israeli leader as in Ari Ben Canaan, or a shipping magnate, as in Ari Onassis, but a recent Greek immigrant, and the surname, Ari, was attached to Michos.

When Ari Michos fell blindly in love with Melissa Steiger, Abigail saw all her dramatic ideas of love fulfilled. They had the clash of cultures, the power of lust, and the trepidation of parents to overcome.

She became the willing facilitator for their secret meetings. He would come to the Lynde house first, to visit, and then sit by the window with his eyes fixed on the street, waiting for Melissa's father to leave for work. When Melissa appeared in the doorway, they would run to one another. If the blinds were pulled shut in her bedroom window, he would know she was unable to get away. Neither of them knew that Abigail was in love as well, a love-struck wannabe.

That was sixteen years ago, a whisper of time. Yesterday. In just a few years it will be Stephanie on a beach somewhere looking for love, Abigail thought. Will I be right along side her, still looking, still wishing?

Tiffany was as love stricken as any young bride when she married Troy Hildenbrand. The wedding took place, as planned, in the November following Abigail's tumultuous summer. What wasn't planned was her mother's surprising October marriage to Davis Corwin, the man she had been dating for over two years.

Cecily and Davis had eloped to Las Vegas without a hint of their decision, and their news upon returning was not well received by either of the girls. Tiffany was the more outspoken. She took their timing as a personal affront, and ranted and raved that it was rotten of a mother to get married right before her own daughter. "You just have to upstage me, don't you? You hate me!"

"I gave you life, didn't I? I don't hate you, Tiffany, anymore than I hate my right arm."

"You do! You always have! You can't even give me one special day. It's always about you!" Tiffany screamed, and swore that she would not say one word to Davis Corwin for the rest of her life. He was not even to come to her wedding.

The harangue should have been forgotten by Tiffany's wedding day, but it was not.

The two women had hit a wall and were only civil on the morning of the grand black and white wedding. But Tiffany had made one major concession the night before at the rehearsal. She consented to her stepfather giving her away. Perhaps, because he had asked her himself, told her what an honor it would be if she allowed him to be at her side. Perhaps it was the twenty-five thousand dollar check he had written as a token of his love.

She said she had wanted to say no, she would have, if she'd had time to process his request, but she was too nervous that night for any more confrontations.

A near disaster struck before the ceremony began, when Grandma Lynde slipped on the stairs going into the church. It was a heart-wrenching sight, the poor little wren, lying perfectly still, flat and gray as the flagstone in front of the church's wooden doors. Tiffany was sitting inside the stretch limousine waiting for the last guests to arrive when she saw Grandma fold into herself like she'd been shot, her feet upended and body rolling down a step to lay face up on her back.

Like a white cloud, the bride flew from the car to her Grandmother's side, sweeping the stairs with the hem of her gown. Abigail ran, too, her hand curled in her mouth. She looked for death in Grandma Lynde's white face, but saw her pale lips tremble and her chest move, inhaling and exhaling, as it should. Knowing how she would be mortified at having her knee-high stockings exposed, Abigail covered them gently by pulling down the long black slip that lined the taffeta skirt on top.

She fought the urge to tell Grandma Lynde how much she was needed, to say she must wake up to do what she had always done. She was the one constant in their lives, the positive force that kept them marching when things were hard. Her enduring spunk gave them strength. She had seen it all. She had learned to match life's sorrows with its joys.

And she was generous about other people's survival, too. When Cecily announced her marriage to Davis, it was Grandma who gave the girls the advice they needed. Your mother is doing what she should do, and you should thank her for it. She doesn't want you two girls taking care of her when she's old. You accept this Davis person. He's been around a long time. Before either of you were born. Before she even met your father. You will be off doing your own lives soon enough. Cecily has to live hers. So, he has a little money. It is as easy to love a man with money as one without.

Grandma had to get back on her feet. There would be no joy at the wedding if she didn't. There would be no wedding at all. "Grandma, wake up," Abigail begged.

A gust of raw wind blew across the steps lifting Tiffany's veil to create a diaphanous tent. Inside their heavenly space, Grandma opened her eyes and looked at the sisters hovering over her. "Am I dead or alive?" she asked.

Someone yelled, "Get Dr. Weary. He's in the church somewhere."

Cecily was the one who went into the church and tapped Dr. Weary's shoulder. He responded calmly, rose and moved slowly so as not to alarm the wedding guests. He knelt at the white wedding veil tent and pushed aside the chiffon to assess the damage.

"What have we here, Gisela? A fainting spell?" he asked. She looked at him slyly. They had known one another over lifetimes, his, hers, theirs, and she had mentioned times when she had to work to keep their friendship alive. It was clear they loved each other.

The church organist pounded away. A crescendo called for someone to do something and caused the ushers and bridesmaids to decide among themselves what that might be. The best man, Corey Buchanan, a very pretty boy from Hollywood, went forward and asked the organist to delay the wedding march. She improvised a version of "Where O' Where is Love" while people waited anxiously, shuffling their feet and shifting their bodies on the hard benches. The maroon carpet, worn thin by years of earnest feet, lay wasted between the aisles for what seemed an interminable amount of time, even the sprigs of flowers tied on the ends of each pew began to wilt. Old friends preoccupied themselves by looking around the sanctuary and appraising one another.

Outside, the drama continued. "Grandma, Grandma, please be all right," Tiffany cried, her mascara becoming muddy rivulets on her cheeks.

Grandma sat up, abruptly. "For heavens sake, why all the fuss?" She shook her head and reached for her hat, shakily placing it back on her head.

Dr. Weary asked her to move each of her parts. She did so, and they appeared to be in tact. Then, despite her protests, he asked two of the ushers to carry her in a fireman's clutch, to the tiny chapel at the back of the church. The two girls started to go with her but Grandma exclaimed, "Tiffany! Your face is a mess! A bride should be sure of herself, sure enough not to need all that soot on her eyes. Go wash your face, like a good girl."

Tiffany's hand reached for her face involuntarily. The mascara soiled the fingertips of her long white gloves. She and a bridesmaid ran into the vestry and downstairs to the church's powder room where she removed her gloves and scrubbed her face until she was without a smidgen of makeup. Skin shining and eyes unpainted, she looked ten years younger than when she arrived.

Meanwhile, Dr. Weary announced that Grandma was fine as far as he could see, but he insisted she remain quiet.

"I'll stay with you, Gisela, until the ceremony is over," he offered.

"Nonsense," she snapped. "Ask Abby to come here."

He obliged.

Abigail moved closer to her Grandmother's side where a crooked finger summoned her to come even closer.

"Closer," Grandma said weakly.

Abigail placed her ear next to her grandmother's trembling lips.

"Darling girl," she whispered, before she stopped and turned on Dr. Weary.

"Go away, doctor, I must talk to my baby for a minute."

Abigail took hold of Grandma's shaking hand. Tapestries of blue veins reminded her of her frailty, but the pressure she exerted proved her determination.

"Stop the wedding! You must go and find your sister. This marriage must not take place. It is no good."

"Why, Grandma? What's wrong?" Abigail asked, feeling the angst in her grandmother's grasp.

"What is your sister doing? Hasn't she got a brain in her head? That young man is a gay if I ever saw one."

"He's a what, Grandma?"

"He's as queer as a three-dollar bill."

"It's not true, Grandma," Abigail protested. "It couldn't be. Don't worry, Grandma, Tiffany is getting exactly what she wants. And she knows all about men."

"She wants to marry a homosexual? What is she thinking?" Grandma's chin stuck out, she had new color in her face. "Go get her and tell her, it is not too late. In an hour it will be. Tell her

Grandma knows. Why, I watched him at the dinner last night, and he was performing for that pretty boyfriend of his like a cock robin. I have not slept a wink. You must stop the wedding, Abby. I don't care whether she was your father's child or not, she is my granddaughter, and I should have some say in this as far as I am concerned."

Abigail had no time to ruminate on her words. "He's a model, Grandma. He can lift a car like a feather. He's in love with Tiffany. She wouldn't settle for less."

She gave Grandma Lynde a reassuring hug and decided the chapel was probably the best place to leave her during the ceremony. At least it would keep her from crying out in protest when the minister posed that rhetorical suggestion, ...speak now or forever hold your peace.

"You stay here, Grandma. Don't worry."

"You talk to her, Abby."

Without looking back, Abigail rushed to the vestry and took her place behind Tiffany. She adjusted the long veil as maids of honor have done over centuries, and to the obvious relief of all, the familiar chords of Wagner's opera sounded and all rose to greet the bride.

Here comes the bride...Abigail sang in her head as the white chrysanthemums and orchids shivered against the black of her satin gown. She was leading her only sibling down the aisle, past Aunt Libby's tearful smiles and Uncle Lyman's thumbs up, past Bo's wink and his dear mother's nod, by Melissa and Ari seated in the fourth row peeking from behind a pilaster, on and on until she saw the altar. That was when she was almost overcome by doubt. What was going on here? As far as she was concerned, if anyone was meant to be at the front of the church taking Tiffany's hand it was Bo, not Troy Hildenbrand. No one in the family knew this man. She was aiding and abetting the marriage of her sister to someone with whom she had never had a real conversation.

Grandma Lynde was aging and had become somewhat prejudiced, and she may have been exaggerating the underlying doubts of the day, Abigail thought, looking at Troy waiting at the altar, but....

If there was such a thing, he was too beautiful. She considered his perfection, the designer cut blonde hair curled around his ears, his automatic smile displayed as easily for strangers as friends, and the cool distance he kept. The day before, she'd witnessed an ever ready tiny comb pulled from his pocket and seen clear polish on his nails as he made sure his hair was unruffled. He was vain, she knew that, but vain and gay were not synonymous. What concerned her most was the coterie of handsome male friends that obviously idolized Troy. Of course, Tiffany had her own fans, too. Abigail reminded herself they were supermodels, public people, and they not only needed to be noticed, they were fed by adulation.

The minister was smiling at Tiffany like an affectionate father. Neither Tiffany nor Abigail had been to the Dutch Reformed Church in the nine years since their father lay beyond the communion rail. If he were alive, this wedding wouldn't be happening, Abigail thought.

"Dearly beloved," began Reverend Vandenhuevel, solemnly placing Tiffany's and Troy's right hands on the pages of an open Bible. He wore a mask of neutrality, one that hid the knowledge of all the pitfalls they would inevitably face. "We are gathered here today to perform one of our most beautiful sacraments, the funeral of Tiffany Marie Lynde and Troy William Hildenbrand.

The gasp was audible, but Reverend Vandenheuvel didn't realize his faux pas. Troy seemed to have missed it, too. He may have been hearing something else in his head, distant sounds, sounds that took him back to a schoolyard he hated or a beach he loved or to a barn in Iowa where he groomed his horse. His eyes shifted to the video camera on the altar. Maybe he was simply wondering if the man making the video was taking shots of him from his good side. However, Corey Buchanan had heard the word funeral and started to chuckle, so did the usher on his right and then the bridesmaids, even Abigail burst out laughing, and by the time the wedding party was snorting and shaking, the congregation had joined them, rocking and rolling with that uncontrollable hilarity only the sobriety of a church can evoke.

The pastor remained clueless, which made it funnier. He looked around, knowing he had missed something, and then raised his head and hand to command quiet. When things quieted down, he began again, this time with stern resolution.

"A wedding is a profound occasion, attesting to the power of love."

He soberly recalled his earliest images of Tiffany, her father's joy at her baptism and confirmation, and remembered aloud the financial contributions Alex Lynde had made to God's work at each of these passages. He said the church that had blessed her way into adulthood would forever be a place where she had a spiritual home.

Grandma was stewing in the chapel. Wanting to know what the laughter had been about, planning to cancel all her pledges to the old church. But, at the altar, Tiffany's face was radiant and the sun seconded the fact. Somehow it managed to stream through a yellow pane of stained glass and land right on her shoulder, outlining her already shining face with a gilded light and turning the tiny pearls sewn into to her veil a shimmering gold.

Abigail's mind moved from the hilarity of the blunder back to the ritual taking place before her. As Troy recited his promises, she only hoped he could keep them.

At some point her mind moved from Tiffany and Troy to herself. She realized she was afraid, afraid no man would stand in front of everyone he knew and promise to love and respect her forever, afraid that there was something terribly lacking in her that brought only the worst in men forward, afraid there was no such thing as happily ever after for Abigail Lynde.

The candles blazed for Tiffany's recitation of vows and blurred as she slipped a wedding band on Troy's finger, the finger whose veins went straight to his heart. Tiffany's eyes were misted with love, sincerity rang in her words, and Abigail made room for hope for the two of them. In that beautiful fleeting moment, she knew her sister was experiencing a dream coming true, and she wanted more than anything else for it to last.

Dr. Vandenheuvel lifted his hands in supplication to the congregation.

"Weddings are an equal opportunity act, a time for all of us to renew our commitments. Husbands, love your wives. Wives, love your husbands." The couples in the congregation exchanged meaningful looks, arms and hands entwined. Davis Corwin and Cecily Benoit Lynde Corwin kissed. The organ pipes sounded, but Tiffany and Troy simply stood facing one another, frozen smiles in place.

"Now then, let me introduce the two who have become as one, the bride and the groom, Mr. and Mrs. Troy Hildenbrand!"

At this point the couple turned and waved at their friends and families. Camera's flashed from all sides at Tiffany and Troy, and the entire congregation stood in a spontaneous outburst of applause. Glowing and confident, the bride and groom began the long trip back down the aisle.

Reality returned with the reception.

It was held in the mirrored grand ballroom of the St. George Hotel, which was decorated smartly in yellow and white bouquets, with black napkins for accents. Tiffany wanted no garter snapping, no bouquets tossed, and definitely no waltz with her stepfather, who was never ever going to be confused with her real father, the late, great, Alexander Lynde. The cocktail hour went on too long due to a plague of photographers. But afterwards, a lovely meal of shrimp and steak was served to music provided by The Fugues, a sedate trio that included a harpist, a violinist and a bass player, all dressed in the same formal black-and-whites of the wedding party.

The one custom Tiffany had not deleted was the toast. Without encouragement, Davis Corwin, as Cecily's slightly inebriated husband, and now the confident stepfather, took it upon himself to rise to present the bride to the groom's family by saying he had watched with awe as her star rose. "Now," he said, "the stars are not dancing above her head, but in her eyes. Troy is a lucky man to have found Miss Subway, and he should know her beauty is more than skin deep. It runs inside and out. She is a daughter any father could be proud of."

Who is he talking about? Abigail wondered. Tiffany had never been Miss Subway and was not exactly beautiful inside and out. Obviously, he wasn't there to hear her response when Cecily had first asked if she would like Davis to escort her down the aisle. He must not have known she said she would rather die than have Mr. Phony Baloney anywhere near her wedding or been told about her attack on Cecily for marrying a geek for his big bank account.

No one was ready when the best man, Corey Buchanan, rose to speak. As he started to toast the newlyweds he broke down in tears, so much so, that Troy's brother Peter had to stand up and take over. Unfortunately, what Peter said was as devastating as the pitcher of martinis he'd sloshed down before he began. "To the newlyweds and my little brother, Troy Boy. Good luck, guys! Here's some advice, Tiffany. Watch your underwear. It wasn't easy being Troy's brother, covering for him and his love for satin and lace. Let me tell you, he looks lousy in a garter belt. I won't miss him strutting around the house in Mom's underwear. No way. Yeah, bro, all that is behind us now. Right? Tiffany, like I said, watch your drawers. I wish you the best, no kidding. I wish you both the best. You sure are pretty together."

Laughter rose up self-consciously, but not enough to dismiss Peter's poor taste. People coughed, rolled their eyes and got up for more wine or the rest rooms. Grandma, who was quite well by then, threw down her napkin and marched out of the room.

Troy and Tiffany proceeded to move in and out amongst the guests like lovely parallel ribbons weaving beauty throughout the hall, only touching one another when the cameras clicked.

Why haven't I been closer to Tiffany? What is it that won't let me get over her mistakes? Altar Ego mocks her wedding, the happiest day of her life. She was no less a victim of circumstance than I. I should have invited her to be here this evening. We hardly know each other anymore. We might be able to talk now, to grapple with how it was as we grew up, look at the way we've changed and what we've learned. We need to tell it like it is, to find one another. Is it possible for us to go there? I miss her. I have always missed her.

17

When In Milano

The gallery grew more and more social as the wine went down. It was clear who was responsible for it flowing. Kendra had a bottle of Merlot in one hand and Pinot Grigio in the other. She deftly moved about refilling glasses, making sure all thirsts were quenched.

In front of *When in Milano*, she spoke to the designer Giorgio Alfoni. "Isn't that clever, Giorgio?" she said, to the beautiful man. "We all know Milano's streets are the sexiest in the world, but contrasting the old and new, c'est trés charmant. N'est ce pas?"

He nodded, and she continued, "The last time I was at the Piazza del Duomo there were more women over six foot than spires, at any given moment of the day. Abigail's sister might possibly have been one of them. You know, of course, Tiffany Lynde is Abigail's sister?" She couldn't resist dropping her name.

"Oh, really?" his face lit up, and he turned to look at Abigail, to see the resemblance. "The model? Wasn't she married to Troy

Hildenbrand?" he asked.

Kendra was reminded once again how easily that illusory world of beauty triggers interest. But she also knew that more people had attended art exhibits than fashion shows last year, more museums than stadiums.

"Do you think she, or better yet, he will be here tonight?" Giorgio asked.

Kendra smiled wickedly, "Anything is possible. The night is still young."

"I haven't seen Troy Boy in years," Giorgio said.

Abigail overheard the exchange and thought to herself, Kendra knows that Tiffany has not been invited and even if she had, a Troy sighting would be extremely unlikely.

Tiffany was still obsessed with her looks and wearing her hips on her lips and in between her eyes the last time Abigail saw her. But she was on a new career path, according to The Star. She had earned a just reward to replace the fickleness of the modeling industry. Trompe L'Oiele, a burgeoning European cosmetic firm, was touting her face and using her as their international representative. It had happened just in time, providing an exciting transition from one life to another, and eased the end of the miserable excuse of a marriage she had endured with Troy Hildenbrand.

It took seven years before she let go. They had each had their share of affairs by then. Only when Tiffany found a man she could love did she admit her marriage to Troy was a hopeless purgatory. Unfortunately, the new love was equally hopeless, as he was a very illustrious married father of four, and his family life almost legendary. End of that story.

Neither Cecily nor Grandma indulged in discussions about Tiffany after the wedding of ill repute. Grandma's sudden illness became suspect in Abigail's eyes, along with the rest of the players. The new Mrs. Hildenbrand shunned her family as well, rarely calling to talk, and then mostly about the weather. Abigail's first glimpse of her sister's new life came more than a year after the "I dos". She was in art school by then and had come home after a long day of classes to find Tiffany sitting in the living room looking half herself, paper thin, pale, and hollow-eyed. California's sunshine was nowhere to be seen. She pretended not to be alarmed by her sister's image.

"And what is your name again?" Abigail teased. "I know we've met before but I can't remember where or when."

"I was in a New York State of mind!" Tiffany said. "I'm here for interviews, but, forget it, they're all cattle calls. It's hard enough to get a job with every blond teenie bopper from Iowa showing up, but now we have to deal with all the European runaways. I'd go blonde but, look, my hair is falling out!" she wailed. She ran her fingers through her once rich brown waves and indeed came up with a handful.

"But why is that happening?" Abigail asked.

I don't know. I suppose I had too much to begin with. Maybe it's my diet."

"You're on a diet?"

"Of course, every model is on a diet. You know that. It's a way of life. The price you pay."

"But you're too thin, as it is!"

"There is no such thing as too thin, Abby. Take a look at *Harper's* if you don't believe me. Please, I don't want to talk about it. I went to Benton and Bowles today. Every model in New York—in the world— was there. It was insulting to be asked to sit and wait for an interview, after all my experience in the business."

Her tiny wrists went to her head, the delicate hands pressed against her ears as if she were bombarded by voices other than her own. A new *Town and Country* magazine lay open on her lap.

"*Town and Country*, eh? What's that about?"

"I like beautiful things, and they are all here."

Abigail suddenly wondered if her sister was pregnant. Was she going to have a baby and a house and a station wagon after all? Despite the fact that no one had been able to forget Troy's weeping best man, she had held onto hope that her sister's marriage, to the man who could lift cars, was real enough to make babies.

"How's Troy?"

Tiffany brightened slightly. "He's doing very well. Working on a Pepsi commercial and then an ad for Soleil. There may be a small part in a Harrison Ford film down the road. But how about you? Are you in love yet?"

"Not a good question to put to a girl whose love life is non-existent."

"Oh, come on, there has to be someone."

"I am in like. There's a great guy I am teaming with at school. He's brilliant— a surrealist painter—and intense. I like them intense." She tried to make their non-romance interesting.

"Intense? What does that mean, exactly?" Tiffany prodded.

"It means, determined, distracted, serious, something like that. He's a strange combination of things—quantum physics, archaeology, art."

"Sexy?"

"I like his mind. That's sexy to me. I'm not sure if we can go the distance, though. So many of the guys at school are gay. I have trouble differentiating straight from bent." She hoped this was something Tiffany could relate to. After all, Tiffany knew better than anyone what it was like to live in New York, and that art schools drew unusual types.

But Tiffany didn't even look up, just continued to flip through the pages, stopping at a French country house. "Well, there are probably many who are bi. Bi is in. I mean, it is in Hollywood." She might have been discussing wallpapers.

"I would think you would have to be one or the other." Abigail said. "Bisexual seems like a cop out to me."

"Lots of the stars are bisexual," Tiffany elaborated. "They take on husbands or wives to protect their careers, look at Julie Andrews and Blake Edwards, or Liza Minnelli and Peter Allen. Rock Hudson and Phyllis Gates. Everyone knows about their understandings."

"Everyone? I don't, I didn't!"

"I mean inside Hollywood. You are not supposed to know, that's the whole idea, Abby."

Abigail wondered if Troy had convinced Tiffany he could love her and give up his boyfriends, or if she agreed to let him have it all. Homosexuality in the world of art and modeling was commonplace. You had to tolerate sexual preferences to be part of it. But how far should a person go? Why would you try to become what you were not? One thing she did recognize, no matter how inclusive Tiffany's lifestyle, something was wrong. She was disappearing; her beauty was at risk and with it, her future.

"Invite this guy home for dinner, Abby, I'll give him the once over."

Abigail wanted to tell her to tend to her own sheep. "No. I would rather keep things platonic than push them. He's a friend, and that's as important to me as anything else."

"Don't settle, Abby. You'll be sorry," Tiffany warned, not knowing she'd said a thousand words.

The following Monday, Tiffany went to an abortion clinic in Manhattan. Cecily went with her. Abigail was surprised that her mother was so ready and agreeable. The termination was a success.

Abigail began to judge her new friends more skeptically. She found their world disconcerting and wished she could make the whole issue of sexual confusion go away. Her friend, J.P., was only a first step. They worked together designing a Fast Track ad, but he began to speak only when spoken to, and to turn left when she turned right. She pretended not to notice and became as remote as he, realizing that it may have been his lack of interest that interested her in the first place. It didn't take a ton of gray matter to know no fledgling romance had been there. She had just wished for some semblance of a relationship. It was their friendship she missed. And she missed her friendship with Melissa, too, who wasn't that far away, but harder and harder to reach.

While Melissa was going to Brooklyn College, in a middle class Flatbush neighborhood and wearing Army pants, studded belts and spiked purple hair, along with rings in her nose and brow, Abigail was floundering at Pratt Institute, in an edgy part of Brooklyn, trying to maintain the cocoon she had carefully woven around herself.

On the morning commute to Pratt, Abigail would bundle up on her walk from the G-Train at Fulton, past the old chocolate factory and the homeless who lived on doorsills, looking too broken to be dangerous. She skirted abandoned cars and rusting market baskets and avoided cutting through the park where drug dealing was more common than children with jump ropes. This was not a neighborhood where she felt safe or certain. Fort Greene may have been next door to Brooklyn Heights, but it was a harshly different reality.

Pratt gave audience to every radical voice in town. Voices like Betty Friedan's championing the National Organization of Women, Louis

Farrakhan's invitation to the Muslim movement, and Paul Gunter's call to stop the spread of nuclear reactors and join the Clamshell Alliance. Abigail felt cloddish and uninteresting compared to the ardor of such people and resisted those who followed in their wake.

Melissa's school had a notorious president trying to bring his college to the forefront of the City College system, at the price of free speech. With her campus far more restrained than Pratt's, the tiger in her escaped its cage. In the name of women's lib, she went to battle against the system, and fought anything that even hinted of prejudice: racism, ageism, patriotism, fundamentalism, chauvinism, every ism but feminism. She said men's love for war and hatred of others destroyed her father and deadened her mother. She received warnings for seditious activities and responded with hundreds of other students, holding "Fuck You" banners in front of the president's office. Abigail knew they had been mismatched in their choices of schools. Melissa belonged at Pratt, and she belonged at Brooklyn College.

Melissa had also become promiscuous. No less than a dozen boys were on her have-done list by the end of her freshman year, and she had little regard for any of them. Call it women's lib in reverse. She would score and move on, sneering at each of the men she left behind. Then Melissa met RayLee. RayLee was a girl in her sociology class who wore sweaters that emphasized her over-sized breasts, dyed her hair red and painted her lips with pink pearl grease. She had beautiful hands that moved constantly when she talked, hands that Abigail learned fondled parts of Melissa, parts, Melissa said, she hadn't known were meant for touching. Abigail was too shocked to ask exactly where they were.

Their friendship became history as Melissa flaunted her passion like a cause. "You can't knock it, 'til you've tried it!" she sang, her arms and legs tangled with RayLee's, in Abigail's living room, on the same couch that Ari Michos had watched her comings and goings. Abigail found the whole scene perversely insensitive. She was both jealous and repulsed by their intimacy and without words to explain it, she and Melissa parted company.

Abigail met Kendra at the beginning of her sophomore year, when she was needing a best friend. Kendra was more independent than she, and usually surrounded by a coterie of admirers. It was her style that attracted Abigail most. She stood up to criticism and rarely resorted to compromise. A few years older than most of the other students, Abigail saw her as a woman of the world.

Kendra operated on another plane, something Abigail couldn't navigate, but admired. Admiration has a way of distancing one person from another, and from the start their friendship was fragile. Abigail never allowed herself to become one of the flock. If and when she and Kendra lunched or brunched, she made sure they would be alone and free to talk about art and family and dreams and schemes. These times were few and far between but significant enough for both to recall over the years. It was with Kendra that Abigail attempted to philosophize and formulate ideas about art.

Kendra had an undiluted vision of art. Art for art's sake. Art as its own metaphor. Color, line, composition, form, texture, art's elements as its purest expression. The non-objective art she later showcased represented this philosophy. Storytelling in art she dismissed, relegating it to illustrators like Rockwell and Kent. She even referred to Michelangelo as that great illustrator, and was just as dismissive of Homer and Hopper. Ironically, the fatuous authority of youth took her to places few aspire.

Her heroes were Vasily Kandinsky and Hilla Rebay, whom she described as the courageous pioneers who paved the way for pure abstractionism. According to Kendra, Kandinsky's intuitive expressions liberated art. He took it to another sphere where the beauty of a piece could only be understood in a spiritual way. Hilla Rebay's championship of the abstract led to the creation of the Guggenheim Museum. Kendra's naming names impressed Abigail, enough so, that she made a point to know their work.

She learned to appreciate Braque, Picasso and Matisse, too, because Kendra exalted their names. She said she loved them because they fooled the public into thinking they were painting subjects, when in truth they were constructing patterns above and beyond the known world.

After graduation, Abigail looked for work in Manhattan while Kendra went to Paris, then Madrid. She tried marriage for three days to a very rich doctor from Barcelona but knew immediately it would not work. To hear her tell, her throat shut down, her ring finger turned black and her back went into spasms. She even thought she might go blind because her eyes ached so. The Pope let her off the hook with a dispensation, and her life went on.

She was working with Peggy Guggenheim's foundation in Venice when she met Garrison Field of the Field Galleries. She fell hard. They were socially, artistically and intellectually aligned. People evaporated in the power of their alliance and new artists were made. As a dynamic duo they fed galleries in New York and Paris, in Brussels and Majorca. Pop artists flocked to them; Warhol was a buddy, and Lichtenstein their friend. Even Motherwell and Pollock were in their stable at one time or another. It was heady and fast and neither slowed down enough to ask where they were going. Garrison ended it. He downed too many pills one night and never woke up. Kendra insisted it was an accident. "No one loved life more than Garry," she maintained.

He left her nothing but an engagement ring, and the Field family was not sympathetic. The SoHo gallery was the one property that had her name attached to it and she held onto it. It was enough.

We were so young, Abigail thought. Pretenders I suppose. She is much more than the woman I knew in college. She hasn't wallowed in her losses or run from the challenges. I don't remember a time when she's been angry or remorseful. She owns her life completely. I can't help but wonder where her doubts hide, and what other things she might long for. Does she live in a perfect world where only those who affirm and protect her are allowed in?

Ah, the skeptic in me is rising, the dark force I can't seem to exorcise. This is so unfair, this looking for the great flaw in everything and everyone. Kendra is the one friend I have that has given me the hope and wherewithal to go on, and I'm not going to waste time analyzing her. I could never emulate the energy that surrounds her. I have no reason to believe she's any different than the person she purports to be.

A new guest arrived.

Abigail moved toward the man she once trusted most. His eyes met hers, and she smiled as he removed his hat and placed it over his heart, bowing deeply. She hadn't seen him for years, although they talked occasionally on the phone and exchanged notes at the holidays. He was somewhat changed, the hair a little thinner, the waist a little broader, but the smile was as ready as ever and the warmth just the same.

"I came to pay homage to the lady of the hour."

"Bo, you came! I only hoped as much!" she cried.

"I should have come earlier; the damn snow is making cabs scarce."

"Well, you're here. That's all that counts. Come, meet Kendra, have a glass of wine. Hang up your coat and promise me you'll stay a bit."

"I can't stay long. I have a date uptown."

"But why didn't you bring Cheryl with you? I am dying to meet her."

"It's over."

"So soon?"

"Just not right. And how's the handsome Hank doing?"

"Oh," she could not begin to explain, "He's fine."

"Where is he?"

"Out of town. Come, you must meet Kendra. I think you two could be great friends." She thought nothing of the sort, not really, not until she saw their eyes meet.

In no time at all her two friends were immersed in a conversation and Abigail took her leave.

18

The Dance

As she moved away from Bo and Kendra, a cold draft hit her ankles. It came through the door with some latecomers who were shaking off their fur coats in an attempt to leave more snow out than in. The glare of the streetlights turned them into silhouettes, but as she watched them climbing out of their coats, Abigail recognized the woman. Holding her sable like a wet dog, was her mother, now exceedingly blonde and bejeweled.

Three years had passed since Davis and Cecily moved south, to some island named Myrtle or Turtle or wherever it is that fifty-somethings go to get a second wind, a place centered around golf and an exclusive clubhouse where they can play out their lives. He was looking satisfied, but then he always had looked satisfied. Abigail still couldn't look him in the eye. His facelift was too obvious, his brows now in perpetual wonder, his cheeks tied tightly to his ears.

Cecily's toned slender arms embraced her.

"Mother! I never thought you'd come. I am so glad to see you. And, Davis, thank you for coming."

"How could we miss an event like this for our little girl?" he answered, specious as ever.

"I'm hardly little, Davis," she laughed.

She had kept her distance from him since the beginning but now he'd apparently adopted her.

Cecily chimed in. "I wouldn't have missed it for the world, Abigail. You're becoming the somebody I always knew you were. Imagine exhibiting here, in SoHo! What's next? Paris?" She looked over the room. "Such a sophisticated group of people...where's our darling Hank?"

"Not here."

"Oh? Babysitter problems?"

"Not exactly."

"Is he ill?"

"Hank's in Tucson, Mother. With someone else's children. He left me a year ago."

"What? You're separated? Dear God. Why didn't you call? You could have warned me! Can't you ever break down that armor of yours and ask for help?

"Armor?"

"Why do you shock me with news like this, now, here, in the face of what should be a lovely evening?"

"Sorry. Honestly, Cecily, I didn't expect you."

"... and Davis was so happy for you, too."

"He can still be happy for me, Mother." Her defense mechanisms shifted into high gear.

"I'm shocked. Absolutely, shocked."

"But Mother, it's you who is the queen of shock."

"I simply wish you had called and told me what was going on," she said more gently, pressing Abigail's hand, the southern tan-in-a-can cheek rubbing her daughter's as she whispered in her ear.

"I saw no need to get anyone else upset. I'm surviving quite well, as you can see." She wished for a conversation stopper. The evening mustn't take this downward turn. "Where are you staying?" she tried.

"But how difficult is it to pick up a phone?" her mother

persisted.

"Mother, I am learning to live with it. Why should I upset you or Tiffany, you have your own problems."

"Tiffany doesn't know either?"

"No. You know Tiffany's life is a rollercoaster ride. She's either high on her way up, or screaming on her way down. A good time to call Tiffany is hard to gauge."

Cecily was clutching her chest as if her heart might escape. "But Hank, how could he? I thought he was a pillar, that you were the perfect couple. I can't believe such a thing has happened. Why did he leave? This is simply preposterous."

"We ended what never began."

"Seems to me quite a few things began, including two beautiful children, a perfectly good life in Montmarte. Oh, men are so stupid!" she blurted before she remembered Mr. Wonderful was at her side. "Except for you, darling," she said, in the event he had taken her words personally.

Abigail had long thought she owed Davis for introducing her to Hank. Hank's departure didn't change that. She would never forget that he had stepped in at a time when she had just climbed out of a terrible depression.

She was twenty-two and should have been on her way with a new job, a smart little studio apartment in Brooklyn Heights, and an uncomplicated social life. She should have been flying, but a failed romance sent her into a dark place.

Grandma Lynde's antennae were the first to pick up the signal. She kept calling, sensing things were not right. When she passed on her concern to Cecily, the lioness mother wasted no time. She arrived to rescue her cub that very afternoon.

"A job is not worth suffering over, Abby. There's always something else out there."

Abigail didn't contradict her mother's guesswork. She just did what she could to look like she was on the mend. She pulled herself away from the couch, and to satisfy her mother, began to reclaim the apartment. Out went the empty boxes of tissues and Cheerios, the Oreo cookie wrappers and empty Coke cans. Dirty clothes were moved from the floor to the common laundry room in the basement, along with soiled towels and sheets. By evening, she went to Bookend's to find a readable book or magazine, and when morning came, she returned to work and tried to concentrate, until an overwhelming paralysis returned and caused her to stay home the following day and the next and the next.

Cecily discovered she was home from work again and called Tiffany for help. Tiffany agreed to try to find out what was going on. She called her sister from California and spoke like nothing was wrong.

"So how is going, working girl?" Tiffany asked.

"It's okay."

"Hey. You don't sound like yourself. What's wrong?"

"Nothing."

"Nothing as in a missed period? Gambling debts? Boyfriend trouble?"

"Not really a boyfriend. Someone I wanted to be with but it ended right after it began."

"Really? Who was he?"

"He was Melissa's old boyfriend, Ari. You probably never met him."

"The guy you met at the beach a hundred years ago?"

"Yes, the same, but not the same, if you know what I mean. Anyway, it's not important. It isn't anything at all."

It wasn't long before Cecily was knocking at Abigail's door again.

"Open the door, young lady," she said as she pounded, "You're coming home with me. You need company. End of discussion."

Abigail pulled back the bolt and opened the door, just to get the noise out of the hallway.

"I don't need anyone, Cecily."

"I think you're pining away here. I called you at work three days in a row and you weren't in. This won't do, and over some foreign boy with no credentials. Really, Abigail. And you don't look well. You aren't eating properly; I will not have you doing this to yourself."

"Foreign boy with no credentials?"

"It's normal for young women to be attracted to the dangerous, but now you should put your energy into something real, someone appropriate. Become a little more practical."

"But how do you know I'm upset about some guy? I think I am

very practical, thank you. I've got a job, an apartment and I just hit a snag, that's all."

Abigail had taken a designer's job at the PureForm Packaging Company, and was walking distance from the subway line that virtually delivered her to the door. Compared to the choices of her mother and sister during the last five years, she considered herself the most sensible of the three. At least she would not choose a man for his portfolio or a set of glorious muscles over a real man with real feelings like Bo. She knew she could go it alone and create an independent life as soon as she got rid of the negative voices in her head and uninvited advice.

"I just need a little time."

"Some beach boy is not worth this misery. I am shocked you would even consider such a person. Really, Abby, he wouldn't fit into your world anymore than you would fit into his. I hope you remember you're a Benoit as well as a Lynde. Your great-grandparents helped build this city. You have a responsibility to your name and legacy."

Abigail's mind flooded with questions. How did her mother learn about Ari? What might explain the spate of venom she was spewing? How could she abort this bizarre tirade?

"What does this man do? Does he speak English? Does he have an education? Sweetheart, he has no credentials and you have so many!"

"Weren't my great-grandparents immigrants, too?" she asked, right before she realized Tiffany had betrayed her confidence, and that she shouldn't have told her sister anything. "Did Tiffany tell you about Ari? She had no right to tell you about him."

"Never mind, Tiffany. I heard it from a little bird. Listen. This man-boy is not worth your misery. I am worried about you."

Abigail was angry at herself for sharing what little she had with Tiffany. She should have known nothing was sacred with her sister. "Tiffany had no right to tell you. I know the whole thing wouldn't have worked out. He doesn't love me, didn't love me and never will. I only wished he was interested in me. And he's not without credentials. He's a businessman and a beautiful person. You think I don't know the arithmetic of love, but I know that one plus one equals everything, and two minus one equals nothing. The someone I chose to love happened to be Ari, but I know it's hopeless."

"Love? Let me tell you something, child of my heart. Love is for the movie screen. You need to think of your lifestyle. What will make you comfortable, provide a decent home, insure your children's education, their place in society. Find a man who loves you more than you love him, not less. Really. These doldrums are nonsense. They're beneath you."

"I don't have to worry about my children's education."

"Nonsense. Of course you will."

"I'm never having children."

"You will find the right man and change your mind. It isn't about romance, Abby, it's about a good life."

"What about you and Daddy? You loved Daddy! I want a marriage like yours."

"You do? Your father lifted me out of a mess because he once loved me. I have that to remember, despite the awful end."

"He died. You can't blame him for that. You had him for awhile. You had his children..."

"Yes, I had his child. You know nothing. I'm telling you, for your own sake, be realistic. Why don't you go out with that MacKenzie boy?"

"MacKenzie boy? I don't even know who you're talking about."

"He's a lovely young man, already part of the family firm, Benoit, Corwin and Schaeffer. They grabbed him right out of law school. If your uncle thinks he's a winner then you might think so, too. Davis says he's utterly decent and still single."

"And what makes you think there would be any chemistry between us?"

"Chemistry? He's a graduate of Columbia, his family name is in the Blue Book and he's not bad to look at either. That's what it takes, my angel, not the stuff of fairy tales."

"You chose your prince. Why shouldn't I have one too?"

"Prince?" she scoffed.

"How can you just forget Daddy? Have you forgotten him? How much he loved us—mostly you? That's what I want. I want the same magic you and Daddy had."

"Magic is for novels. Better yet, novellas. Magic is illusion. Poof and it's gone."

"But, Daddy..."

"Your father died in a hotel room with another woman."

She brandished the words like a sword. They made their mark, cutting Abigail's heart in two before entering her mind. It wasn't true, she thought. She remembered the phone, the dangling phone.

"I don't believe you. There... there was the phone. He wouldn't have been making a call if someone else was in the room."

"The woman ran, of course. She didn't want her name mixed up with his."

How could her mother know such a thing? Her poor father accused that way, with no one to defend him. She wished she knew who he was calling. Was he afraid? Was he sorry? Was he trying to reach them? Before words surfaced, tears began popping out of her eyes.

"I hate you!" she cried. "How could you say such a thing about Daddy?"

"When we know what's real, we can sort out the rest," Cecily said. "Maybe I waited too long. Perhaps, I should tell you now what I have never wanted you to know. Your father married me when I was pregnant with another man's child. He saved me from making a terrible choice. To have a child out of wedlock or to marry a man I hardly knew. Your sister was the product of a wild weekend in Newport with a married man. She never had to know about her real father because from the day she was born, your father claimed her as his own. He never acknowledged she was anything less. But he paid me back in the end, didn't he? He must have felt justified."

Pain and outrage made Abigail's bones weak; her mother's face blurred before her eyes. How dare she corrupt the one incontrovertible belief that had sustained her, the belief that the only man who ever truly loved her, her father, was perfect? Did she want to completely obliterate any hope she had for love? Her father had been the standard bearer, the man who once wanted only to protect her, to protect them all, and now...now even her sister was someone else.

How many years had she spent wondering why she and Tiffany were so different? How many times had she felt guilty about her grandmother's favoritism? Now she understood. Did this also explain the special love-hate thing that existed between her mother and sister, the emotions that excluded everyone else and made them more intimate, even as they remained apart?

Two weeks later, still numb with hurt, Abigail met Hank MacKenzie. Cecily had engaged Davis in her matchmaking scheme. It was Davis who sent Hank to meet her on the 26th floor of the Williamsburg Bank with an important document; and Davis who provided a guard so they could have private access to the old observation deck. New York was bathed in pink and purple and edged with gold that evening. It was so clear they could see most of Brooklyn, the Manhattan skyline and a piece of the Atlantic.

Maybe being four hundred feet in the air set the mood or, maybe it was fate, but she felt something special happen in that tower. She wasn't the only one who was surprised. When the tall attractive man carrying a brown envelope stepped out of the elevator, and she smiled at him, she could still remember how relieved and open his face looked as he introduced himself.

"Well, hey," he said. "Are you Uncle Lyman's favorite niece?"

"One of two," she said.

They weren't particularly smooth as they fumbled around for the right words, but he graciously asked her to go to dinner at Gage and Tollner's on Fulton Street, a famous place, known for its thirty-six gas lamps and excellent cuisine. Of course, she said yes.

In the soft glow of antiquity, he ordered a bottle of St. Emilion Bordeaux, and tested its aroma and flavor before letting it touch her glass. She was impressed.

After they had properly toasted one another, she opened the brown envelope to read the supposedly urgent letter inside. It was a card that read:

Remember Abby,
Love is a choice. Let this fellow court you. Just because things
may not always go as planned, enjoy the life you're offered!

It was signed with a grand C. She knew it wasn't Cecily's logo, it had to be C as in Corwin. She didn't share the message but it turned out to be the best advice Davis ever sent her way.

Their courtship was smooth and pleasant. In a year and a half, she was pregnant and married, in that order. Tiffany approved, Cecily was relieved, and Abigail was prepared to make a life that would look like everyone else's. It may have been 1987 and the rest of the world swaying to Graceland, but her head swam with baby names, the most outrageous being Forsythia, the flower of Brooklyn.

She looked around the room for Bo. He seemed to be caught up in a serious conversation with Kendra. She couldn't help but contemplate what that might mean.

By her side, Cecily coughed, again and again, tears reddening her eyes. From the depths of her cupped hand she said, "… just recovering from a bout with bronchitis, and this news seems to be bringing it up again. I don't know if I can stay, really. This is just too much of a shock."

Abigail didn't know what to think. Her mother had never seemed very interested in her life or her marriage. She wasn't at all sure what Cecily was thinking, who she was really worried about.

"Mother, relax. Come inside and see the show. I am trying my best to enjoy the evening. Please. Let's talk tomorrow or the next day, or next week, okay?"

"I will never understand you, Abby. But do show me your latest things. I am truly curious. Davis seems to be absorbed. That's a good sign."

"Go join him, Mother, and be your own judge. I'm curious what you see in my work."

Abigail watched Cecily glide into Davis' side, shaking her platinum head and leaning against his narrow shoulder. That's how it had been with them since she first attached herself to his arm at a mortgage and loan affair at the bank. It was close to eighteen years since she took him to the altar. His millions surely hadn't interfered with their happiness.

Abigail might have been behind a one-way mirror observing the couple's act as they upstaged the room. Davis was the great conciliator patting her mother's arm sympathetically, while she dabbed her eyes without regard for the paintings. Just as it crossed Abigail's mind that her mother's upset could be legitimate, Bo broke in.

"That isn't Cecily?" he asked.

"It is."

"Well, I'll be damned. She looks great!"

"She always did."

"I have to say hello, before I go."

"You're leaving? I want you to stay. You know, you're the best friend I have here."

"Not as good a friend as I'd like to be."

"Your date, is it with someone special?" she asked.

"Well, I am afraid the law corrupts. You learn all the ways to get in and out of things. Special gets harder and harder to find."

Abigail laughed, not knowing what he meant but thinking he was still lovely. "I don't suppose you would want to know that Tiffany has finally left Troy? She has a new career in the cosmetic industry."

"That's good. It wasn't the best match. Where is she living?"

Abigail doesn't see the reaction in his face she anticipated.

"Still in L.A., but she's on the road a lot. New York, Chicago, Paris—the circuit."

"Abby, you are more beautiful than ever. This is your night. I am so glad I made it." His words were said easily, as to a sister, and she blushed, regardless. He was the sweetest man she had ever known—so kind, so present. She held his arm and planted a kiss on his cheek. "Bo, I have always loved you," she said.

"It was pretty damned cute when you were fifteen and trying so hard to be a woman."

"I was scared to death. Still am."

"Bo!" Cecily called. "What a pleasant surprise. How did you know about tonight? My goodness, it's been ages...."

She stopped abruptly and gave Abigail a strange look.

"I had to see my favorite girl doing her thing," he answered.

"Yes, well...."

They had an inane exchange of superficial information with Cecily acting oddly distracted, not herself.

"Abby, I think Davis and I must go. I will discuss things with you tomorrow. The snow seems to be picking up and...." She was obviously dismissing Bo, almost to the point of rudeness. "I can see you are both preoccupied and it isn't a good time, anyway. I will come back to the gallery another day without the crowd. You give those dear children a hug from me, won't you?"

"Abby, I think you and your mother need to talk," Davis said before he left. He managed not to see Bo, froze him out of the picture. If he could have furrowed his Botox-laden brows, he would have.

After they left, Bo asked Abigail if the two were all right. He couldn't help but notice their upset.

Privately, she knew he had been maligned; that they had seen him as the interloper, the destroyer of the happy marriage of Hank and Abigail. But starting down that road was pointless. Instead, she simply reminded him she had never quite understood her mother and vice-versa.

"Tell me about Kendra," he said.

She fought a silly jealousy as she answered. "She's a special person, always has been. I think we're are becoming friends on a whole new level."

"Is she involved with anyone?" he asked, not even trying to be subtle.

"Do you like shitzus?" Abigail asked.

"As long as they know their place," he said.

"Abigail," Kendra interrupted, suddenly at their side. "You're a success in the making. Everyone adores your work."

She turned to Bo. "Bo, did you know this woman was creating these things in a coal bin?"

He laughed and shook his head no. "I knew the day would come though. She was always lost to her art and books. I'm glad she didn't start living through her kids like most women do. Too many female talents are squandered that way!" he said.

Kendra agreed, sliding her arm through his and leading him to the guest book. "I think you should sign in, right here. Name, address and phone number."

"I'd be pleasured, Ma'am," he said, pulling a pen from inside his dark gray suit jacket along with a pair of horn-rimmed glasses. After he put them on, he looked back at Abigail and winked.

He was a man of the world now, confident, groomed, but his basic nature seemed unchanged. Kendra and Bo would be an equal match, she thought; a balance of power.

The room felt emptier after Bo left for his date uptown. A few others started to leave, and she was not surprised, seeing as it was snowing and they were running out of food.

Barney re-entered her periphery. "I wonder if you could help me?" he asked. I am curious as to what poem goes with this painting?" He was pointing toward *The Tango*.

"I think this is more of a musical piece," she said.

He moved closer. "I think I love you," he said in her ear, his warm breath sending ripples of want traveling down her spine.

She smelled his aftershave. He was outrageous. It had to be the wine speaking. His glass was half empty, and it wasn't his first or second, and yet, her glass was half-empty, too.

"That's good enough for starters," she laughed.

"No, I mean it. I think I love you."

"Is your wife here this evening?" she asked, knowing if he had a wife somewhere, this would straighten him out.

"Was she here again? She does that thing sometimes, hovering around, checking up on me."

"Excuse me?"

"I suppose she might be taking in this exhibit, but I don't feel her here. Margie? You here?" He was looking up and around. "She's been gone eleven years."

"You're separated?"

"You could put it that way. Margie died in '86."

"Oh, you're a widower then?"

"God, that word stings. It sounds ancient, like I should snort oxygen."

"I'm sorry. It was just, just that I thought you were coming on so strong, and I …. I'm not good at it."

"It?"

"Flirting."

"I wouldn't say that. I'm turned on."

"You really don't know me at all."

"Ah, but I do. I know more than you think. You're bouncing off these walls."

His eyes were smiling at her. They were climbing inside her head. She wanted to have the assurance he assumed she had.

"I would prefer not to bounce."

"Let's try dancing, substitute bouncing with dancing. You're dancing in this room. You're dancing on these walls. We're dancing, that's it. Can you hear the music? I can almost see the rhythm in this painting."

"I think you've been duped. You can't know me through this work. In fact, I'm not sure any of these paintings are authentic."

"Forgeries?"

"In a way."

"What way?"

"They all lie."

"What does it matter? You were just doing your thing and now others are having the fun of deciding what that is."

"So who are you, Barney or Nietzsche?"

"I'm Wade, for starters. Your servant and admirer. Do you prefer Abby or Abigail?"

"Wade? Wade not Barney. Oh no. I think I get it. Wade Barney. Barney for Barnstable. You're the private investigator, aren't you?"

"The snoop? Yes."

"Why didn't you introduce yourself earlier. That wasn't fair."

"My devious nature. No, actually, I hoped you would remember my voice, and then you didn't. Besides, it's lousy work, I do."

"It served me well."

"You think so?"

"I do. How else can I move on?"

"You're doing it royally, tonight."

"This is the last place I expected to start my life over—here in SoHo. I've never thought my work to be So-Ho material."

"Your work is very different from Kendra's typical stuff, that's for sure. Her affair with black-and-white dabs and doodles must be coming to an end. Maybe even she is getting tired of it. All those stripes and splashes were lost on me. I used to try to think of something intelligent to say about them. Good try? Interesting angle? Nice splash?"

"Kendra and I have been friends since art school. How did you two meet?"

"She took a kayaking class I taught in Rockland County—Nyack, to be exact. I rent kayaks in Nyack. Euphonious, huh? Stephenson would have made the most of such a rhyme. Oh how I'd love to go out in a kayak, out in a river so blue, Oh I do think to kayak from Nyack would be ever so fun to do!"

"Not bad," she said, thinking he was looking more and more appealing.

He shoved his hands in his pockets, retrieved a flyer and handed it to her. She read the large print. The Hudson School of Kayaking.

"The Hudson is a great place to learn kayaking as long as you don't swallow the water. You know Nyack?" he asked.

"You know I live in Montmarte, up river."

"Do you ever escape and explore? That town is so exclusive you might as well be on an island."

"I have to admit Montmarte is not Nyack. I think Nyack has more character, more room to breathe. I wish I had moved there instead of Montmarte. A person needs contrasts to remember what's real."

"Are you for real?"

"I live and breathe, sweat and take mega vitamins. But no, no I am not real. Not yet."

"I've been watching you all night. You're more interested in your art than anyone in the room."

"I've never seen it as a body of work. It's as if I am reading my own biography. I have to admit I'm finding it fascinating to hear the comments."

"I told you, I think I love you." He holds up his hands and his shoulders in a shrug of helplessness. "Who's the guy?"

"What guy?"

"The one that got you to place those pretty lips of yours on his cheek."

"An old friend."

"How old?"

"You know, I would rather hear more about what you think of my paintings."

"I don't know anything about art. I told you."

But he told her what he thought some of them were about, anyway. She ignored her aching legs, forgot about Cecily and Davis and Bo, and listened to his interpretations.

The only one he understood was *Chaos*—he was dead wrong about the others. If art was communication, she had failed.

"How am I doing?" he asked.

"Not bad!" she fibbed.

"I may make you wait for the rest of my interpretations until we see each other again. We are going to see each other again." He put his hand on her back and led her closer to the painting of the dancers.

"Do you tango?" he asked.

"Hardly!"

"Well, then tell me about this painting?"

In the painting, two dancers moved as one and made a valentine of their bodies, the trees around them arched as well as the spaces in between.

"This isn't about me, it's about someone else, about another tango, one I watched. I've never danced the tango in my life. A dancer, my friend, I am not."

"There, you have said it. Friend. Now we're friends, at least. We're moving right along. We've shared poetry, art and now dance. This thing is happening faster than I expected." He looked up at the ceiling, "What do you think, Margie? Is it a go?" He turned back to Abigail, "I should warn you. Sometimes she manifests herself."

Abigail thought he was too glib. "How can you get over losing someone so completely that you can joke about her?"

"I'm not over her. She's with me. I incorporate her into my life. We never had secrets before, and we don't now."

Abigail decided to stop judging, she couldn't know what that kind of connection could feel like.

"Do you have children?"

"No. Well, there's my dog Zipper. He's a hound of some sort. Margie and I decided not to have kids once we realized things were looking bad. Now, I regret it."

They walked side by side to the foyer and filled their glasses. She looked out the window and saw the snow had started to stick. Fat, flat flakes were floating slowly down, the kind that melt into each other.

"You know, it's not going to be easy to go over the river and through the woods."

"Not too," he grinned.

"My Dodge caravan doesn't like the white and drifting snow. In fact, I would be better off with a horse. I think we should consider calling it a night."

"Freeze," a voice yelled.

"Hands on your heads!"

19

The Hold-Up

"Everyone to dah back a dah room. Move!" yelled a squat man dressed in black. It was a horrible party joke, if it was one. He was one of two men pointing at the crowd with what looked like toy guns, intending to herd them to the back of the gallery like cattle.

Sounds of gasps and murmured expressions of surprise gave way to the movement of feet and the rustle of dresses as everyone swished by in deference to the command. Wade, meanwhile, turned himself into a human shield, temporarily obstructing Abigail's view of the men with his shoulders. She knew enough to be grateful.

"Move it, asshole," the frenzied man shouted at him as they stumbled along with the others into a tight cluster at the far wall, outside the storage room.

"Take everything off. Throw your clothes in the middle of the room," the other bandit ordered. Abigail thought he couldn't be serious. She peered around Wade to see the man more clearly and checked his eyes for a twinkle, but no humor was evident. His eyes were as dark as the ski mask he wore. He was the shortest man in the room, but with his gun he was tall. People actually began to strip.

"Everything!" the man ordered, ripping the buttons right off the blouse of one of the older women. "Now!"

Clothes started to fly; dresses, jackets, ties, shoes and socks. The pile in the center of the room grew as each piece was added. Simultaneously, the other thief extricated wallets and change from pockets, and dumped the booty into one of two gray suede bankroll bags. As Wade stripped, he could no longer cover Abigail.

"Everything, fucker!" The man said to Max, waving his gun like a whip.

Abigail, meanwhile, did nothing until the cold nose of the gun was on her cheek. "Take off your clothes or I'll do it for you, Blondie."

She shakily began to undo the pearl buttons of her sweater and pulled it over her head, then unfastened her black velvet skirt, let it drop to the floor and kicked it away. It was toasty in the room but her legs became wobbly as Jello. The same gun grazed her face as she was told to remove her grandmother's opal earrings, the sapphire ring and the watch on her wrist. "It's only a Timex," she protested.

"A Timex keeps running," the little guy said, taking it from her hand and tossing it in his bag. This has to be a hoax, Abigail thought. What thief makes jokes in the middle of a heist? But, the rest of the crowd was not laughing, and the gun looked more genuine up close and personal.

They all stood in a pathetic huddle, silent, except for the woman whose blouse had been torn. She was weeping. The crowd that had been so social only minutes before was now lewdly exposed in a most peculiar array of underwear; reduced to effete voyeurs of one another's intimate apparel and helplessly mortified by the men who stole their jewels, their wallets and identities.

"Get over there, all of yahs, get over there and if you make one fuckin' noise you're dead. You got dat? Down, down on your knees you motherfuckers. Better yet, lie down!"

The little tough guy went over to Fred. "Maybe we'll do you a favor and bugger you tonight, Sweetie. Catch them satin panties will yahs?"

Fred Farber's shiny red bikinis were in direct contrast to Wade

Barnstable's baggy boxer shorts. Fred had turned a ghastly gray. He wrapped himself up like a sparrow and lowered himself to the floor. Wade bowed to the floor next to him. "Don't worry, Fred," he whispered. "These guys are lunchmeat. I can take them out if I have to."

"Shuddup!" the larger crook said.

The group moved closer to the wall where Kendra lay, disrobed, eyes closed, in a fetal position. Somehow she managed to look like an ad for Victoria's Secret, which made Abigail question again if she could possibly be guilty of staging the unfolding nightmare.

Abigail lay close to Wade, could feel his warmth, hear his heart pounding. She wondered what he was thinking and hoped he wouldn't do anything stupid. A few stolen items were nothing compared to bodily harm. She tucked herself into the arch of his spine so they fit like spoons and rested her hand on his arm where the soft hair was electrified, standing at attention above sinews of tensed muscle. His hand folded over hers and their fingers tangled.

With her eyes closed against the embarrassment of the room, she buried her head in the groove under his shoulder blade. There was a mole on his shoulder the size of a penny. She would ask him later if he was born with it. If not. She would remind him to have it checked. He squeezed her hand, reassuringly. In her mind she pictured his palm and wanted to see if his life line was deep and unbroken. She would remember to check the creases between his third and fourth fingers and see if he was going to have more than one wife. His leathery maleness filled her senses. She trembled. He whispered, "Don't be afraid."

"Shuddup! You think we can't shoot you in da mout?"

Abigail realized she was not afraid. She felt sure these characters weren't going to shoot anybody, sure about her survival and sure about Wade's. What she couldn't believe was the unexpected rush, the burning sensation, the desire to press her body against the man beside her, to feel his flesh respond. The closeness of him made her head swim. The room disappeared and the sobs of the old woman became a lullaby as she leaned deeper into Wade. If not for the crowd she would have pulled him into her, taken him all the way in.

The whole scenario may have lasted all of five or ten minutes but it seemed like hours before the men retreated. Like a pair of stealthy

Santa Claus's, money bags thrown over their shoulders, they warned the group not to move. To an invisible lookout man at the door, the short man called, "Don't let 'em move. If they do, just let 'em have it." To the huddled mass, he said, "Keep your asses down or you'll get a new hole to brag about."

The prostrate, almost-naked victims, couldn't see the door and couldn't know for certain who or what was there. They obediently lay mummified and waited. When silence had prevailed for a few minutes, Kendra stood up and wailed, "Those bastards! At Christmas, too!"

One by one, the rest of the group started grabbing their clothes. Abigail stood in place until Wade brought back her things. He delicately turned his eyes from her chest. She, on the other hand, regarded his, noted the tightness of his abdomen the burnished tones of his skin. His body was younger than his face. His dark blue eyes looked even darker now. She didn't want him to be angry, to do anything irrational.

She said, "I hoped it was a joke."

"Not very funny if it is," he muttered. "I'm going to call the police."

"The phone's in the storeroom," she pointed to the door of the closet.

Different expressions of disgust came forward as the group got dressed. Then Maynard Darling started to giggle. His partner joined him, and before long the laughter erupted into hysteria. Tootsie was loosed from the storeroom, and she started barking as if she was part and parcel of the group. Even the sobbing woman had pulled herself together, recognizing the ludicrous nature of their circumstance.

The joviality did not last, however, because a new voice yelled, "Down on the floor!" and the group gasped and dropped like plumb lines to the carpet. Kendra threw herself on her little dog.

Abigail managed to look up and see two policemen, who could have been Keystone Cops with their hats on backwards, guns drawn, bulletproof vests exposed and arms flailing about.

"Where are they?" one of the cops shouted, throwing open the door of the storage room. Wade was standing in his shorts with the telephone in his hands and turned to see the policeman raise his pistol.

"What the Hell?" Wade said.

"Don't shoot!" Abigail screamed from the gallery.

The cop didn't. "Where'd they go?" he asked, instead.

"Out the front door," Fred yelled.

"Don't anyone move," another cop ordered.

Semi-clad, they remain huddled again, until another policeman arrived and allowed them to continue dressing while he took down whatever information he could glean from the disheveled group.

Simultaneously, the thieves were caught in the subway underpass at the end of the street. Their tracks in the snow had been conveniently obvious. In less than an hour, the suede sacks with all the possessions were returned to the room where the police had to begin the long process of reclamation, including the photographing and recording of stolen properties, and names, addresses and telephone numbers of the victims.

Something close to bonding set in, and soon more wine bottles were opened as they, the liberated, celebrated their survival. It would be an opening no one would ever forget, an opening that would be reinforced in the next day's news as Max and Fred were taking copious notes and lapping up the whole scene.

Wade, at ease now, brought Abigail another glass of wine. She held it up and, uncharacteristically, toasted everyone for coming to her grand opening. More laughter ensued. The merriment continued in a kind of survivors' joy, as each recounted their thoughts during the robbery.

It occurred to Abigail that perhaps all men should be stripped down first, and checked for telltale tattoos on their tushes, satin thongs or flowered long Johns. It could be a litmus test of sorts.

Finally, the new friends bid one another farewell and headed for home. Fred and Max, Wade and Kendra and Abigail remained. Kendra embraced Wade and looked at Abigail like a cat. "I was hoping you two would find each other tonight. Wade and I go way back, way down by the riverside you might say."

"So I've heard," Abigail smiled. "Kayaks in Nyack."

"Of course we go way back, too, don't we, Abby?" Kendra added.

Abigail felt Kendra's affection as never before and her own in return.

Max approached. "Kenny, Sweetheart, you managed to stage the most fascinating spoof I've ever seen. What a way to bring your patrons together! A true New York experience. You are a clever wench."

"I should only be that clever!" Kendra laughed, downing the glass of wine from her crystal glass.

"Look, why don't we go over to Wolfe's and have a hot pastrami sandwich?" Fred suggested. "The appetizers didn't do it for me. I'm suddenly starving."

Max laughed. "I'm going home to write, we have a scoop."

Wade turned to Abigail. "How about it, Abigail? Want to grab a bite?"

"Can't," she said.   "I have that grueling ride back up to Montmarte."

She didn't mention she was afraid she would be driving blind, that she might stay at a motel on the other side of the bridge. "You all go ahead."

Kendra shook her head, "No. Another time, Fred. Tootsie is not allowed in Wolfe's. They'd just see her as meat. I wouldn't put it past them to slap her between two pieces of rye."

"I think I better follow Abigail," Wade said. "We'll have to fight the snow to get to the Tarrytown Bridge and then God only knows what we'll find in Rockland County."

"Fred, love, forego Wolfe's and let me cook something for you back at your place," Kendra said. "I really think I'd like to stay in town tonight."

"My pleasure," Fred replied enthusiastically. He seemed fully recovered from the humiliation.

Abigail peered out the window. The snow was falling in big wet flakes; the streetlights were fuzzy moons above the white streets. Traffic was negligible. The large flakes were usually the last before the snow turned to rain.

Wade said. "Leave your car and let me drive you home, Abigail. I mean, I owe you. You saved my life."

"Yes? How so?"

"You told those clowns not to shoot me. They were trigger happy, sure as hell, scared to death."

"You can't blame them. It's hard to know where the enemy might be hiding."

"Will you trust my driving?"

"I probably shouldn't. But, I would just as soon have you at the wheel, I hate driving in snow. I'll take the commuter train back in the morning to pick up my car."

"Gawd, what a night!" Kendra sighed. "I'm so thrilled for you, Abby. It went better than I expected, right up to the strangest shakedown in SoHo history. Did you ever hear of anything so crazy? I didn't think they were serious at first. Did you?"

"I didn't, not until I realized how frightened everyone was and saw they were actually stripping. Wade was my hero."

"I noticed," Kendra said.

"I think I love her," he confided.

"Whoa, boy. You betta getta grip until she's ready. Timing, you know, is everything. But here's a hug for good luck." Kendra embraced him. He returned the gesture.

They proceeded to straighten out the room and find coats and hats, etcetera. Abigail was the only one who had brought boots, the mother in her ready for all occasions.

Wade warned, "You should call a cab, Kenny."

"I already did, but God knows when it will get here."

That's when they heard the taxi's horn give a double beep and saw its top light shining dimly. Kendra placed Tootsie, snugly in her golden satchel, and said, "Good night and good luck, you two. Take it slow and call me in the morning!"

Fred slipped his left arm through Kendra's right, Max put his right through her left, and the three friends skipped out the door into the white night with Toto riding high. You would have thought they were heading for Oz.

Abigail kicked off her heels and slipped her stockinged feet into the down-filled boots. "So glad I brought these old things," she said.

"Are you tired?" Wade asked.

"Not in the least. I'm more awake than I was two hours ago. I'm not sure if I have ever been so awake."

"I still can't believe the whole thing, can you? Are you sure a video camera wasn't hiding somewhere?" He put on an old Army parka.

As Abigail stood up, he helped by taking her hands.

"Listen, Abby, I want to kiss you. I need to kiss you. After all, I've been almost naked at your side in circumstances far more intimate than a kiss. I just want to know the kiss part. One kiss. That's all.

One. ”

She knew she shouldn't make a big deal of a kiss, it seemed sophomoric. And she had wanted to kiss him, in fact seduce him, only an hour before. He wasn't dangerous. An outrageous flirt, yes, but also the friend of a friend, after all. She knew she would look silly saying no. Besides she needed a kiss, she wanted a kiss. It had been too long.

Like an adolescent, she said, "Okay, just one."

He pulled her to him, her hips meeting his, the heat of their lips immediate. Blue light flooded through her and lit the edges of her skin. Her whole body burned. She was weightless. It was a kiss unlike anything she had ever known. It took all her strength to extricate herself from his arms, but she did.

"Phew. I am not ready for this," she said, knowing her voice was unconvincing, even to her own ears.

He buried his lips in her hair. One hand was on her neck, the other somewhere else. "Let go, Abby. Take a chance. You never know, we might be able to go the distance."

"I'm not ready."

"You're going to free yourself, one of these days, and I want to be there. I want to help. I know we're right. My intuition is pretty well honed. We're good."

"Not yet," she said, even though she felt like dancing.

20

Les Confidentes

Something skittered across the floorboards overhead. A faint smell of red wine lingered in the air and, outside, the snow continued to fly.

"All right," he said. "You don't fool around with strangers. Let's have a nightcap then."

"I think we better cut the drinks. The snow is going to be enough of a challenge as it is."

"The snow should be stopping soon, it wasn't even predicted."

"But what if it doesn't?" Abigail asked. "What shall we do?"

"It's just a flurry, better to wait it out. It will let up; but, right now, the visibility must be zero."

She retreated to the storeroom to call Marlene for a clue as to what was happening upstate. Marlene said she couldn't tell how much snow had fallen but it was building and then she added, "Mr. MacKensie called."

"Hank? I suppose he wanted to talk to the children."

"They were in bed. I told him about your whereabouts. I hope this is all right with you?"

"It's fine. Did he leave a message?"

"No. Just that he will call again tomorrow."

As she reentered the room, Wade was saying, "Did I tell you it was your voice that attracted me? It's soft, kind of musical."

She thought if he heard her when she lost her patience, he would think differently.

"The snow is still falling in Montmarte. However, the kids are asleep and the babysitter's not flustered."

She crumpled to the floor in a heap and leaned against the wall. "What I wouldn't do for some chocolate."

"Hmmm," he smiled. "Let me see what Mr. Fix-It can do."

He walked over to Kendra's sleek rosewood desk and opened a drawer meant for pencils, erasers and notepads. "She has a stash in here."

He disturbed the drawer a little and pulled out a red tin box. Abigail saw it as proof that he and Kendra knew each other better than she had thought.

"Try these chocolate-covered cherries. They ought to do the trick," he said.

"How did you know where they were hiding?" she asked.

"I gave them to your friend on her birthday and watched her hide them from herself."

Abigail wanted to know what else had he given her. Kendra was obviously fond of him, but she hadn't sensed a romance. She mused, "I can't help wondering what Kendra is denying herself in addition to chocolate. I don't think she has a lover. I know she doesn't want children and only flirts with the idea of a real home. She doesn't have any of the things, other than the gallery, that make life meaningful to most women. Do you think she's holding out for Mr. Perfect?"

"Well, it obviously wasn't me!" Wade laughed. "I think she's a pretty self-sufficient woman and doesn't waste much time on worrying about what isn't."

"That's what she projects, at least. Maybe she was too hurt the first time around to move on. I don't want to let that happen to me."

"It won't. You already have the things you think make life

meaningful, as you say. That is, if you want them. The kids, the home, the lover when you're ready."

He sat next to her on the floor, and they unwrapped their cherries. She watched his deft fingers crush the red foil, form a tiny ball and toss it into the waste basket by the desk. He looked around the room again.

"I like your work. It's fun, Abigail. Happy, no matter what you say."

She bit into the dark chocolate. The cherry juice oozed out, reddening her lips and satisfying her tongue.

"But the kiddy colors are just a cover-up."

"I wouldn't call them kiddy colors.

"I wasn't telling happy fun stories. I am not a happy fun person. My colors are a cover-up."

"Are we happy tonight?" he asked.

"Close!" She suspected he knew that already. It had to be evident her body was awake and hungry. What he couldn't know is that she never had felt so truly alive.

Not only was her art accepted, but it had spoken to her and helped her to understand and feel.

"But it isn't happiness I'm after," she explained. "It's about living a life where I take risks, that stretches beyond convention. I don't want to pretend any more."

"I hope that kiss wasn't faked."

"You're scary. You know that, don't you?"

"This from a woman who wants to take risks?" He laughed.

"It's your familiarity, as if we have known each other for a long time. I don't trust it. I...I still need to protect myself."

"Don't be too protected, Abby."

"I should go," she said, and started to get up.

"Hey, don't do that. I'm not dangerous, certainly not as dangerous as the roads out there. Christ. It was just a kiss. I don't usually act this way. I swear it's not my style. I often don't see women when they're right in my face, but I recognize something about you, something special. I can't name it. I'm sorry. I....I've been waiting a long time."

He turned into a pretzel, folding his arms and crossing his legs. She could feel him withdraw. She feared she had ruined what hadn't even begun.

"Well, I am not saying we can't get to know each other better," she said. "We'll take it slow."

"Yeah."

She didn't move, instead, she took another cherry from the box.

"I've been a jerk. Let's start over," Wade said.

"How?"

He put out his hand to shake hers and in an official voice, said, "Hello, I'd like to introduce myself. Name's Wade Barnstable. I investigated your husband's whereabouts. You may remember?"

"Why, yes. Yes, I do. And let me thank you for helping me understand my marriage was truly dead and that Hank MacKenzie was just one more person I never really knew."

"Oh hell, more than likely he's someone who changed. A guy who runs off to a townhouse in Tucson, with some little woman and her two kids, can't be the same guy you married."

"No. No he isn't. Thank you, again, for pointing that out."

"You're welcome. Listen, I came here tonight because I liked the sound of your voice on the phone, and I guess I have to admit Kendra said you were beautiful." He leaned into her side. "And she was right. You are."

"You haven't told me very much about finding Hank. How did you learn about his life in Tucson?"

"It was easy. You've heard the expression follow the money. I called his office in the city, made like I was following up on a bogus order for an air-conditioner, got his address and hopped a plane. Is that all you want to know?"

"Do you always lie?"

"I'm afraid it's part of my business. I am very good at it."

"How can a person trust you then?"

"I hate lying. I only do it when it's necessary."

"Will you tell me the truth?"

"Always."

"I still have so many questions about Hank, but I don't think you can answer any of them. Only Hank can explain, and we're not talking. You see, I never knew what happened, what really went wrong with us. I'm still not sure about the whys—why he left, why Jane Browne, why he didn't talk to me, try to fight for the marriage?

How he could abandon his children?"

"Look, guys are animals. They see an opportunity, turn on and move in, and its curtains for the women they leave behind. I see it every day. It's nothing personal."

"How can you say nothing personal? It's the most personal, the most devastating thing that can happen to a woman. And it was nothing like Hank, an aberration of who he was."

"Women get swept away, too, not just men. Someone comes along offering easy sex when they're in neutral and unsuspecting, and wham, they're throwing their lives away. Saw it happen to my old man. Saw my mother take off with a mechanic from Suffern and never look back. The only thing my mother and that guy had in common was their love for an old Corvette, as far as I could see. But she must have found something she wasn't getting from my dad."

"What was he like?"

"My father was a quiet man to begin with, but after my mother left, he didn't speak for years. In fact, I would say he went to the grave without talking about it."

"How sad."

Wade stretched out his legs and shook his head. "We humans are not much different than apes. But, I have to admit my mother was happy with Greg Waters, she stuck with him to the end."

"What end?"

"They died in a car crash up on Route 17. It was a hell of a thing."

"That must have been terrible for you. You know, I thought my mother and father were incredibly in love. When my father died none of us could speak about it. We felt deserted, like he had done it on purpose, and, who knows, maybe he did. The doctor had told him to stop drinking, and he died with four martinis in his stomach. Worse than that, there was a woman in bed with him, and she wasn't my mother. My mother's hurt filled the whole house. I took his death badly, too. I still ache if I go there, so I don't."

Wade nodded. "At least you cared about him, that's important. My father hid in books. He read the entire set of the *Encyclopedia Britannica*, his answer to getting an education. I resented it until I found books for myself. In the end, they were about the only thing we ever shared... probably the reason I want to write."

"I lived inside books, too, until I found painting. I think it's giving me my sanity. Especially, lately, when I've wanted to run."

"Where to?"

"From, not to. I feel like I've been on the run for most of my life. I've always wanted to run away from something, but it's not clear to me what it is. You see? I'm not the person you think I am."

She unfastened the clips in her hair and let it tumble to her shoulders.

"I distrust people, their motives and their sincerity. I see masks everywhere, masks of caring, of importance, of satisfaction. I wear a mask on my own face most of the time. Now, I have to deal with the fact that my paintings are masks, too. Honestly, I don't have any idea what makes people tick. I used to fantasize about hiding in a bubble, where I could float around and watch what goes on behind closed doors to help me figure out what is real and what isn't. I don't think my marriage was real. I don't think I ever loved my husband. He probably left me because he was the least appreciated man on earth."

She thought she may have just said the unspeakable.

Wade turned and his fingers pushed the hair back from her face. "You're too hard on yourself for such an intelligent, talented woman. There are always two sides to a story."

The noise scratched over their heads again. "Did you hear that?" she asked.

"Night critters. You need to start letting go or end up stuck like your girlfriend, Kendra. She might as well join a convent."

"Painting is enough of a love affair for me. Like a love affair, it calls for trust and it's full of risk."

"After Margie died, I had to come to terms with living, take a hard look at the good and the bad. I've decided life dishes out the good and bad equally. Life, for example, is just the other side of death. And death only exists because of life. They are eternally wed, co-dependents, one of no less value than the other. Just like good and evil."

"That's the opposite of what I was taught. My father always said we could avoid the dark if we stayed in the light."

"Ha. Well I hate to argue with your old man, but what's wrong with the dark? Look at the beauty of a night sky and think how clouds relieve the sun."

"I'm afraid of my dark side. The few times I went there, I had a hard time getting out. I felt disappeared, lost. Everything in life looked like a great tragedy."

"It is! But it is also a comedy and a thriller and beautiful. Take your paintings. Why do you say your paintings aren't, aren't…."

"Authentic?"

"Right. But they are! They are authentic. The paintings are you, at least where you were when you painted them. They are you, heads to tails. They are vibrant, funny, sad, a love letter from Abigail to life. They talk."

"What did you say your name was?" Abigail asked.

"Barney. My friends call me, Barney."

"Hi Barney. That's a nice, homey name."

"Hi Abby. That's a nice four letter word."

"I like you, Barney. Have we met in another lifetime, maybe?"

"Do you believe in love at first sight?"

She shrugged. "I don't know that it makes any sense at all. Do you know the boys called me the Ice Queen in college? Will you promise never to call me that?" She looked to see the answer in his eyes and noted they reflected more Merlot than promise.

"Sounds cruel and ignorant. They weren't your friends, or they would have known better. Your lips told me nothing could be any further from the truth."

"It was a cruel name, wasn't it? Kendra told me about it just the other day, for some odd reason. I tried to explain that I was intimidated by most men back then. I couldn't relax at parties or dances, no matter how much I wanted to."

"There's nothing wrong with being shy, if it's your nature."

"It wasn't exactly that."

"So, you were hard to get?" he asked.

"I didn't say that either. When I was a teenager, I had no crowd, no clique of girls to cover me. I thought the groupies at the beach or on the streets were from another planet. I wasn't connected."

"Were boys falling at your feet?"

"Hardly. It was my sister, Tiffany, and my best friend, Melissa, that boys gravitated to. But there was one boy…"

"Uh-oh. Why do I think you are going to tell me about him?"

"I won't if you don't want me to. I made him up from the start, but we do have time to kill."

He leaned against the wall, and put his head back. His eyes closed. "I like listening. Shoot."

"Okay." She looked at the ceiling. "Once upon a time, when Abigail was sixteen and ripening like the fruit on the trees... No. No. Wait," she laughed, "I can do better. I'll try again.

"Summer turned her skin as golden as a Bartlett pear..."

"How about just getting to the facts, Ma'am. Just the facts. Who was the guy?"

"Abraham. He was Jewish. A good person for a nice Jewish girl, but not for me."

"A kosher romance. Short and sweet?"

"Short, but not sweet."

"So, he was your first love?"

"In a way. But right on the heels of Abraham was Ari and I would consider him my first love, although he had no idea."

"Did you forget to tell him?"

"He preferred my friend, Melissa. He wanted her from the start. Ari Michos, that was his name. He was Greek, an immigrant."

"And who was Melissa?"

"Melissa was my best friend, my alter ego. She lived on my street in a house across from her grandparents'. I met her grandparents first—they were really nice people—but Melissa's parents were weird. Her father looked like a bulldog and was a miserable sort. She never said a word against him. She said he was a war veteran and suffered from flashbacks and terrible nightmares. His jaw was shattered in combat, so he couldn't smile and always looked angry. To make matters worse, he killed one of his own men in a cross-fire. I think it was in Korea."

She rested her chin on her knees and longed for a blanket.

"Come here," Wade said, making a pillow of his shoulder. "So what's the big deal about her father?"

"I don't know. He had nothing to do with Ari and me."

She looked at the painting of two women talking at a small round table. "That picture, *Les Confidentes*, could be a portrait of Melissa and me. We talked about everything. In the beginning she told me more than I wanted to know, at the end she didn't tell me enough."

"So, Ari and you loved Melissa?"

"Yes. I adored her, but Ari was my secret love. It was schoolgirl stuff, I suppose, looking back at it now. I had an empty little bundle inside me wanting to be filled. I stuffed it with other people's experiences because I never had anything of my own, anything I could count on. And that first juicy summer when love seemed possible, and loving Abraham was not, I just projected all my thwarted love to Ari."

"Did he appreciate you?"

"We were just friends. I got to know him because he would come to my house to meet Melissa. Whenever he knocked at the door, I ran to answer his every need. He let me use him to practice talking to a man. He would hold my hand and confide his wishes, lies and dreams to me. I tried to tell him mine, and sometimes he hugged me, but never the way I wanted. He was a pained person who wanted so much. I imagined that someday he would see me instead of Melissa and unwrap the package I was saving. I lived for his visits and hoped that if he and Melissa broke up, I would be standing in her place. It was so foolish. All we talked about was Melissa. She was our link. It was always Melissa."

Abigail looked at the painting again and saw how the one girl was more engaged than the other. She saw herself in the blonde girl, ostensibly listening but thinking about something else.

"Did she come tonight?" Wade asked.

"Melissa? No, we grew apart. There were the little differences and then some big ones. Bizarre things happened, and now that I think of it, it may have been because of her father. The Steiger's house was silent and sad. Melissa's father, worked nights distributing papers, and her mother sat alone, day after day, at the kitchen table, practically catatonic. Her parents didn't talk to one another as far as I could see. But Melissa and I always had so much to say to one another. We could talk all night."

Wade put his arm around her and stroked her hair while she spoke.

"One night Melissa told me Ari was always wanting to make love, and she was bored with it. She said she was thinking she would have to end their relationship soon. I couldn't believe it. She could talk love and romance one day and break up the next. I knew how much Ari loved her, but I was secretly happy when they broke up and ready for him, willing to be his second choice."

Wade had closed his eyes again. She saw the graying stubble on his chin, the furrows in his forehead. His face was nowhere nearly as gentle as his words, his lovely hands.

"Oh, you must think I'm a nitwit telling you this kid stuff."

He straightened and tightened his grip on her shoulder. "No. No I don't. I told you I like the sound of your voice. Come on, let's get to the rest of the story."

"Well, okay. I'll wake you if you fall asleep, alright?"

He laughed. "Not a chance."

"Okay, but you tell a story next."

"Fair enough."

"Of course, I thought that I would become the love of his life. I was sleeping, maybe dreaming of him at Melissa's house one night, when I felt a hand sliding up my leg and under my nightgown."

"Oh, now the plot thickens," Wade said.

"It wasn't funny. I opened my eyes and saw a bushy-haired man with twisted lips standing over me. When I sat up and let out a sound, he fell back and hobbled out of the room."

"Her father?"

"Yes. How did you know? It didn't cross my mind, not until Melissa apologized for him. She said sometimes her father drank too much and went into the wrong bedroom. She was sure he must have been very embarrassed and left the room to be with him."

"Incest."

"Do you think so? I knew it was something strange, but incest was too foreign and repulsive for me to imagine back then. Now I know it might have been possible. It would explain a lot of other things."

"The poor kid."

"It would explain the frustration of Ari's feelings. He said he could have her, anyway he wanted, but he couldn't have her at all. She was not allowed to date. Her father forbade it, and so their comings and goings were all very secretive. They sneaked around making love anywhere they could.

"And, here's another thing, I remember. Ari was very understanding when it came to Melissa's father; he didn't blame the man for coming between them. His father had been killed in a coup in Athens. He and his brothers had watched their father and uncle slashed in the living room, not only cut open, but salt poured in their wounds to augment the pain. Ari said the soldiers laughed when their bodies went into spasms."

"Jesus!"

"He understood that for Melissa's father there would be no peace, just as there would be no peace for him. He saw it as the horrible cost of war, the reason why a man would want to keep the person he loved most locked up. I think part of Ari's love for Melissa was that she had to live with this price everyday."

Wade shook his head. "Seeing his father killed that way could have robbed him of his manhood; being helpless is a hard thing for a boy. I should know."

"Yes. Yes. That's almost what he said. He said Melissa made him feel like a man. That she was so giving. So wonderful. 'She asked for nothing, only gave,' he said. It was this sensitivity that made me love him. That, and his long fingers and the little overbite that made him look ready for a kiss, and his way of talking to me as if I was a great friend and a wise woman. He seemed to think I understood much more than I did. He didn't know how I ached for him."

"And you didn't let on because of Melissa?"

"I didn't let on because I wasn't Melissa. I thought she had some witch's power, something unknowable. I was shocked when she confided they were having sex everywhere and anywhere they could find some privacy."

"I hear you," Wade says. "You were still a virgin."

"Almost."

21

Snow

Abigail stood up and stretched. "I sure am dredging up ancient history here tonight." She looked out the door. The blowing flakes had turned tiny and dry. A hush was taking over the city, the way it does during a serious snowstorm. She wrapped her coat around her like a shawl, wishing it was Cecily's sable.

Wade got up and looked for the thermostat.

"I'm afraid we made a mistake to wait out the snow," she said.

"I wouldn't be so sure. From what I see, we called it right. The roads haven't improved any. We'll just wait 'til this thing blows out of here and the snow plows show up. Besides, I want to hear the rest of Ari and Abby's love story."

She poked him. "It wasn't a love story. It was a rites of passage story."

"You mean that was the end of it?"

"Well, it's your turn. Who was your first love?"

"You."

"Oh, please. Remember we were starting over, you were going to tell the truth."

"I was mad for Miss Munger."

"And what happened?"

"I moved on, to first grade. By the end of that year, I was in love with Mrs. Williamson."

"Always the teacher's pet?"

"No. I don't think it was mutual admiration. They were careless with me, passed me on like bread, and I became the fickle bastard I am today."

"Ouch. I don't like the f-word."

"So tell me, how does your rites of passage story end? Did that Greek goon ever marry Melissa or turn you into a maid of dishonor?"

"Ari might as well have fallen off the ends of the earth after Melissa broke up with him. The pastry chef at the St. George Hotel was her next victim. It didn't take long before he realized he was just a playmate, too. I, meanwhile, longed to see Ari, even to talk about him, but she didn't want to mention his name again. For her, over meant over."

"Did you ever see him again?"

"Not for a long time. I suppose I was just as distracted that autumn as Melissa. We both started college, and while I couldn't meet anyone who was right for me, she went through more lovers in her freshman year than most women have in a lifetime. The strangest thing was, she ended up with a woman!"

"Not you?"

"I might have been better off if I'd loved women. I went to art school, remember, where a lot of the men were gay or thinking about it. Whatever. They weren't thinking about me. Since I had no one to love, I would think about Ari and imagine our meeting again, and his recognizing that he had loved me all along."

"You're shivering. Come closer, we have to be each other's radiators. The thermostat seems be on a regulator."

A lonely plow groaned through the street, sounding like it was losing the battle.

She snuggled into Wade's side and put her head on his shoulder.

"So when did you see the Ari guy again?"

"Do you really find this little story even remotely interesting? She didn't wait for him to answer.

"I was fresh out of art school and had just started working and living on my own. Grocery shopping down on Seventh Avenue, I saw the sign, Michos Roofing. Michos was Ari's last name. Ironically, the store was in the old Connors Real Estate Building where my mother once worked. I had to go in.

An older version of Ari came toward me, at least he had the same dark eyes. I was flustered until I saw the real Ari on the phone at the other end of the room. He turned, smiled and waved, and I didn't have a chance. He was more beautiful than ever."

"Hey. Let's not get carried away with details."

"No problem, I can hardly remember them. I do remember that I asked him out to dinner right in front of his brother, and he never hesitated."

Abigail knew that this could mean little to Wade, but for her at that time, Ari was the height of romance, and the one she wanted, regardless of the consequences. She had never asked a man out or been so aggressive.

"We stayed in the neighborhood, went to a typical neighborhood bar, the kind with black glass on the walls and red plastic leather in the booths and a dated jukebox. Of course, we talked about Melissa and then about his family. He said his mother still spoke only Greek and his nieces and nephews spoke only English. It divided the family into two worlds, the old and the new. He was self-conscious about his English, enunciating every syllable very carefully. It always touched me how hard he tried."

She stopped talking, knowing her drivel was sop to anyone else. Who, but she, would care to know how it was when they started slow dancing to "Hold Me", with his arms and hands moving around her like they belonged, and the hot breath in her hair that made her body liquefy? Just remembering, made that night alive again. She was so ready, so completely swept away that night she practically dragged him home to her sweet little apartment to offer him the great gift of her virginity. She was twenty-one, and he was shocked that she bled. She was embarrassed and tried to make as little of it as possible, but he did not. He became more tender and more ardent, and they made love over and over again all night. "We shall make this right," he had said.

Wade interrupted her reverie. "Where's the storyteller gone? Hell. I want to hear what it took for the Ice Queen to melt."

Startled by his choice of words, she moved away from him. He had thrown the Ice Queen label back at her right after his promise. "You used the very words you called ignorant and cruel," she said.

He recognized his mistake, looked contrite and apologized. "I will never say it again, Abby, I promise. Go on."

She sat on her knees. "We should leave. At least try to go. But, now, I think I may have had too much wine on top of everything else."

"Maybe, it was those cherries," he said, and then started singing, "The weather outside is frightful, and the fire inside delightful. I don't care if we ever go, let it snow, let it snow, let it …."

"Stop! Really, I have to get home."

"But the point is you have to get home in one piece. You're on the brink of a great career and a spectacular romance. A skid on the road could spoil all that, and I don't think taking such a risk makes sense. Let's wait awhile."

She walked over to the window, but it had become frosted on the inside. She scratched out a peephole. "My God. Look at that!" The wind made the snow look like it was snowing up as well as down. "It looks like snow replicating snow. We'll never get out of here." She started to pace. "I should call home again, but Marlene has to be asleep by now. I don't want to wake the kids, either."

"Look, we can make do. Hell, we have wine and caviar…good company. We can sleep on the floor and keep each other warm. What else does a person need? Are we going to put Ari to rest now? Have you gotten over that guy yet? Is he out of your system?"

"I only told you about him because he was the one. The only man that made me forget myself. To act before I thought. I suppose you were never so foolish."

"I lost myself to Olivia Newton John and before that to Kim Basinger and before that to Melissa Gilbert. I told you, I was a fickle bastard."

"Not fair. I've told you a true story and you give me your fantasies."

"I've been celibate more years than the Pope!"

"I doubt it!"

"More years than I want to admit. Okay. Yes, I loved. I loved once or twice, and then I married someone who loved me more than I loved her, or so I thought. I was naïve and stupid, but I'm not stuck in the past."

"So, there's no one out there waiting for you to get home tonight?"

"No," he said. "Come here."

She sat down again, put her arms in her coat sleeves, pulled up her hood and tightened her coat collar. She fumbled with her gloves and wrapped herself in her own arms.

"Warm enough?" he asked.

"I am now," she said.

They sat quietly. Wade had gone somewhere inside his head and so had she.

Abigail remembered how she had waited for weeks on end for Ari to call after that first tumultuous date. She made excuses for his dalliance, thinking perhaps, he was shy, or worse. Maybe he thought she was just a foolish American girl, not knowing she had thought of him for years.

She made up scenarios of the two of them in a little walk-up just blocks from his store. In the mornings she would open her eyes and see his dark head on her pillow, his arms would be around her. They would make love before they rose each morning, and tell each other their secrets before they went to sleep at night. They would grow wiser and wiser; he believing in his potential, she, giving him a new confidence, lifting him with her own history.

She would learn to cook mousaka and dolmades. They would drink wine with dinner. He would grow to love her more and more, and she would always show him compassion and take courses in Greek and love his mother. She could almost hear Yanni playing in the background.

With her heart full and needs great, she gave up hoping for Ari to make the first move and finally, fatally, took it upon herself to connect with him again. She did not call ahead. She just showed up.

When he greeted her at the door of his office, she experienced none of the instant affection, none of the familiarity she anticipated. "Come in. Have a seat, he said," pointing to a chair by his desk, treating her like a customer, without a clue that she was on a precious mission. She remained standing, intending to make a date for the evening.

On the other side of his desk sat a dark-haired girl with eyes like question marks. At first, Abigail thought she was a secretary, then, noticing how much they resembled one another, thought she might be his sister. But what did she know? She had no idea if he had sisters; for all she knew he could have been a quintuplet.

Of course, Ari was ignorant of why she was there, and couldn't know the love only she could fathom, or that she was ready to claim him for her life, ready to fulfill the most immature set of dreams a girl could invent. He couldn't see the pictures she had in her head, or their future domestic bliss, of their mornings and nights. No. It was quickly clear, no such thoughts had crossed his mind.

"Abigail, you must meet Adelpha," he said. "She has this week come from Crete, and she is here to stay. Adelpha, this is my fili, my friend, Abigail. She is very good friend to me during hard times."

"Ise omorfi," the girl said softly, but Abigail didn't acknowledge the compliment.

"She says you are beautiful," he said.

And you call me a good friend? Abigail thought, standing perfectly still as her brain turned into cotton. Was he dismissing what she thought had transformed their friendship into love? His words became indistinct as they spun around the room, flying off the walls, the shelves, his metal desk and the face of the solemn foreign girl. Somehow she grasped that he and Adelpha were to be married by the end of the month. He may have explained that his family and Adelpha's family were longtime friends from the same village, and they had shipped her to America to marry and be safe.

Abigail looked at the young woman, whose large hands were folded prayerfully on her lap. The girl was not to blame, she was only claiming what she probably thought was hers all along. She wondered at her own incredible ignorance. She knew so little about Ari, just scraps of information about his family and their ways. She knew only his struggle, his passion for another woman, the wanting him that made her want to give herself away. She felt like a fool who loved a man for no good reason on earth and had imagined he would love her.

She fought to keep her composure, to wish Adelpha well and walk away with her back straight, through the office, her feet attached to her legs, pushing her legs beneath her, one step, then another, and another until she was around the corner at a distant doorway and free to weep.

And this was how things began and ended in the brief, passionate love life of Abigail Lynde. She willed herself to forget Ari and decided that she would never, ever, love anyone so recklessly again.

At work, she functioned by pure will until she started to slow down. Then little by little her energy ran out. She was so depleted she couldn't get out of bed in the morning.

When Cecily interfered, inflamed by the information she had coaxed from Tiffany, it severed any connection the two sister's had left and managed to devastate an already faltering respect she had for her mother.

Those days of heartbreak were weighed down further by a mysterious dread and overwhelming loneliness. Her hormones turned against her, withholding her period and complicating the misery she already found too much to bear, a misery that incorporated all the disappointments, poor judgments, abandonment and hopelessness of her short life. A shadow self toyed with her psyche, and cruel and judgmental voices inside her head relentlessly attacked for her for being not only a romantic fool but a stupid one as well.

On the day she spotted and suffered the cramps that heralded her period, a sense of redemption began, and brought with it a gratitude that broke her dark spell. She immediately returned to work and soon found designing very satisfactory. It was precise on one hand and inventive on the other, requiring the attention of her left brain and her right. It may have lacked the potential of a large income, but it gave her life structure and engaged her mind. Work also allowed her to let go of her dreams and live solely in the moment for the very first time.

Abigail also found a short-term peace in the solitude she found reading and painting in that first place of her own, the cozy nest perched high enough to see the lady of the harbor again, back in the neighborhood where she had liked herself best. She vowed that, as soon as she was able, she would buy a bicycle and start traversing the Promenade.

But instead of buying a bike, she met Hank, and very soon he told her he was ready to settle down and said she was the person he saw himself with for the rest of his life. She was complimented. He seemed to be normal and safe, a perfectly nice man.

Her first doubts about their future surfaced when he told her he wanted to have children. She couldn't see herself as a mother, wasn't sure if she could conceive, and more than that, thought motherhood was a commitment beyond her ken. She told him they really should wait until the time was right, but the time arrived sooner than she expected. Then, she put off the wedding until she knew the baby was firmly planted, its heart beating on its own, well beyond the first trimester.

Despite her caution, after a late wedding and an early, healthy birth, she had to struggle with an overriding sense of doom once again. She obsessed that what was given could also be taken away. She feared joy would bring disaster and tried not to love Stephanie too much. The God of her own invention was a cruel trickster. He had taken her father, sent men to torture her, deprived her of family and friends and left her to fend for herself. This God was not about to lift her up and give her grace.

Abigail must have drifted off there, on the floor, listening to her own thoughts. It was Wade's soft snoring that woke her. She tiptoed to the window and realized there had been no choice, after all. It was the right call to stay in the gallery, and they would probably be there for the night. The snow had covered the streets that now looked pure and unspoiled. Its whiteness hid the wounds beneath, the broken sidewalks, the wanton garbage, the excrements of dogs and humanity. She thought how remarkable were the clouds that had unexpectedly delivered their celestial blanket, cleaned the city, and tied it together like a lovely gift, making the old, new.

She navigated to the tiny bathroom and rinsed her mouth, used the toilet, and washed her hands and face. In the storage room, she looked for something to serve as pillows. The only thing she could find was a Kendra's thick wool sweater. She rolled it up and put it under Wade's head, which he dopily allowed, and then lay a roll of bubble wrap next to him for herself. They would need more than their coats as the night wore on. So she moved the trays from the tablecloths and turned the heavy cloths into covers. She flicked off the lights and lay beside Wade, tucking her back into his front, insuring them both the comfort of one another's warmth.

His arm moved across her waist and pulled her closer. She listened to his breath, deep and relaxed. She considered the weight of his arm, until she fell asleep again—a sleep that took her to an ice palace where icicles hung tentatively, dripping and breaking, some dangerously falling like knives from the high beamed ceilings. She had to run through the rooms to keep from being struck. In the last room, the icicles were gone, and she discovered a beautiful golden throne lit by the sun. It glowed in front of huge open doors leading to stone terraces and a lawn where barefooted children, wearing haloes of buttercups and daisies were playing in the grass.

She ran outside and saw they were Stephanie and Alex and realized they were looking for her. The three of them started to dance. Whirling and twirling in a circle, joyously dancing until they fell down laughing. Suddenly, the children's laughter turned into tears. She told them that it was all right, they could cry as much as they liked. She cried with them, only the tears that rushed down her were sent by a divine joy. "It's all right to cry!" she said to the children again. "It is all right," and the children embraced her as they formed a happy bundle. The sun escaped the clouds and came closer and closer until it hovered right above their heads, lowering itself to smile, a warm, tender, forgiving smile.

22

Morning

It must be morning, Abigail thinks as she feels two arms tightening around her. She remembers the man, the smile, the *I love yous.* She wonders if he will remember his words from the night before. The bubble wrap is stuck to her cheek. Has her cheek conformed to the plastic? Are its little bumps now impressed on her face? Her face must look like a waffle iron.

Her body is warm. Considering the lack of a mattress, she's not that uncomfortable. She tries not to awaken Wade, but turns slightly to check for indentations. Little bumps press against her palm.

He mumbles something like, "Are we there yet?" But she thinks it's dream talk.

Are we there yet? She thinks about it. She is somewhere but is she there? Maybe the expression, "there is no there, there" is true. There is no place to go. It's all in the process. Last night had been better than she dreamed, but it was only a point in the road. She has to head home now, take up where she left off, although that is looking a lot better than it did a few days ago. She can't wait to see the children. She'll take them out in the snow and go sledding up on Nob Hill. They'll build a snow girl and she will show them how a little water can turn snow into ice they can sculpt.

She doesn't see any daylight through the frozen windows, but the radiators start to hiss.

She stays as still as possible. Why hurry? They will not be able to get out of the city easily. She's sure of that. It's so still. Not a motor, a rat, a clanging thought to disturb them, just the promise of heat.

"Are you awake, Abby?"

"Not quite," she says.

"I'm not either. I have a conch shell on my head. It's noisy as hell in here."

"I'll get you a glass of water, that should help."

"I also have a mouth that belongs in the trenches. God, it's foul."

"I have a toothbrush—want to use it?"

"Are you kidding? I didn't think you were that kind of a girl."

"And that's just for starters. But then, you don't know me very well."

"Well, I'll take you up on the toothbrush, if you tell me where it is. And I will get my own water, thank you."

"It's in my purse, over on the desk." She turns her mottled cheek from his eyes, hoping in a few minutes or so her skin will recover its shape. She hears him urinating, then the flush. She doubts he put the seat down, too many years alone.

He brushes his teeth, and she gets up and goes to the door to see what has happened during the night. It is a wonderland outside. The snow sits on the iron gratings like frosting on a wedding cake. The window sills of the buildings are wearing white smiles. The sky is lighting itself, but Venus is still spectacularly bright, and the moon, a mere sliver, rests fingernail-thin in the west.

"How bad is it out there?" he asks.

"It is glorious, a winter wonderland. Come look."

He crosses the room, and they stand together looking at the

morning, the messy foyer behind them.

"You know, I think our first date should be sledding. When we get back, why don't we pack up the kids and go play in the snow?" he suggests.

"They will wonder where I found you."

"I won't tell them we've already slept together, I promise."

She laughs, then turns and hugs him. The sun hits the tops of the buildings across the street. "You know, I'm famished."

"You are ravishing," he says, looking at her pocked face and the crusted mascara on her eyelids.

"And you are a liar," she says.

"It's my art, how I survive in the trade. But I don't take my work home with me."

She looks across the mounds of snow that represent cars. "Do you know which one of those mounds is yours?

"Nope."

"Oh, this should be fun. We better start now so we can find it by noon."

They bundle themselves up. He tapes bubblewrap over his shoes, and tears cardboard boxes into makeshift scrapers. Then he waterproofs their gloves by lining them with plastic bags. With his pea hat pulled well over his ears he opens the door and points down the street, "I think it's that way!"

Outside, they trundle through the snow, which is no more than eight inches on the road. "I think this might be it," he calls over his shoulder. She goes to his side, and they start scraping at the driver's window.

"What color are we looking for?" she asks.

"Gray," he says.

"Boring," she replies.

"You're right, and this one is not it—it's cherry red—probably some kid's."

"How about this one?" she asks pointing due south.

"Could be!"

They plow through more drifts and scrape the second car, side by side. Her black velvet skirt is now white.

"Blue! Jesus! This may be harder than I thought," he says.

It's true. All the cars look the same, each crammed into spaces too small for much manipulation. All of them tucked into banks left by the last night's plows' early efforts.

"Hey, I think this is it!" He points to a license plate's partial number.

"That's something like my number, anyway."

They scrape and find gray. "Looking good! And it's a Volvo, my favorite make. Let's go for it." He pulls out his keys and they claw at the snow around the door like two desperate polar bears.

"But how can you ever maneuver out of here?" Abigail pants.

A cold sun rises in the brilliant blue sky overhead and, where it can reach beyond the long shadows of the buildings, turns the snow into a dazzling glare that is hard on the eyes.

They hear the sound simultaneously. It is a plow pushing snow over the sides of the cars, burying them deeper for what will probably be days to come. The red car takes on two more feet. "I hope the kid is with someone decent," Wade says.

They move into the center of the street, waving at the snowplow's driver. His machine moves slowly, a great rusted dinosaur at work, until it slows to a stop before reaching them. Wade calls, "Hey man, could you help us out of here? Is it worth a few bucks?"

"Sure!" the driver says, "but I don't take money. I'm just doin' my job." The plow creaks and groans forward and back and carves a road around the parking space so they can get out. And then he goes beyond the call of duty, gets out of his cab and helps Wade rock the car backward and forward until his wheels get a footing, and the nose of the car points away from the rear of the car in front. The man directs Abigail, and they put their hands on the trunk of the Volvo and push with all their might until the car rolls onto the street.

Wade begs the man to take some money, but he walks away. "Have a good trip home," he calls, "and a Merry Christmas."

"Gee, that sounds nice. A good trip home," Wade says, as he helps Abigail get in the car.

"But do you think there will be anyplace open for some coffee and a quiche?" she asks.

"Hmmm. I think I'll have the sausage and pancakes," he says.

"Maybe some French toast, with hot maple syrup," she says.

"A German waffle with fresh strawberries and whipped cream," he says.

"Hot cereal with brown sugar, raisins and cream," she says.

"A veggie omelet with Feta cheese and mushrooms," he says.

They turn the corner onto 2nd Avenue. Not another car is in their path.

"Maybe the kids will take to kayaking."

"Maybe you won't like them."

"I like them already."

"You're a dreamer."

"Yes ma'am, I believe I am. By the way, good morning."

"Yes, it is," she says, relaxing into her seat, the seat belt tight in its socket.

He looks straight ahead. One by one, the lights turn green, all the way down 2nd Avenue.

About the Author

Brooklyn born and raised, Carol Egmont St. John is an educator, poet, author and workshop leader. Her first book, *Taproots: Where Ideas are Born*, consists of poetry and homilies designed to show the role of metaphor in the visual arts and the written word. Her novel, *Anchors of the Soul*, explores an unlikely friendship between two women. Both books are about empowerment.

St. John's workshops, by-products of 25 years of teaching, have been experienced by hundreds of workshoppers from across the country. They include "InnerReach: a creativity workshop for everyone", "Writing for the Joy of It", and "Paint as Play".

Public talks on "Art for Everyone", and "Owning Your Creative Self" have been heard on television, radio and in clubhouses in both Eastern and Western United States.

The Carol St. John Studio is located in Tubac, Arizona. Through her monthly column in the local paper, St. John reminds her readers that life is an art and all of us are artists creating ourselves.

For more information about St. John and to find out about upcoming workshops visit www.carolstjohn.com or email her at tusaints@aol.com.